Stuck in Downward Dog

Stuck in Downward Dog

A NOVEL

Chantel Simmons

KEY PORTER BOOKS

Library and Archives Canada Cataloguing in Publication

Simmons, Chantel
    Stuck in downward dog / Chantel Simmons.

ISBN-13: 978-1-55263-832-3, ISBN-10: 1-55263-832-4

    I. Title.

PS8637.I474S78 2007   C813'.6   C2006-905958-6

The publisher gratefully acknowledges the support of the Canada Council for the Arts and the Ontario Arts Council for its publishing program. We acknowledge the support of the Government of Ontario through the Ontario Media Development Corporation's Ontario Book Initiative.

We acknowledge the financial support of the Government of Canada through the Book Publishing Industry Development Program (BPIDP) for our publishing activities.

This book is printed on acid-free paper that is Ancient Forest Friendly (100% post-consumer recycled paper).

Key Porter Books Limited
Six Adelaide Street East, Tenth Floor
Toronto, Ontario
Canada M5C 1H6

www.keyporter.com

Text design: Marijke Friesen
Electronic formatting: Jean Lightfoot Peters

Printed and bound in Canada

07 08 09 10 11 5 4 3 2

For Brent and for my dad

"Yoga exists in the world because everything is linked."
—T.K.V. DESIKACHAR

"I wish I had a twin, so I could know what I'd look like without plastic surgery."
—JOAN RIVERS

Prologue

ASHTANGA: A SERIES OF FLOWING POSITIONS.
This "road map" leads us to the state of "yoga" (union with the Infinite).

I was lying face up on the cork floor, legs straight out, feet to the sides, palms face up, eyes closed, not moving. Everything hurt. And this was the easiest part.

Savasana, or Corpse Pose, was the reason I practiced yoga at all. The chance to lie as still as possible, flat on my back, while keeping an empty mind and calling it a workout, was something that no other form of exercise came close to offering. It was the rest of the ashtanga yoga class that wasn't so superb, but that was probably because I wasn't so superb at it. And I didn't seem to be getting any better, at least not compared to everyone else in the room.

Each class went something like this: as we'd start out with the basics, I'd feel like a master of movement. In Upward Dog, my back was arched nicely and my arms weren't shaking (at least not as much as they used to), and for a flash I'd get this feeling, as though the two new girls behind me (in matching Lululemon outfits with coordinating hair ties) might be looking at me, wondering how long they'd have to come to class to be as good as me, and realizing that their expensive, trendy outfits did not a yogi make. But as soon as I moved into Downward Dog, a pike position where my arms and legs were supposed to be straight and my butt high in the air, it was as though I exhaled any semblance of confidence. Through my legs I'd catch sight of those same girls and see that they were already much better than me—and it was only their first week. Their butts were higher and their heels were flat on the floor, and they looked *comfortable*, as though the position wasn't difficult at all.

And it only got worse.

As the instructor led us into One-Leg Down Dog, directing us to raise our right legs to the ceiling, I was so focused on everyone around me that I lost all control over my limbs. My arms would start to wobble, and I'd lose my balance and slam some body part (an elbow, a knee or my head) into my mat, experiencing an excruciating blow both to my body and my ego.

The instructor always reminded us that it was okay to fall, that everyone falls at some point. But it wasn't okay with me. It stank.

This wasn't just the way it was going for me in yoga class. It was the way my life was playing out, too. Even though I kept going to the yoga studio of life, trying to move to the next level, I couldn't seem to get out of that just-graduated-from-university-need-a-job-and-money-and-a-home-and-a-boyfriend phase, even though I was years past being a student. And when

I looked around me, I was surrounded by people who, regardless of age, seemed to far surpass me not only in yoga, but in all aspects of life.

The day I turned twenty-eight, my mother told me it was my year. Rather, she wrote it—*It's Your Year, Mara!*—in big, loopy letters with sunny yellow icing on an extra-large chocolate chip cookie she'd baked that morning at her shop. My mother was convinced it would be my monumental year, just as it had been her monumental year. Twenty-eight was the year in which she'd given birth to me, her second daughter, and completed her family with my father. It was the same for my now-thirty-five-year-old sister, Victoria, who, the year she turned twenty-eight, made partner at her law firm, gave birth to her second of three children, and got a full-time housekeeper, much to the envy of all the neighbors, and me.

I, on the other hand, was dumped by my boyfriend just days after I turned twenty-eight, making me not only unmarried but apparently undesirable, living alone in a basement apartment I could barely afford, with a job I hated and a cat I loved. My mother, ever the one-woman positivity parade, insisted it could still be my year. That my luck was going to change. That I would get unstuck.

I wasn't so sure.

Chapter One

OM: A SIMPLE CHANT WITH A COMPLEX MEANING.
This mantra represents body, mind and spirit on the pathway to overcoming obstacles and achieving a goal.

*O*livia Closson, one of my two best friends, insisted that every woman happily cohabiting with a man needed a roaster. Olivia had been advising me on topics from guys to grouting since the sixth grade, so I wanted to believe her, but I suspected she was just trying to clear out a space under her kitchen sink for her new deluxe, five-setting rotisserie roaster. Also, I wasn't sure that I, a woman who didn't even own a cookbook (unless you counted the recipes in the back of the *Reader's Digest*— a subscription my mother paid for because, apparently, my life would be unfulfilling without the "Humor in Uniform" jokes), needed a contraption for cooking whole chickens. Still, I was open to the possibility that at some point my boyfriend, Sam, would stop working long hours and want me to create a meal that didn't require sandwich bread or dried pasta. If only I had known that Sam was going to break up with me that very day,

I could've saved myself the hassle of maneuvering the lethargic roaster from Olivia's King Street West penthouse condo to my basement apartment.

I was carrying the roaster (Olivia had insisted I pay her twenty dollars so I wouldn't feel like a charity case) up Clinton Street, where I'd gotten off the 506 streetcar on College, right in the heart of Little Italy, when I saw the moving van parked on the front lawn of the semi-detached, gremlin green, sparsely shingled house where Sam and I had lived in a subterranean apartment for the past six months.

Clinton wasn't the prettiest street in the neighborhood— that honor went to Palmerston, with its billowy maples and lampposts straight out of *A Christmas Carol*. But rent on Clinton left me with just enough extra cash for my yoga membership, which, in my mind at least, was why we lived there instead of three streets over. And we still reaped all the benefits of the area. Situated just north of Little Italy, south of Koreatown and walking distance to Chinatown and Little Portugal, it was rich with culture, history and stray cats that kept Pumpernickel, my cat, thankful for his indoor abode. When I'd found the place, I'd overlooked the obvious—that it was below ground and would be damp, dark and cold even in summer. Instead, I'd been swayed by the fireplace in the bedroom, thinking it would be romantic. It turned out it wasn't a fireplace at all, but a flue-less alcove with a mantel. I could barely afford half the rent as it was, and Sam refused to cover my share, so until I could get my bed, wardrobe and cat above ground, I had to accept that Clinton Street was as good as it got. At least I was living downtown and not in the suburbs, like Scarborough or Vaughan.

When I reached the house, dubbed Gremlin Manor by the other three sublets, I placed the roaster, neatly packed in its original box, complete with owner's manual, on the pigeon-pooped front walk. A fortysomething fat guy, wearing a bleach-blotched orange Bart Simpson T-shirt circa 1990, and a skinny, balding guy about ten years younger with low-slung jeans and a bungee cord holding them up greeted me on the front steps.

"You . . . Mara Brennan?" the skinny guy asked, looking down at an orange plastic clipboard and then back up at me. I nodded, confused. He walked over to me and handed me a pink waybill that had Sam's signature on it. "The landlord supervised—he just left," he said, adding, "I think you've just been dumped." Then he and the fat mover guy went into the apartment and returned with Sam's couch.

I watched as they loaded the white pleather couch into the moving van. Sam had bought it because it had great design even though it squeaked when you sat on it and got cold in the winter and sticky in the summer. Sam, who had a well-paying job plus bonus as a Bay Street banker (the Wall Street of Toronto), hadn't offered to pay more than half the rent. So we couldn't get a nicer place, above grass level, like normal couples. But he had spent $5,000 on the couch, which he bought at one of those very important furniture stores on King Street East that offer furnishings in obscure shapes and uncomfortable fabrics and call them *love seats*. We'd never made love on it. I wasn't even allowed to put my socked feet up on it because it could crease, crinkle or catch my cooties and pass them on. Now, I wondered where the couch was headed, and what would've happened if I'd arrived home ten minutes later.

When they were done loading the couch, the fat mover guy climbed into the driver's seat while the skinny mover guy tossed me a set of keys, shrugged helplessly, and got into the passenger side of the van just as the horn beeped twice.

Bessie filled me in on the rest. Bessie had been Sam's assistant at the bank as long as I'd been his girlfriend, which was almost a year. She'd left a message on our answering machine (a graduation gift from my father years ago), and the light was flashing when I pushed open the front door, which led directly into the middle of our living room. The room was now empty, except for the tiny TV Sam had left behind, now sitting on a stack of old phone books. The kitchen table and chairs were gone, as well as the floor lamp that illuminated our place since there were no ceiling lights. I looked into the bedroom (not difficult since it was only two steps from the living room) to see the green futon, which had been Sam's in college and which we had stored under *my* double bed in case of overnight guests (who never materialized). My bed (the one I'd bought when I graduated from university before even meeting Sam) was gone, and the futon was now in its place. I was beyond stunned. Pumpernickel was a brown ball of fur curled up in the corner of the room, behind the futon, since the movers had removed any other items under which he could have typically hidden. He saw me, made a tiny mew and sauntered, unconditional love in tow, out of the bedroom toward me, stretching his paws up my leg once he arrived at my feet. I picked him up and walked over to the answering machine, pressed Play and listened as Bessie explained the situation. Sam had accepted a job in Calgary as an oil stock analyst. He'd bought a house. He would send a check for his share of the month's rent—which had been due five days earlier—by mail. She said, "I wish I wasn't the one telling you." I thought, *I wish I wasn't the one she was telling*. Even though he'd taken my bed, I had to believe it was a misunderstanding—that the movers had packed it by mistake. That he wasn't actually that much of a jerk. That maybe even Bessie had gotten it wrong, and that *we* were moving to Calgary, Sam and me, *together*.

I immediately picked up the phone and punched in his cell number. I had to talk to him. This couldn't be it. This couldn't be the end of everything. My call went straight to his voice mail, and I hung up.

Sam and I hadn't been getting along that well lately, but when he'd left for Calgary the previous week, it was just for an interview, and he promised he'd be back by the fifth of June to take me out for my twenty-eighth birthday, even if by then it would be three days belated. Sam had mentioned the idea of moving to Calgary, but I'd nixed it. So what if I had a job that wasn't exactly in my field (working as a receptionist at a cosmetic surgery clinic didn't really require the geography degree I'd acquired at the University of Toronto five years earlier), and which I loathed to the very depths of my dermal layer of skin. I didn't plan to work at Face Value forever, and while I figured out what I really wanted to do, I needed to be in Toronto, where every family member and friend of mine lived within a 100-mile radius, in case I needed to complain about my setbacks in person.

So if we had differing opinions about living in Calgary, it wasn't the first argument we'd had and I certainly didn't think it would be the breaking point. Lots of couples were unhappy, but they went on to get married. I just assumed we'd be one of them.

When the phone rang (Sam had generously, though not surprisingly, left the landline—since he never answered it, only ever using his BlackBerry), I still thought it would be Sam, calling to explain that *we* were moving to Calgary, *together*, which, given the alternative of living alone in a tiny apartment that didn't even have a couch and that I couldn't afford on my own, I might have considered. I didn't get the chance.

Instead, it was the hostess from Via Amore, calling to confirm our reservation for two that evening. I canceled the reservation and looked at the roaster in its box. Even in June, the apartment was damp and chilly, reminding me why anywhere outside of Toronto, people called this a cellar, not a home, and used it to store homemade wine, old records and hand-me-down china. I placed the electric roaster on the spot on the floor where Sam's pleather couch had been and plugged it into the outlet in the wall. It roared to life. I tossed the owner's manual in the garbage in the kitchen (I lacked stamina when it came to instructions), returned to the living room, turned the empty roaster box upside-down to sit on it and let the amber glow from the ceramic roaster comfort me as Pumpernickel curled up in my lap.

⌐

Miss Fit was a women's-only yoga studio a block north of College and Yonge that my two best friends, Olivia and Mitsuko (aka Mitz), and I had been going to every Tuesday since 2002, when it had been a boxercize studio. It had been converted into a yoga sanctuary about a year later, causing women to closet their Nike cross-trainers in favor of bare feet.

The studio resembled a box of organic bran flakes—crisp and clean on the outside with hundreds of identical-looking women I called the Bran Flakes mingling inside. They were thin and wispy, in coordinating yoga outfits afforded by their well-paying jobs or husbands. Many of these women had belonged to Miss Fit since its high-low impact days, but had seemingly tossed those recollections along with their high-top Velcro Reeboks, slouch socks and thong bodysuits.

Now, these women wore Nuala yoga wear to shop at Whole Foods for fair-trade coffee beans, free-range eggs, wild salmon and organic apples, and attributed their shiny hair to macro-biotic shampoo and the flaxseed they sprinkled on their morning cereal. Or so they professed to each other.

My theory was that most of them shopped at Whole Foods for the overpriced but tasty prepared meals they could eat while watching *Desperate Housewives* after their nannies put their kids to bed. Plus, there was free parking with purchase (unheard of in the city), so they could drive to upscale Yorkville in their gas-slurping suvs straight from their plastic surgeon's back entrance (it would say "facial" in their day planners). And the shiny hair? A ninety-dollar transparent gloss treatment they got on their lunch hour from their hairstylist, using chemicals that were hardly organic.

There were exceptions to the Bran Flakes. I was one of them, with my size 10 bottom squeezed into generic stretch shorts from our step-class days, a sports bra that could pass for lingerie (its fabric was so intermittent) and a simple T-shirt I wore not only to yoga, but for sleeping and sometimes even for walking to the Dominion down the street, where I bought white, completely unhealthy bagels in bulk and conventional apples that tasted better and crunchier than organic ones and were half the price.

Lisette Liposuction could have been the poster girl for the Bran Flakes. Lisette was thirty-seven (but told everyone she'd just recently turned forty) and pretended that her body (after three kids) was a size 2 because she drank four gallons of water a day, ate only raw food and did yoga daily and twice on Sunday. What no one knew from looking at her was that she also shopped at the Nip and Tuck Shop—and not the type that offered Fizz Wizz and candy necklaces. No, Lisette was on the preferred client list at Face Value Cosmetic Surgery Clinic, where I just happened to be the receptionist and where I had filed and unfiled Lisette's overstuffed folder so many times it should have had its own frequent flyer miles status.

Our relationship—Lisette's and mine—was understood yet unspoken. Smiles and nods were exchanged at both the yoga studio and the surgery clinic, but a reference to one was never made at the other, and I sometimes wondered which she'd be more embarrassed to admit: that she got a little not-so-natural assistance, or that she went to a B-list surgeon off the beaten track.

I suppose I was a nip (or tuck) resentful, since I wanted to feel that I was working out for a purpose, and if the best-looking women in the class weren't in top shape because of weekly yoga sessions, then maybe it was all futile. Or maybe it was that, deep down, I knew I could look better too if I got surgery, only I didn't have the money. I wondered if that was the only thing stopping me. But I was sure there was more to it than monetary hindrance: I didn't want to feel as though I was cheating. I wanted to get a body I'd earned through hard work.

When I looked at my two best friends, who were both perfect and didn't have to succumb to surgery—Mitz, always in Roots yoga, and Olivia in her trademark Lululemon—I had to believe there was hope for me, even if I did wear fading cotton shorts to yoga, and even if they did bunch up between my bum cheeks and lock the sweat against my body. And even if, more importantly, I had always been just a little too pudgy in all the wrong places.

I was thinking about this as I shifted, while sitting, into *purna titali*, Butterfly Pose, placing my feet together with my knees out to the side and looking down to see a tiny, but still very noticeable hole right in the crotch of my shorts. It never ended. I felt like I was always attempting to appear a certain way, but the reality was that I never quite succeeded. Like my hair. I'd spent more than twenty minutes before leaving work trying to perfect a sideswept ponytail, but once I got to class, I felt self-conscious, sure that I appeared as though I'd forgotten to tie the other half. That was when our instructor, Air (whose name used to be Arielle when she taught boxercize), announced that the yoga studio was transforming into a surfer-cize studio to "get us in shape for surfing season."

I pulled my legs together and hugged my knees to my chest. It didn't surprise me that Miss Fit was swapping yoga for the next new trend; the whole reason Olivia, Mitz and I had started doing yoga in the first place was because our memberships to the boxercize classes were still valid when the studio decided to reinvent itself. What surprised me was that the studio thought anybody in Toronto needed to get fit to surf, given that the city bordered on the most polluted of the Great Lakes and that swimming in it was about as healthy as fat-free candy or chewing tobacco.

But the real problem was that I didn't want to stop doing yoga. Even though I had in no way mastered it, I wasn't ready to give up. In all my fitness years, it had been boredom that had led me to quit, not failure. How was I going to get better at yoga, or bond with my friends, if we no longer had a place to practice our *pranayamas*? I felt like the air was being sucked out of me.

"Maybe it's time for a change," Olivia mused aloud (which meant she was in the process of making a decision for the three of us) once we were in the locker room. She slipped out of her stretch capris and into her designer jeans. She was a size 2 but always had to buy larger sizes because she was so tall, then alter them to fit her twenty-four-inch waist. It was hard to feel sorry for her, even though I'd been asked to for years.

"You know, this place isn't as convenient as it used to be when we all lived and worked nearby," she said.

Even if Olivia no longer lived in the apartments above the yoga studio as she had when we joined, she still worked only two subway stops—a ten-minute walk—south at the offices of the Bay department store. And Mitz still lived in College Park (the apartments kitty-corner to the studio), though I supposed she'd soon be moving over to King West (right near Olivia once again), where her fiancé, Amir (who'd proposed just days earlier), lived in a townhouse. Still, it was hardly inconvenient for them, and it was as convenient as it ever had been for me.

"Why don't we do our own thing for the summer, and find a new studio for the fall?" Olivia suggested, pulling her long blonde hair back into a new ponytail and smoothing non-existent fly-aways. "There's a cute little studio near my place that offers rooftop yoga all summer long. I might give that a try."

I stuffed my shorts and T-shirt into my yoga bag. Olivia patted my hand and pointed at the ground, where I'd dropped my sports bra in a puddle.

Mitz slipped on her stylish, if somewhat sensible, Cole Haan pumps and nodded.

"Sounds good. I really need the summer to plan the wedding anyway, since I don't want to be traipsing around Niagara-on-the-Lake in the winter, knee-deep in snow, trying to find the best place for photos and a reception. I'll likely just take the summer off and resume in the fall. By that time I can see whether I've lost the necessary ten pounds from stress alone. If I have, maybe I won't need to work out ever again," she added with a laugh.

If Mitz needed to lose ten pounds, I needed to lose twenty. At least.

"What about meeting for tea?" I asked.

Olivia grabbed her green-and-blue version of the argyle yoga bag Mitz had made for both of us last Christmas and slung it over her shoulder.

"Let's be flexible, okay?" she said.

I felt crushed.

I followed my two best friends, Mitz Moretti and Olivia Closson, out of the purple pod and across the street to the little tea shop on College we'd met at every Tuesday even before joining Miss Fit during our boxercize phase. Over the years, we'd moved through *20 Minute Workout* reruns in the early '90s to step classes in our university years, and dabbled in Pilates and Body Pump trends, but we'd always gone for tea afterward.

Mitz ordered her usual—Lemon Peppermint Bliss—which she claimed soothed her ulcer, and moved aside.

"Did I tell you I'm testing out new cleaning products?" she announced. For Mitz, this was a big deal, considering she cleaned some portion of her apartment daily. "Now that I'll be moving into Amir's place, I've got a whole new range of surface textures and woods that I need to accustom myself to." Although this was big news for Mitz (so she *would* be moving to King West), I decided my own news was big enough to justify the abrupt change of subject.

At home and on the way to yoga, I'd rehearsed how to announce it. Version one involved a pity-inducing soliloquy about how Sam was a selfish jerk who'd left with all the furniture but without a word of explanation. Version two featured me as the dynamic dumper who'd seen that Sam wasn't right for me, that we had different life goals, and I was so relieved to have my personal time and space back after giving it up for the past year. Both were big proclamations, but I settled on neither and mumbled out a terse, pathetic mix of the two: "Sam left."

Olivia looked sufficiently alarmed, which made me feel a bit better, though I had to wonder how alarmed she'd look if she also knew I was sleeping on a futon.

"For good?" she asked. Just as I nodded, she declared confidently, "He was never right for you," though I felt that what she really meant was that he wasn't right for her, since she'd never liked him.

Mitz nodded in agreement, but seemed to be paying more attention to the plastic honey container she was holding. She gave it a squeeze to coerce a trace of liquid down toward the spout. I wished she'd give me a squeeze instead. I felt like I needed it. Part of me just wanted to cry, but I had to keep remembering that any jerk who would take my bed was not boyfriend-worthy. Thinking of the bed was the only thing keeping me angry—instead of just sad—about the breakup.

"You know, that's why I'm so glad I never lived with a guy before getting engaged," Mitz stated in her casual way, as though she was revealing her plans to make linguini for dinner. "It's just such a hassle if you break up," Mitz continued, in effect moving on to the cons of marinara sauce (it stains) rather than Alfredo sauce (it doesn't). "It's like going through a divorce without the ring or the alimony." She shook her head for effect, then picked up her mug of tea. Olivia ordered a Numi Red Mellow Bush (a blend I couldn't even begin to understand) and followed Mitz to find a table. For the first time in months, I'd had the chance to make a noteworthy contribution to the conversation, and the discussion was over before I'd even ordered my tea.

After changing my mind three times, I pointed at a random tea jar on the counter, and waited as the Buddy Holly–type counter guy in a brown "Don't Hassel the Hoff" T-shirt prepared my lapsang souchong in a Styrofoam cup, explaining that they were out of ceramic mugs. I took a sip and spit it back into the cup. It tasted like a forest fire. I grabbed a few packets of sugar and went to find Olivia and Mitz.

Although the three of us had grown up in Niagara-on-the-Lake, a quaint town near the New York State border defined by the Shaw Festival (a theater company dedicated to the works of George Bernard Shaw and his contemporaries), Fort George and an abundance of tourists staying in an overabundance of bed-and-breakfasts, we were quite different.

I was the second and final child born to my parents, Catherine and Mitchell (aka Cookie and Mitch), who were also born in Niagara-on-the-Lake. They met in the fourth grade, married after the twelfth and became teachers at the only public high school in town. Life was simple and uncomplicated in our three-story white colonial house with the wraparound porch and rocking bench. There was comfort in knowing that each day started with oatmeal and brown sugar, and ended with defrosted chicken breasts tossed in homemade bread crumbs, accompanied by wax beans and Tater Tots—or some minor variation. Now, of course, my parents went to Tim Hortons in the morning and ordered Pizza Pizza on Saturday nights. But back then, in the mid-'80s, it was different.

In comparison, Olivia and Mitz were worldly.

Mitsuko Moretti was half-Japanese, half-Italian, and was the eldest child in her family (four sisters and one brother). She grew up in Niagara Falls (arguably the Italian capital of Ontario) where Mitsuko became known as Mitz. By the time she was eleven, they had settled in Niagara-on-the-Lake, and she joined the girls' softball league in town the summer before we entered the sixth grade. Since our team (Pinky's Pizza Pink Flamingoes) was the worst in the league, it prided itself on accepting any new players regardless of their ability to throw, let alone identify a softball in a lineup at SportChek. Mitz and I bonded over Grape Crush and the boys' team that practiced on the field after us.

Mitz had naturally wavy, deep cranberry hair, olive eyes and skin that made her look tanned even in winter. In a word, she was mesmerizing. When I didn't look in a mirror to compare myself with her (I had the same beige-brown hair then that I have now, neither curly nor straight, that cowlicked the circumference of my overly-large-for-an-eleven-year-old head, and the same pale and blotchy freckled skin that burnt within seconds), I couldn't get enough of being around her. By the time the September school bell rang at Our Lady of Fatima, we were best friends.

That same summer I met the Clossons, a Dutch family comprised of Olivia Closson and her mother, Sally, a real estate agent who, upon hearing that the Niagara-on-the-Lake market was hot, had packed up their clogs and bicycles and had moved them into a decrepit estate house, abandoned for more than a decade, right on the Niagara River and across the street from us on Willow Lane.

Olivia was the only child of a single mother who'd decided at twenty-one that she wanted a baby, traditions aside. Having grown up herself without a father, Sally Closson couldn't be bothered with having one involved in raising her own daughter, which seemed to be more common now, but wasn't quite so much in the '70s, except for Cher in *Mermaids*—and that film had come out in 1990.

Apart from their long, naturally straight and buttery blonde hair, Sally and Olivia could've been Cher and Winona, because of Sally's blithe ways and Olivia's incessant need to agonize over every minor detail and to keep her mother in check when she became too erratic. As Niagara's top real estate agent, Sally was constantly hosting open houses, so Olivia, Mitz and I ate our way through that first summer, devouring shish-kebabbed hors d'oeuvres while fawning over the pages of *YM* magazines, deciding which boy (Corey Haim or Corey Feldman) we would date and planning our fall wardrobes (often inspired by Alyssa Milano).

Although Sally was Niagara's top agent (with *Sally Sells!* bus-stop benches to remind us), she could hardly afford to send Olivia to private school. But she did anyway, insisting that life was all about appearances and if you didn't act the part, you'd never get the role. So Olivia took a bus each morning to Sandy Acres, a private grade school, and then to Dunfield College, a boarding high school (where she was a day student), and Mitz and I graduated from Fatima to Niagara High School—home of the Niagara Newts. But the three of us stayed friends through it all, evolving from eating ice cream on our bikes to working at the Avondale Dairy Bar, where we scooped strawberry ice cream into sugar cones and then scooped dates with the boys who worked the banana split station. But if Olivia and Mitz were the ice cream and the chocolate sauce, I was the bowl that cradled our friendship and held us all together. The one that kept us friends.

Then something changed. I suppose, if I look back, the changes had just been waiting to happen. Mitz went from playing sports to playing the happy housewife long before she was set to be one, making sushi and spaghetti noodles from scratch in the second kitchen in the basement of her parents' home, and Olivia evolved from decorating her bedroom with boy-band posters held up with strawberry Bubble Yum to sewing window treatments and sticking faux marble tiles on the moldy bathroom floors of homes her mother was preparing to sell on the Niagara real estate market.

When we all moved to Toronto for college (Olivia and Mitz enrolled at George Brown College for interior decorating and culinary arts, respectively, and I joined 2,500 students in the department of geography at the University of Toronto), Olivia found us an adorable apartment near the university in the Annex, an older neighborhood that mixed single-family homes, frat houses and duplexes divided into student apartments, but my parents insisted I get my bearings by first living in a dorm. By the time I convinced them to let me move in with the girls, it was third year and Olivia and Mitz—OM— were well established. They had schedules for bathroom cleaning, meal preparation, boyfriend sleepovers and even their menstrual cycles, which coincided with guilt-free Sun Chip binges.

"You're better off," Olivia said now, as I sat down on the third stool, equidistant from Mitz and Olivia at the round stainless steel table by the window. I placed my cup and white sugar packets on the shiny, spotless surface, surprised that my situation was still top of mind.

Olivia didn't believe in marriage. She thought it was full of anti-feminist values. But she did believe in the social benefit of coupledom, and was a strong advocate of common-law marriage. As a buyer in the home decor section of the Bay (home to the most popular wedding registry in Canada), Olivia had honed her anti-marriage philosophy and had several theories, one of which was that most people got married so they could get free gifts and snag a large discount on anything they wanted to purchase for themselves. Since she also believed that no woman would ever get the engagement ring she actually wanted out of her man, she decided last year to purchase her own 2.3-carat Tiffany Lucida solitaire and live common-law with her boyfriend, Johnnie Cutter, an aspiring musician who'd auditioned for MTV's *Making the Band*, only he hadn't made the band.

Mitz, on the other hand, had gotten engaged to Amir Summers, a thirty-nine-year-old dentist with dull eyes and gleaming veneers that he whitened nightly (an act that was completely unnecessary and the reason why Olivia and I secretly called him "Amirror").

"This will give you time for *you*," Olivia went on. She extracted her tea bag from her mug by artfully looping the string over her spoon and squeezing any excess moisture from the bag before resting it on a side plate, which she'd apparently picked up for precisely that purpose. "Men are so demanding. Now you're free to accomplish all of your own goals instead of being inconvenienced by their insensitive inclinations and putting up with their shortcomings."

She illustrated her point by describing the latest debacle with Johnnie, which involved guitar picks in the washing machine, socks on the sofa (when his feet weren't in them) and listening to his latest anxiety (that his lack of height was hindering his musical career; apparently, all real rock stars could've been basketball players, if only they'd been sporty). When she finished her discourse, she pointed at my tea, to which I was in the process of adding a second sugar packet in the hopes of making it more of a smoky sugar bush than a full-on forest fire.

"You shouldn't drink out of Styrofoam, Mara," Olivia said, looking disdainfully at my disposable cup. "For one, it's bad for the environment, and two, it secretes all types of toxins. You'll never get pregnant, and if you do, your child will have two penises—regardless of the sex."

The word "sex" only reminded me that I wouldn't be getting any anytime soon.

"Right. Thanks for the tip." I tore the second empty packet into tiny pieces and placed them in a neat pile beside my evil cup.

Mitz took a sip of her tea, then nonchalantly explained that if tea is brewed properly it should be perfect as is and shouldn't need sugar, milk or honey, whereupon Olivia reminded me that sugar has thirty calories in just two teaspoons and I'd have to do thirty sun salutations just to burn that amount off. I wished I'd just tossed the tea, Styrofoam cup and all, in the trash on the way to the table and avoided the topic altogether. Although I was sure there was some sort of composting-equivalent program to prevent Styrofoam from degrading the environment, I had no defense against the queens of etiquette and cuisine.

"You can really focus on your career now," Olivia said. I hadn't made the connection between getting dumped and getting a new career, but, of course, Olivia would think about things like that—which was why she was making nearly six figures between her day job and her hobby of buying, remodeling and selling condo units as she moved around the city. She'd also been asked to guest lecture at her alma mater on more than a handful of occasions, less than five years after graduating. I could hardly say the same, though it wasn't surprising that my own alma mater didn't look to me as a practicing geography expert, given that I was working as a receptionist at a cosmetic surgery clinic.

"You should decorate," Olivia was now saying. "I've got some great ideas I've been wanting to try out, but you know, I keep running out of space to try new schemes."

"Or throw a dinner party," Mitz interjected. "I find that's the best ego booster when I'm feeling down."

Of course she did. She was a personal chef whose ideal downtime was spent cooking, followed by cleaning and doing laundry. She was a wife and mother just waiting to happen.

"But the most important thing to remember is that you will find another guy who will love you—the new and improved you—and you won't be alone." Mitz patted my hand.

"There's absolutely nothing wrong with being alone," Olivia reminded both of us, though I couldn't remember the last time she was boyfriendless. "But a dinner party is still a good idea. You could use your new roaster," she added, nodding, and in doing so caught sight of her watch, took a final sip of her tea and stood up. "I've got to run. I'm interviewing a new house cleaner at seven."

There was, apparently, nothing wrong with the cleaning skills of Olivia's current house cleaner (aka cleaning lady to most people, but Olivia refused to perpetuate the stereotype that only women were capable of cleaning homes for a living, even though she'd yet to hire a cleaning man), but apparently the current cleaner had high demands that weren't sitting well with Olivia.

"I am more than happy to stock the kitchen and let her help herself to whatever she likes—fruit, bagels, salad, biscotti— but to blatantly ask me to pick up specific items like white cranberry and peach juice and Perrier when there's San Pellegrino and orange juice right there in the fridge just seems ridiculous."

"Why don't you tell her she has to bring her own beverages?" I asked.

"Because—you can never be sure about manual labor. For all I know, she could smile and agree, then spit in my soy milk."

Olivia brushed a non-existent strand of hair off her forehead. "I just need to find someone with both manners and attention to detail. Is that too much to ask?"

Is it too much to clean your own condo? I thought as Mitz stood up, too.

"I'll come with you," Mitz said. "I've got to pick up the Save the Date cards for the wedding at Paper Ideas."

"Already?" I asked. She'd been engaged only three days, and the wedding was still a year away.

"Olivia said I should send them out immediately," Mitz said, looking to Olivia for confirmation.

"Definitely. It's only proper etiquette not to give your guests last-minute notice for a summer wedding. Plus," Olivia added, "the sooner you send the Save the Dates, the sooner you'll be able to redo your kitchen with all the new accessories you registered for."

"Good point," Mitz said, then turned to me. "And while I plan my wedding, you can plan your dating strategy. You could use my wedding as a target. If you start now, you might time things just right to have a new guy propose to you at my wedding."

"Or not," Olivia said. "Mara doesn't need a guy to be complete. I certainly hope you don't think that I'm who I am because of Johnnie." She turned to me. "Just think of all the things you could accomplish now that you're a free, empowered woman."

I looked back and forth at them as Olivia patted my hand. "I'll call you tomorrow and make sure that you're on track," she said to me. "Remember, I know what's best for you."

Mitz gave me a quick kiss on the cheek. "We're here for you, and we'll help you get through this. Just remember, even if you do meet a rich guy on the way home and fall madly in love"—she waved her finger at me—"no getting married before July 21 even if he tries to fly you to Vegas. I don't want anybody trying to steal my bouquet, so to speak!" Mitz laughed and Olivia joined in. I had to wonder if they were laughing at Mitz's joke-with-truth or at the ridiculousness of the possibility that I would meet a man and fall madly in love when I had just been unsuccessful at securing the guy I'd dated for nearly a year—which was definitely a sufficient amount of time when a girl is twenty-eight and a guy is thirty.

I stood in front of the tea shop, watching Olivia and Mitz as they turned to walk south back to the corner of Yonge and College to grab a cab together, yoga bags slung over their shoulders. Mitz was like a tiny, perfect housewife doll in a floral Ann Taylor Loft skirt and cream twin set with even creamier pearls, a gift from her grandmother when she turned twenty-one. Her fake but reasonable-length acrylic nails and her perfect, naturally wavy hair, enhanced with rollers every morning to make each curl more precise, made her classic and classy.

Olivia, by comparison, was just short of five-foot-nine in sneakers, which she wore only to yoga or while out running, making her five-foot-eleven the rest of the time in one of her signature pairs of Christian Louboutin heels.

Olivia was adamant about not altering her appearance for a man, but that was a cinch for her since there was nothing that needed altering. Everything about her appeared to be effortlessly chic, from her chemical-free long blonde hair that hung without a single kink even hours after being tied back in an elastic, to the two-hundred-dollar tank tops she could wear without a bra, to the Prada sunglasses she sported while driving her silver Saab 9-3. She didn't really exercise, but she was also prepared to skip breakfast if it meant she could fit into the last pair of Seven jeans at a sample sale. She had a year-round tan, thanks to lunch hours spent shopping on shabby-to-chic Queen West and winters split between Under the Tuscan Sun Bed tanning salon and last-minute trips to Johnnie's mother's current residence, a beachfront property on Venice Beach where she was living with her fourth husband.

Although Olivia refused to marry Johnnie and claimed to be an independent, unmotherly type, I had to think she liked having a guy who didn't make as much money as she did, and who needed her to take care of him, both emotionally and financially—which she did seemingly without effort. Both boutiques and banks sent her holiday cards, which she'd hang over the mantel of the latest condo she'd purchased—she was on her third since graduation and was currently seeking out a fourth. Each one had netted a heftier profit than the last, thanks to the cosmetic upgrades she'd done herself.

How did my two best friends—the girls I'd once done everything with at the same time, from getting our ears pierced to getting our periods—get so far ahead of me and so sure of themselves? Okay, so they had their differences. Mitz was a traditionalist. Although she had a very good career, being a chef and caterer only better prepared her to cook meals for her family-to-be in her future role as a full-time housewife and mother. And while Olivia might not make pesto from scratch, she knew which of the city's caterers did. In the end, their dinner parties were both successes, each in their own way. And while Mitz might wait for a man to open a door and Olivia would open it herself, they both knew which door needed to be opened—the one that led them right to the next opportunity, whether it was a new client, a new promotion or a new, better, more beautifully decorated home.

I looked down at my split ends, my chipped nail polish and the thin layer of brown cat fur that didn't blend into my blue sweater vest. Where my friends were decisive, strong and perfect, I was indecisive, weak and so full of flaws that I didn't even know which to start fixing first.

I thought about this as I made my way west on College, through the hospital district to the base of the university campus, where students filled patios and emptied their beer steins. I walked along the edge of Chinatown to Little Italy, the most romantic neighborhood in the city, where couples strolled after intimate dinners, stopping on the sidewalk for gelato or a spontaneous kiss. A community made for coupledom. A place I no longer belonged.

I opened the door to my basement apartment, and Pumpernickel jumped down from the window ledge in the kitchen, galloped over to my feet and reached up to put his paws on my thighs. I dropped my brown-and-orange argyle yoga bag and reached down to pick him up. I carried him into the bedroom, grabbed a notebook and pen from under the futon and then returned to the roaster box, where I sat, putting Pumpernickel at my feet, which he sniffed and then flopped on top of.

If my friends were perfect and I was stuck in a rut, what I had to do was become more like them. I wasn't about to plagiarize them, but a little harmless imitation-as-flattery couldn't hurt.

I needed to start with our similarities and build from there, but as I thought about all of their accomplishments, I realized the only thing I had in common with my two best friends was the yoga class we had, until today, attended together. Getting better at yoga was a start—at least that way, when we joined a new club in the fall, anyone in the class watching us chant "Om" in unison might think that if we were at the same level in yoga, maybe we were at the same level in other areas. Maybe no one would ever know in how many ways I lagged behind my two best friends. But I wanted more than that. I wanted to *be* just as good as they were at everything else in life.

And then I had an idea. Since I had nowhere to go but up, all I needed to do was create a list of the ideals that Olivia and Mitz embodied, the rules they lived by that made Olivia and Mitz—OM—so perfect, and then methodically implement the list, item by item. I would give myself a deadline and, I thought, suddenly feeling it all come together, a party at which I would have all my friends over to witness how much I had accomplished.

Which is how, four days after my twenty-eighth birthday, I put pen to paper, and came up with the OM list.

The OM List

By Mara Brennan

1. Get a perfect body.
2. Get a promotion or a real job.
3. Become a fabulous chef with my own unique dossier of recipes.
4. Keep an immaculately clean living space.
5. Unleash my inner decor diva on my apartment.
6. Improve my time-management and multi-tasking skills to appear busier to others and create an air of importance.
7. Become an etiquette expert so as not to embarrass myself in social situations.
8. Be well read and knowledgeable in order to engage in enlightening conversations.
9. Stop dressing in Gap and create my own signature style.
10. Throw a dinner party to display my accomplishments and the successful implementation of my OM list.

Chapter Two

KARMA YOGI: A PERSON WHO IS SELFLESSLY DEVOTED TO WORK.
The present state of work is a result of cause and effect, past
actions or inactions.

*F*ace Value Cosmetic Surgery Clinic (where I was not usefully
employed but employed nonetheless as a receptionist) was
located on Bloor Street East in the final row of businesses before
the rather desolate Bloor Street Viaduct with its suicide barriers,
erected to prevent depressives from jumping onto the Don
Valley Parkway below. At first glance, Face Value's address might
suggest that the place was located in the midst of both the crease-
less foreheads and the couture that comprised Bloor Street West
(Toronto's version of the Champs-Élysées). But it wasn't.

Most of the other lucrative cosmetic surgeons in the city
were tucked in behind Holt Renfrew (in the heart of Bloor
Street West shopping) in renovated Victorian brick houses or
inside Hazelton Lanes, a boutique-filled shopping complex.
Face Value was located on the wrong side of Yonge Street,
which acted as the meridian, dividing the city into a west side

and an east side. As far as Bloor Street was concerned, west was haute and east was hoax, but my boss and the owner of the clinic, Dr. Marjorie Wickham, liked it because the rent was cheap. Like her. And so, since opening more than five years ago, the clinic had occupied a unit on the second story of Goodluck Strip, or so I referred to it because good luck was what you needed to find anything decent for lunch (once you'd exhausted the five choices—Subway sandwiches, Starbucks, Swiss Chalet, Nijo Sushi and the Panzerotto Pizza joint) but also for the Goodwill used clothing store that acted as a hub for the homeless, unemployed and bored.

It was a lengthy walk from my apartment to work, but one I undertook every morning and every evening anyway, because it was free and because taking public transit meant walking south from my apartment to the streetcar on College, taking the streetcar over to Yonge Street, transferring to the subway to go north to Bloor, then changing subway lines to go east one stop to Sherbourne, all in all a feat that ended up taking just as long as walking the whole way. Walking also saved me $2.75 each way, and I got to wander through the Annex, and past Chanel, Cartier and Holt Renfrew on Bloor. Some nights I even stopped for kimchi fried rice at Ka-Chi in Koreatown. Through the uninteresting blocks, I usually attempted to devour the beauty pages of *Allure*, *Flare* or *Vogue*, while trying not to bump into telephone poles, newspaper boxes or parking meters. I figured it was good exercise, too, though it remained a mystery to me why I was still a size 10 after years of the twice-a-day trek.

Annie Markowitz called at 9:35 a.m., just as I was opening the door to the clinic. This involved using four different keys to unbolt four locks to the second-story office, which was located just above a street-level chotchke store that featured holiday ornaments in the front window display year-round. I lunged for the phone, fell into my chair and kicked off my shoes. Annie wanted to book another follow-up appointment to her third rhinoplasty, which she had had last month. Since the first surgery, she hadn't been able to breathe while lying down. This was a problem for obvious reasons, although Marjorie—who was also the cosmetic surgeon and only other employee of Face Value—said Annie was most upset because it meant she had to be on top whenever she was "making whoopee" (Marjorie's words, *not* mine). With a husband plus a boyfriend on the side, Annie wasn't pleased. Since neither Marjorie nor Annie wanted to have to redo the nose job, Annie came in once a week and Marjorie took a CT scan each time to see if things were getting any better.

"What's the latest appointment available tomorrow?" she asked.

I told her, penciled her in and started my morning routine, which I had down to a fine-tuned procedure (think mini-liposuction: ultra-thin cannulas leaving no marks and causing no downtime). I was technically paid to arrive and start this series of menial tasks at 9 a.m., but I could get everything done—coffee started, stereo turned on to pump elevator-music renditions of popular '80s theme songs from *L.A. Law* to *Family Ties* through the surround-sound speakers Marjorie's brother had set up last summer, mail sorted into six very specific and color-coded folders, and Marjorie's slightly burnt (just the way she liked it) coffee poured into her stained 97.3 EZ Rock mug—in less than half an hour and before she arrived at 10:03 a.m. So I usually aimed to be in the office by 9:30 a.m. And since I was making $15 an hour, starting half an hour late slightly increased my wage-per-hour ratio and made me somewhat less embittered that I was approaching my third anniversary working for a woman I despised.

I didn't have time for distractions before Marjorie arrived, so when the phone rang again, I debated not answering it, but did anyway because I could see by the caller ID it was Bradford. Distractions from friends were the jujubes of my working day, so although Marjorie puckered up at personal calls, I told him to hold while I started the coffee. Then I came back to talk to him, since I still had fifteen minutes to spare.

I met Bradford Lynch on a cruise ship the year after I graduated from university. Both of us were traveling with our grandmothers, who were widowed and happened to be friends from the Fonthill YMCA morning aquacize class. I agreed to accompany Grandma Gerta for several reasons, one of which was that I really liked her and not because I felt I had to, but more importantly because she chose me over my sister and had offered to pay. Given that I hadn't found a career that would do the same, I took her up on it.

After three days on the Caribbean Sea, while Grandma was at origami class on the lido deck, I headed to the fitness room for the first time. I was on the treadmill, wondering how long I had to walk to call it a workout, while watching a *Love Boat* rerun on the overhead TV, when tall and gangly Bradford, who had hands as big as his feet and was festooned in a blue Maple Leafs hockey jersey and burgundy-and-gold plaid flannel pants—managing to be overdressed (for the July heat) and underdressed (for a Princess Cruise Line) at the same time—

asked me if I had any lip balm. Although I wasn't attracted to him (for reasons obvious to any girl who doesn't wear Sorels with a sundress), I was thankful for an excuse—any excuse—to get off the treadmill. We went back to my room, where we divulged our mutual love for The Body Shop's Born Lippy lip balm. Later, we drank Bellinis and then bonded over napkin-folding classes for the same reason: the hot napkin-folding instructor, Dylan. Which is when I realized that Bradford was gay, despite his horrible fashion sense and love of hockey.

At first, Bradford tried to discourage me from being his friend. He warned me it wouldn't be good for my ratings, since he claimed that too often the single woman on the brink of fabulousness meets her downfall by getting wrapped up in a gay male friend. And he did not want us to be thrown in with the Bridget Jones and Tom, Will and Grace or Julianne and George in *My Best Friend's Wedding* couples of the world.

"The gay guy will be handsome, kind, wise, witty, fashion-savvy and the perfect boyfriend—if only he weren't gay. And the girl will lose all sense of self—and opportunity for dates—by relying too much on her gay friend, then complaining that she's going to die alone and near killing the gay friend with her incessant moaning until she snaps out of it. Count me out. I don't want to be responsible for your downfall, nor put up with the agony, which could last a good six months or more," Bradford had said to me.

Once I reminded Bradford that (as if his non-existent sense of style and my questionable fabulousness weren't clues) we weren't fictional characters in books, on the syndication circuit or the TBS movie of the weekend, he agreed that we could give friendship an audition once we debarked and got back to our lives in Toronto, where we both lived. He, in the heart of the gayborhood at Church and Wellesley, and me, in the Annex, where I was then sharing a second-floor apartment with Olivia and Mitz.

Five years, two fights and a million martinis and late-night bonding sessions later (often over Molly Ringwald movies, for which Bradford had a soft spot), Bradford was my confidant. Olivia and Mitz were still my best friends, but Bradford was the one with whom I could really be honest. He was the first person I had called on Monday night. After *it* happened.

"You can have my apartment," he now said on the phone. "I've called my landlord. It's a go. If I were straight, I'd tell you to bake me cookies in nothing but an apron as a thank-you, but alas, I'm not turned on by such frivolities. And I've been hypersensitive about hygiene lately. So please, fully clothed culinaration only."

"Cookies or not, I can't take your apartment," I told him. "I'm planning to clean my living space, and if I'm going to embark on a cleansing ritual, I want to do it to banish my own ill remains, not yours." Besides, moving was not an item on my OM list, and I wasn't convinced that Bradford wouldn't break up with his current boyfriend, Tobias Strolz, a hot Austrian decorator and pseudo-celebrity (with whom he lived in a house in High Park), and move back into his apartment on Isabella Street—otherwise, why was he still holding on to it? I told him so.

"I'm about to be the uncle of my own sperm baby. I hardly think that's the sign of a flighty relationship-goer." It was true. Tobias's sister was also gay, and she and her partner were about to have a baby—one that was conceived thanks to Bradford's sperm donation.

"I'm a creature of habit, you know that," Bradford went on. "I've had the same apartment for twelve years and the same boyfriend for three. I've gone to the same barber for eleven years and have had the same haircut for ten. I eat one hard-boiled egg and two apples for breakfast every morning, and I drink three cups of coffee every four hours throughout the day. I could go on, but then I'd just be getting into bowel movements, and I'm sure you don't want to hear about that."

If only I could be so sure of myself. But that wasn't the real issue. What concerned me most was that Bradford was constantly solving my problems for me, and if my goal was to become more like Olivia and Mitz, then I had to be adamant about refusing his handouts. He couldn't have been more the opposite of Olivia and Mitz (only one of the many reasons they made every effort to avoid each other), and I needed to avoid his influences.

Also, Bradford had given me his job at Face Value, and paycheck (and ability to pay my rent) aside, I don't think I'd ever entirely forgiven him for it.

Four years ago, at the height of the guy-craze for butt implants, Bradford took a job as an accountant for Marjorie. But a few months into the job, Bradford realized she had no interest in listening to him about her financial situation, and recognized his post as an overpaid, overly bored receptionist. When he couldn't settle for just the perks any longer (more than half of Marjorie's clients in the early millennium years were vain and lovely-looking gay men who made for great eye candy but who showed no interest in Bradford given his own lack of vanity), he quit to get a job on Bay Street, where the salary and the eye candy were better, even if the odds were slightly less favorable that the men were interested in him and not their female assistants. But not before Marjorie made him find and train his own replacement. He immediately asked me, since it was then two months since I'd quit a job as a teaching assistant in the geography program at U of T and was working in the travel section at an Indigo bookstore instead.

I agreed, thinking it would be temporary, until I found a real job in my field. High school guidance counselors should tell students that being a master of the Laurentien pencil crayons used to color maps in school—Peacock Blue, Deep Green and Photo Brown were key—did not lead to unlimited job possibilities.

And so, I was indebted to Bradford because, even though I hated my job, I'd been paid every two weeks for three years now. Which certainly helped out—particularly with food and shelter, if not with personal fulfillment.

About a month into the job, I had developed a love-hate relationship with cosmetic surgery. It was like squeezable cheese—obscure in concept, but strangely enticing. I'd never get it done, and I didn't agree with it, but I recognized that it was a lucrative business. And as far as being a doctor went, I could see why they'd rather suck the fat out of a patient's thighs than listen to her moan about her arthritis.

The problem with my job was threefold: the pay was lousy, there was no room for advancement, and every time I tried to succeed I just got more duties dumped on my to-do list. When I'd taken the job three years earlier, I was required to answer the phone, book appointments, clean treatment rooms after procedures and convince clients that no, their lips didn't look lopsided, and yes, DD was a perfectly reasonable breast size for a five-foot-two frame.

The extra duties were my own fault. A few days after I started, I made the mistake of bringing Marjorie back a grilled panini when I'd taken a long walk at lunch. Now, every time I left the office at lunchtime, Marjorie expected me to bring her back a takeout container of brown-rice hand rolls, yaki soba noodles or some other dish that required walking at least twenty minutes west on Bloor and back. She always repaid me, but it was the inconvenience and the chance that she might or might not like the lunch I chose for her—because while she enjoyed spicy tuna rolls she didn't like tuna sandwiches, and pad Thai was okay but any other dish made with glass noodles was not—that made the trek all the more unpleasant.

Just then, Marjorie Wickham bustled through the door, clanging the chimes overhead. I told Bradford I had to go, but not before agreeing that if I wouldn't take his apartment, I would at least let him buy me a Crummie cupcake at the Cupcake Shoppe, and he'd help me figure out how I was going to get a perfect body now that I didn't have a yoga studio to go to. I likely couldn't afford Olivia's rooftop yoga studio, given that our Miss Fit membership rates had been frozen since we joined, while out in the real world prices had no doubt climbed.

Marjorie fixed her marbly eyes on me, unleashed her Armani Exchange nautical silk scarf and flung it over the coat rack.

"Did you pick up the *Post?*"

Everything about Marjorie was a little too cheap 'n' chic for the cosmetic surgery world, from the signature Armani scarf she wore every day (around her neck in the summer and over her black, wash-and-wear haircut in the winter) to the free *National Post* newspaper she made me pick up at Timothy's in the morning when I bought her a raisin bran muffin to go with the Nabob coffee. Then there was the reliable, four-door taupe Chevy Impala she drove down the street to the office (passing two Timothy's and fourteen *National Post* boxes on the mile-and-a-half route from her rundown, two-bedroom apartment on Madison Avenue, where she lived alone, a 47-year-old woman who'd never married or had a known date in the three years I'd worked for her—I booked her entire schedule, from haircuts to the hypnotherapy sessions that kept her from smoking, so I would know). But Marjorie knew her market, and it was all part of her business plan. These less-than-high-class details spoke louder than she did, saying: "If I were overcharging you for my services, I'd be wearing Hermès, lunching at the Four Seasons and driving a Mercedes."

Marjorie adjusted the tacky aquamarine-encrusted peacock brooch on her lapel, then smoothed what she probably thought was an edgy haircut but what always looked to me like bedhead. Then (sounding just like the white Shih Tzu she forced me to walk when her dogwalker was sick) the yapping started:

"Did Deirdre O'Donohue call yet with her Visa number because we've been holding that personal check for more than two weeks and I thought you told her that we can't accept her personal checks if they're going to bounce and I just saw her last night at Young's Flowers on Avenue buying a bouquet that costs more than a photo facial and I know she saw me so if she doesn't call then you can tell her that I'm not going to give her any more photo facial sessions and I don't care if her face is blotchy."

Marjorie didn't get the classiest clients in the city, but what they lacked in wealth, they made up for in pure volume. Instead of snagging the Bridle Path celebrities and Rosedale ladies who lunched, Marjorie got the working woman who was a little overweight, didn't wear much makeup and didn't have that much money but was willing to shell it out on a quick-fix tummy tuck instead of a gym membership.

I didn't actually know if Deirdre O'Donohue had called. She could have, but given that I'd been on the phone with Bradford, she could've been any one of the flashing lights I didn't answer. Really, the trouble with the phone system was that the call display worked only if you weren't on the phone, but not for second calls coming in when you were already talking to someone, which, unless Marjorie was standing right beside me, seemed to happen a lot.

"And the paper? Where is it? Apparently Eleanor Overholt got a full-page write-up about her practice this morning."

Truthfully, I hadn't picked up the *Post* because I hadn't had any cash in my wallet, and I didn't feel like paying a $1.50 debit charge to get Marjorie a $1.50 muffin just so she could get a free paper. Particularly when I never even afforded myself the luxury of an oversized slice of banana bread or cup of tea. So I said what I said whenever I didn't get the paper. "Sold out."

"Great. Well, there'd better be a drug bust or celebrity scandal. If those papers are selling out because of that damn article—" she paused and sniffed loudly, making a face. "Is something *burning*?"

I looked toward the kitchen, where I could see the coffee pouring down and sizzling on the empty burner. I'd left the carafe beside the sink.

I raced around the end of the desk and into the kitchen.

"For the love of injectables. Is it too much to ask that you pay attention to what you're doing? If I were as negligent as you, I'd be putting implants in people's asses instead of their chests."

I knew better than to offer a lame rebuttal. Instead, I tried to coax the hot coffee toward the sink with the dish cloth, but it was outrunning me, all over the counter and dripping down onto the floor.

"When you're done cleaning up that mess, come and get the files for April off my desk. You're already a week late in sending out invoices," she said. "And make a fresh pot of coffee. In the pot would be a nice touch."

"You bet," I chirped with the enthusiasm of a liposuctioned patient about to have a latte.

Marjorie gave the coffeemaker her scalpel stare and then looked down at my feet, which I remembered were shoeless.

"Are we wearing shoes anymore or is that too much to ask?" She didn't wait for an answer and continued on into her office. By the time I had a fresh pot of coffee ready, Marjorie was on the phone, yelling at her publicist, Didi Sky, a woman often even more overbearing than Marjorie but who still listened as Marjorie reamed her out when she was upset. As she clearly was now. Apparently, Marjorie had also seen Dr. Eleanor Overholt on *Talk Toronto* that morning, showing off a new laser machine and plugging her profile in the *Post*. Marjorie wanted to know what Didi was doing for her at that moment and, more importantly, what had been stopping Didi from getting her on *Talk Toronto* or talk radio or anywhere else that she could talk. About herself. And get more clients.

"Are you sick? Are you hurt? Are you dead? Am I hallucinating that Eleanor is getting *all* the publicity and *I* am getting nothing? Am I missing all the newspaper articles about me?

Are people secretly filming me while I'm working and I'm unaware that I'm being broadcast on the nightly news as the top surgeon that I am? Am I? Hello?"

I snuck out of her office, closing the door and breathing deeply. If she was hollering at someone else, then she wasn't hollering at me. At least for the moment. It was like a waiter telling you that they'd just served up the last of the side salad so you'd have to order fries—guilt-free!—as a side, I thought, as I logged on to the Internet and began my favorite pastime: online Windows shopping for beauty products. It always made me feel as good as the creams, lotions and potions promised I would look after using them.

While Marjorie was a whiz with laser machines, she had no patience for the Internet (her website consisted of her photo and the clinic's address, telephone number and e-mail address), so she was constantly hounding me every time she caught me online—I could hardly claim I was updating her site—which made surfing a challenge, but not an insurmountable feat.

Marjorie Wickham was like the cellophane-wrapped mint you got at the end of the meal. Even if it was white, you couldn't tell if it was going to be a chalky English mint or a stale Scotch. Or if, just maybe, it would be the kind with the chocolate center, even though you knew that the chocolate centers were only one out of every fifty mints you got—just like Marjorie's nice moments. The rest of the time she was simply different versions of menacing, chalky, stale and bitter. Still an icky mint.

Thankfully, most of the clients at Face Value were great, which I attributed to one of two scenarios that most of them seemed to fall into: if they'd been nice when they were ugly, they remembered what it was like back then and were still nice even though they were now prettified; if they'd been bitter when they were ugly, they were now happy to be pretty and so had had a personality turnaround.

In any case, clients were rarely in a bad mood. After all, would you be in a bad mood if you were in a candy store finding out you could have whatever candy you wanted—and not get fat or develop zits?

Seeing the confidence and joy Marjorie instilled (or injected) into her clients, and the way they acted after a treatment, was enough to boost me out of even the foulest mood. Even though I didn't really play a part in people's happiness, I also wasn't a target when things went wrong. And at Christmas and Easter, I usually went home with several boxes of Pot of Gold and Laura Secord.

Which is why my temporary job had gone on so long and why, as a size 10, I was always the chubbiest person to leave the clinic. Fatter people waddled into the clinic, sure, but they always left lighter, sucked down to at least a size 6.

My mother thought I was much more accomplished than I really was. Which worked in my favor not least of all in that she didn't often call me at work because she assumed I was much too busy to chatter. It wasn't that I didn't keep myself busy during the day, but it was mostly self-induced online browsing for beauty products (to which I admit I was slightly addicted), as opposed to actual office duties. I loved my mother—and my father—that goes without saying, but I sometimes found it hard to live up to her overwhelming positivity.

So when she called just before the end of the day, as I was virtually purchasing a container of Cake Beauty Satin Sugar (it promised to suck the grease right out of my hair, no water required, which was key given the unpredictability of hot water flow in my apartment), I wasn't surprised when she followed up her "Hi-hi!" chirp by telling me she had very exciting news to share.

I finished my transaction, popped a black jujube in my mouth, then googled yoga studios in Toronto as I cradled the phone between my ear and shoulder.

"Tell her the news, Cookie," my father interjected, apparently from another extension, "so we don't hold her up."

"Do you have an operation this afternoon?" my mother asked. "What is it?"—she lowered her voice—"Foobies?"

I couldn't get upset with my mother, whose cluelessness at thinking my schedule was at all affected by Marjorie's surgeries was endearing, as was her use of my lingo for fake boobs in an attempt to be cool. My mother wasn't dumb. She taught high-school physics and chemistry for years, and when she took early retirement she got a degree in art history before starting her own business. My mother knew I wasn't a surgeon, but sometimes she seemed to believe I had a lot more responsibility than I really did. She was constantly asking me about in-store appearances with Marjorie as though I, and not Didi Sky, was her publicist. Although it was sweet that my mother thought my job was so important, I sometimes wished she would realize what was really going on—that I worked at a job I hated, using absolutely no skills I had acquired during university and getting paid poorly to do it. It sometimes made me sad and lonely that she didn't understand, and I wondered whether

I'd be better off if she did realize just how unsuccessful I was. Maybe she'd offer me a job in her business, which was a local success story.

I told my mother no, that the office was quiet and I was just doing some research—not a lie, I thought, since I *was* researching yoga studios (though it was hardly work-related). Still, if I was going to get a perfect body, I needed to continue working out. While it would've been easier to just quit yoga altogether, there was something that was keeping me interested. Perhaps it was my tendency to catch on to trends years after they were first popular (I'd started watching *Seinfeld* only when it went into syndication, and hadn't bought pedal pushers until they were known as capris). But maybe it was something more, though I wasn't sure what.

"You sound overworked," my father said, then made a noise he reserved for two occasions: when he'd tasted a new flavor of cookie my mother had made, or when he was feeling sorry for me. I knew he was on the extension in the basement. He spent his afternoons there, on the computer, while my mother bustled around the kitchen with *Wok with Yan* reruns playing on the mini TV on the shelf where the microwave used to sit until she read that microwaves could harm an unborn child. With my sister being the successful child-bearer for years and my mother's hopes for my ability to procreate still not dashed, she'd sold the microwave at the street yard sale a few years ago.

"But you're enjoying it, right?" he added, as always. It was both sweet and the reason I could never tell them how exactly the opposite was true.

My parents have always loved whatever job they've had at any given time in their lives. And because of that, they wanted to believe that I loved mine. I could see their point. Doing something you loved was a priority to them. They'd never traveled outside of the country, and they'd never eaten at a four-star restaurant. But they were absolutely happy because they'd never had jobs where they'd had to count the days until the weekend, or work overtime so that they could go on vacation. If they figured they hadn't passed down to me the concept of doing what you loved, then they'd have thought they'd failed, in part, as parents. And I couldn't bear that.

"Well, I hope you're still going out with that handsome boyfriend of yours. What are your plans in the big city for Friday night?" my mother asked.

I couldn't remember the last time I'd made plans for a Friday night on a Wednesday, but more importantly I couldn't recall the last time I had Friday night plans at all. But that was lost on my parents, who, until it went off the air, religiously watched the *Electric Circus* dance party while sipping mugs of warm milk with cinnamon sticks, thinking they would catch a glimpse of me shaking my butt and making them proud.

I didn't want to disappoint them, but I didn't want to lie, so I said, "Oh, I'll probably just have a quiet night in," which was the truth, given that I didn't have cable anymore (Sam had canceled it before he left, since he'd been the one paying for it). What I wasn't telling them, which was slightly more significant than not having cable, was that I didn't have Sam anymore.

"Well, Cookie, get on with it," my dad interrupted.

"Right-o! So, we've got big news," my mother said. I wasn't surprised, since even the arrival of the mail gives my mother an adrenaline rush. "I'm putting your father to work."

"Homer, too," my father added, referring to his red Honda Odyssey.

"I thought Dad had a job," I said, mostly to chastise my mother, who left him a daily list of chores (which seemed to focus mostly on finding spots for my mother's dollar-store stash and removing spots from the rarely used silverware). He completed these tasks between trips to and from St. Mary's elementary school as a short-bus driver, a part-time gig he had picked up after taking early retirement from teaching a few years earlier.

"He's going to be the man about town," my mother continued.

"The man with the van," my dad boomed.

"The man with the cookie van," my mother added.

"Very exciting times," my father concluded. "Mrs. Higgins is going to have some stiff competition."

"I thought Mom already *was* her stiff competition." In fact, I thought my mother was Mrs. Higgins' only competition, aside from store-bought Oreos.

The previous year, my mother had started Cookie's Cookie Bouquets—a tribute to my father, who'd called my mother "Cookie" since their first date in the sixth grade, when she baked him a chocolate-chip cookie in the shape of an M for Mitch.

Unfortunately for my mother, she didn't realize that cookie bouquets had peaked in popularity in 1993. Fortunately, neither did many of the aging residents in the Niagara region, so my mother's business had been a sweet success so far.

Now, my mother explained, she was going to be so busy baking—as a result of her new marketing plan—that she wouldn't have time to make deliveries, which was where my father came in.

"We're going to paint the van pink!" she said, clearly thrilled.

"And the town red," my father added with a chuckle.

"While taking away the blues," my mother added. I was about to interject (my parents could go on like this for longer than a lipo session), but my mother moved on to explain to me her well-baked strategy.

"Mrs. Higgins only focuses on the good times. And with our aging community, there are a lot of sad times. And sad times are especially when people need to be cheered up—with cookie bouquets!" Her excitement was escalating. "So I'm going to focus on the sad times. I've made a list," she said. "Do you want to hear it?"

"Of course," I told her, unsure what this list would involve—types of cookies, ingredients, people who were about to die . . .

"First, there are the unfortunate events: getting in a car accident, getting dumped by your steady, breaking your arm, getting carpal tunnel syndrome. You know, that's quite a serious concern with the theater workers."

"Really," I commented, wondering what these theater workers were doing to get carpal tunnel syndrome—handing out programs too swiftly?

"Then there are losses that are deaths: losing a parent, losing a child, losing a best friend. And there are the losses that are unfortunate, but not life threatening: losing your keys, losing your job. The best part is that your father is creating cards to go along with the cookies. He's come up with a template, such as 'Sorry for the loss,' and then we just have to add—"

"Of your pet?" I suggested, knowing how my mother liked it when I was on the same Brennan brainwave as her.

"Exactly!"

"How are you making the cards, Dad?" I asked skeptically, because when my mother had launched Cookie's Cookie Bouquets she'd made her own stickers for the boxes on the relic dot-matrix printer until my sister ordered shiny round stickers for her from a stationery store in Toronto.

"On the Apple IIc," my mother answered assertively. "You remember that program we got you the year Victoria got her retainer and you cut off that big chunk of hair in the back because you had a cowlick?"

Of course I remembered. It was the same year I was cast as Alfalfa in my school's *Little Rascals* Christmas spectacular. Given the unusually high ratio of boys to girls in my fifth grade class, it was not a coincidence.

"Print Shop?" I asked. I couldn't believe the green-screen Apple IIc still worked.

"Yes! Well, your father was cleaning out his office in the basement and he came across it. Gosh, we'd forgotten all about it, hadn't we? There was still paper in the box! What a lucky find."

"Wasn't that paper orange?" I could still recall the card Victoria gave me the year I turned ten. "Double digits? Double Wow!" And the cards we'd made our parents: "Orange you glad . . . to have a daughter like me?" My sister always personalized the back of the card with an insignia that read "Queen Cards. Fit for a queen." But nobody regal ever had the name Mara, so my cards were always blank on the back.

"And some of the losses have double meanings," she went on. "Losing a child."

"Like in the grocery store?" I wasn't sure who was going to send cookies in such an instance, but my mother was open to opportunities.

"The trick is to be able to get orders out within an hour, which is where your father comes in."

"I'll be so speedy—"

"Now, not too speedy, Mitchell," she said in a tsk-tsk sing-song voice.

"The speed limit, of course."

"We've already got a tall order. The second grade class at St. Stephen's lost their turtle."

"Physically or spiritually?"

"Both. Getting stuck under the rad for the weekend didn't prolong his life. They found him dead Monday morning. I'm going to make shortbread turtle-shaped cookies for the class."

"Sounds great."

"Anyway, we should let you get back to work—"

Just as they were about to cut me off, I figured I'd better tell them about Sam. I needed their sympathy if I was going to hit them up for rent money.

"Oh, Mara..." My mother said with disappointment, her voice trailing off. I could actually hear her shaking her head, presumably because she was wearing her signature dangly, shellacked cookie earrings.

"Do you think he'll change his mind? Or maybe there's something you can do to win him back? I mean, surely this isn't final."

Of course it was. Sam had left me because I was defective at the wife level. I had capped out at girlfriend.

"It's okay, Mom. I'm not going to be a spinster." Though I had to admit, living in a basement apartment with a cat got me closer to spinsterhood than being listed in any guy's black book.

"Of course you're not. I'm just saying, you're twenty-eight. This is your year."

My mother was full of monumental moments: the hour she gave birth to me (though I'm sure she told my sister the same thing); the day she bought her first pair of heels; the second my father asked her to marry him; the year she had a great haircut for eleven consecutive months; the minute she discovered how to make cookies in her slow cooker. But above all, her most monumental of all moments was the day she turned twenty-eight because every day after that was near perfect. Her whole life fell into place. She had a full-fledged family (two daughters and a pet rabbit), a nice home with furniture in each room, a job she loved and a garden with a goldfish-filled pond. Since my sister's twenty-eighth year had also been a grand success (though she'd been faultless, as her name implied, since birth, so I couldn't say for sure which of her years had been less than perfect), my mother only expected that I, too, would be blessed by the good fortune of this Brennan tradition.

But I was learning I wasn't my mother, and I definitely wasn't my sister. At this point I probably needed to pick up the pace if I hoped to stay one step ahead of my niece and nephews' talents.

Although Victoria was seven years older, she had always achieved everything at an earlier age than I had, rather than vice versa, as is common with two sisters. She'd started walking sooner, talking sooner, and riding a bike and learning to drive at a younger age than I had. She'd kissed a boy sooner and had made the honor roll every year of high school (I got high enough marks only in my final year, when it mattered). She'd even gotten her period earlier than I had.

Now, she was a perfect wife, a mother of three—Aidan, nine, Stansmith, seven, and Serena, three—and a lawyer, though she was too busy to actually practice. She was president of the PTA at the private school both Aidan and Stansmith attended, sat on the board of the children's hospital and went for Zen shiatsu and Qigong Beauty Rejuvenation Energy Facelifts twice a week, all of which took up so much time that she had to employ in her palatial Bloor West Village home both a full-time nanny and a cleaning lady (unlike Olivia, Victoria wasn't averse to gender-specific titles). She didn't need to work, though, since her husband, George (formerly known as Big G to his football buddies at Queen's University, where Victoria met him), was one of the top lawyers in the city and preferred to be the bread- and case-winner of the household.

Ten minutes later, I was fairly certain I'd convinced my mother that I would survive, boyfriend or not, and by the time I'd hung up and was ready to leave work for the day, I'd actually convinced myself that I'd manage, too.

Unfortunately, my mother and father seemed to believe one of three things: that I made more money than I did, that the television reporters had it wrong and the cost of living was not as sky-scraping ridiculous in Toronto as the media claimed (even if one wasn't living in a skyscraper), or that I really had learned how to budget from the days when they paid me thirty-five cents a week to clean my room. So they didn't insist that I move, or even ask how I'd be able to afford double the rent now that Sam was gone.

Maybe they'd just been distracted from the practical aspects of the breakup by the overwhelming excitement I'd projected about my prospective dinner party. Perhaps I'd done *too* good a job convincing them that I'd soon have skills—from hosting to culinary—to showcase at my summer soiree. A soiree that would help me usher out the old (rather useless) Mara and welcome in the new, improved and self-sufficient (not to mention sassy) Mara.

After I got off the phone, I realized I'd just made my OM list real by sharing some of its items with my parents, and that if I was going to follow through with my plan, right down to actually hosting a dinner party, I should make sure I had some guests. It seemed to me that if I was going to work hard to complete the OM list, then the ideal time to showcase the effects of my self-induced workload was on a day of rest, which is how I came to decide that the Saturday of the civic holiday weekend in August would be the perfect day. I searched EmilyPost.com and eHow.com to see if there were any etiquette rules on how far in advance you should send invites, but the varied answers justified flexibility, and, given that Mitz was sending Save the Date cards for an event more than a year away, I decided there was nothing wrong with sending my invites now, even if the party was nearly two months away. Everyone knew summer was the busiest season for social events, and if I wanted a good turnout I needed to give my guests time to plan.

After work, I walked to Yorkville and headed to the Papery to purchase invitations. Once I determined that a pre-engraved invitation would set me back the equivalent of a day's work, I decided that simple, blank cards would be just perfect, and would still allow me a budget to actually buy supplies for my dinner party.

While waiting for Bradford to show up for our cupcake date, I began filling out the invites by hand, using my favorite teal gel-ink pen and following the etiquette rules I'd printed from the Emily Post website (tackling Item Number 7 on my OM list: Become an etiquette expert):

All formal invitations, whether they are to be engraved or to be written by hand (and their acceptances and regrets) are invariably in the third person, and good usage permits of no deviation from this form.

And so, I wrote the first invite to Bradford, since I knew he wouldn't mind if I made a mistake:

> *Miss Mara Brennan*
> *requests the pleasure of*
> *Bradford Lynch's*
> *company at a formal dinner*
> *to celebrate the civic holiday,*
> *on Saturday the fifth of August*
> *at seven o'clock*
> *524 A Clinton Street*
>
> *Kindly send response to*
> *524 A Clinton Street*

Emily Post said I was supposed to ask guests to respond to the name of the estate, such as Garden Estate or Darling Acres, but I thought that seemed a bit foolish, given that I lived in the basement of a rundown house.

Then I made my guest list: Bradford and Tobias, Mitz and Amir, Olivia and Johnnie, and Victoria and George. And me. Nine people, which according to Emily Post was too many, since seven was the maximum number of guests I was supposed to invite to a formal sit-down dinner without hired help. And hiring help for a dinner party I was throwing to show how accomplished I was at cooking and hosting seemed rather ineffectual. But I could hardly uninvite myself—and even if I did have only seven guests, I would still be short eight chairs and a table—so it seemed useless to worry about having one extra dinner guest. Besides, Emily Post probably insisted that there be equal numbers of men and women, and I wasn't about to order any of my guests not to bring their significant others to comply with some strict party rules.

My gel-ink pen ran out of ink halfway through Victoria and George's address. I wasn't sure which was the lesser of two etiquette evils—to toss the envelope and hand-deliver the invite the next time I saw my sister, or to swap the gel-ink for a ballpoint and continue addressing the envelope. I decided on the latter, and nabbed a ballpoint off the counter.

Then, since the point of the soiree was to showcase my skills, it seemed reasonable that I should begin to tackle the OM list, and since Bradford still hadn't arrived, I pulled the list out of my bag and gave it a once-over.

I would start with Item Number 4: Keep an immaculately clean living space. I knew it probably made more sense to go in order, but seeing as Number 1 was Get a perfect body (and taking into account that I was sitting in a cupcake shop with the very probable possibility of indulging in not just one, but two calorie-infused cupcakes), cleaning seemed more realistic. Keeping five hundred square feet clean was a more manageable and tangible goal than achieving my image of a perfect body, which involved unrestrained boundaries and an unclear sense of completion, particularly because I was no longer exercising and was currently classifying a cupcake as the perfect dinner appetizer.

At least with cleaning, I'd know when I was done.

"Tell me again why you're cleaning?" Bradford asked, two cupcakes each later, when I explained why I had to go home and couldn't be distracted with his movie marathon—even if he and Tobias were having a Jennifer Grey pre-nose-job double bill night at their place. I hadn't told him about the OM list. Part of me thought he might be offended that I was using Olivia and Mitz as inspiration instead of him, but the other part thought he would just think it was stupid—which pretty much summed up his opinion of Olivia and Mitz.

"Is this something Mitz put you up to?" he asked and shook his head while taking a sip of chocolate milk from a red-striped straw. I loved Bradford because he knew me so well, but at the same time he didn't always understand me.

"Of course not, it's just that my place is dirty . . ." Surely that was good enough reason to clean. "And besides, it gives me something to do," I continued, then reminded him that I was no longer doing yoga, and that Mitz was planning a wedding and Olivia was house-hunting, and before I knew it Mitz would be trying to have babies and Olivia would be the new Debbie Travis. Considering that I didn't know how to cook and didn't have a good job or any money to take up other hobbies or join another yoga studio, was it so bad that I tried to clean my apartment?

"What you need," Bradford said, losing patience, "is a good dose of self-esteem, which I thought yoga should've been doing for you. But then again, you were taking it at that 'we're-too-cool' club. If you really want to learn to do yoga, why don't you go to a real yoga studio?"

Bradford pulled out a twenty and put it on the table. "You know, Tobias's sister, Sofi, and her partner own a studio on the Danforth, and Sofi's constantly looking for someone to work Friday nights. They run classes until midnight, but they can't get any of the instructors to work the desk that late. I don't know what they would pay, but I'm sure it's just taking names and handing out towels, and maybe you could suggest they pay you in free classes."

"Friday nights?" This was insensitive even for Bradford. He could at least pretend that I wasn't going to be home alone eating ice cream and painting my toenails.

"Yes, and this way, you won't be bewailing your lack of dates. Which works especially well for me if I'm going to continue being your friend."

I knew he was joking, but still, I felt torn. I didn't usually have plans on Friday nights, but not getting paid to work a second job when I could barely afford to live on the money I made at my day job didn't sound appealing. And aside from that, Bradford was helping me out—again. It was like second nature to him. I blurted out a problem and within seconds he had an answer. Still, if I wanted to be better at yoga than Olivia and Mitz by the fall, I needed to at least start doing yoga again. Maybe Bradford was right. Maybe joining a real yoga studio was the way to go. After all, it was on the Danforth, where people not only recycled the already-recycled containers of their pesticide-free produce, they *composted* the produce parts they didn't eat. It didn't get much more authentic than that.

The waitress returned with Bradford's change, and we got up to leave, Bradford promising to ask Sofi about the studio that night and see what he could do to get me a position—and free classes.

Deep down, I knew that Bradford was right, that I needed a boost of self-confidence, but a part of me felt like I would always be the same person I was right now. I'd always be a little overweight, a little self-conscious and a little bit of a failure in any goals I set for myself. Still, I had the list, and that had to count for something. I had to believe that the formula that made Mitz and Olivia so perfect could work for me, too.

And so, even though I was letting Bradford help me once again, I tried to convince myself that it wasn't taking me off track but, rather, that it was helping me become better at yoga and, at the same time, start the process of checking Item Number 1—Get a perfect body—off my OM list. Which meant, I thought, as I headed to Canadian Tire to pick up cleaning supplies, that I was undertaking two tasks at once. Which was, in fact, multi-tasking—Item Number 6 on my OM list.

Chapter Three

NATARAJASANA: COSMIC DANCER'S POSE.
The dance creates and destroys with each step.

$\mathcal{J}$n theory, cleaning seemed like it would be therapeutic. I wasn't sure how I thought I'd feel about it, though I didn't expect I would be annoyed. But so far, the process had been quite aggravating, and I hadn't even begun to scrub or scour anything.

First, I'd consulted Mitz about cleaning products. She quizzed me on surface textures—rotting painted wood, chipped ceramic and peeling linoleum—rattled off a list of supplies I'd need, and then modified the list once I told her I was standing at a pay phone inside Canadian Tire, where I planned to purchase all the items that day, and would not be making four stops around the city or a trip to Target in Buffalo for a brand carried only in the U.S.

More than an hour later, I finally lugged three bags full of products home, only to find that, before I could put the cleaning products to work, I needed to clear out Sam's stuff. Surprisingly, even though he'd taken all of the furniture (I still couldn't believe he had taken the bed. Seriously, didn't they have beds in Calgary? New ones, that wouldn't remind Sam of me when he was making out with my replacement?), there still seemed to be a substantial amount of junk. In the closet, I found a Cougar boot box filled with comics, a roll of Imaginus posters left over from his dorm days and a box made of faux-wood paneling containing mixed tapes and random papers. And that was just a start. I pulled one of the tapes out of the box. In Sam's recognizable penmanship (while still precise it was slightly loopier than usual, indicating youth and a some-what less meticulous nature), "White Hot Summer" was written on the back of the case. It was a tape he'd obviously made back in high school, and the theme was bands with the word "white" in their name or in a song, so the tape was heavy on the White Snake and White Lion. I dug my Walkman out of the bottom of the closet, where I tended to stash unused work-out items such as ankle weights and my ab roller, and popped the tape in, slipping on the headphones. White Lion's "When the Children Cry" started up. I lay down on the carpet and stared up at the ceiling. Pumpernickel sniffed the box of tapes and then curled up on my chest, purring.

Both sides of the mixed tape later, I felt drained emotion-ally, if not physically. In an old orange Nike box, I found every letter, card and photograph I'd ever given Sam. He'd kept them all, even the note I'd left one day telling him I'd gone to get Nutella and marshmallows so we could make s'mores together. I remembered that night. We'd been in our place for only two nights, and I'd wanted to do something romantic. But when I'd returned, Sam had informed me that marshmal-lows were on his banned list since they were made from animal cartilage and, of course, he couldn't eat products made from animal cartilage, or any animal parts, since he claimed he was vegetarian (and, in all likelihood, was now the only Calgarian who was). He wasn't a very good one, though, because I'd seen him eat jujubes and his mother's tomato aspic at Christmas, both of which contained gelatin. The part that upset me most was that I was just trying to be romantic, and if he'd been trying, he would've offered to make his s'mores with only the Nutella and wafers.

Next, I opened the cupboard and started to pull out items, including Sam's granola. I felt a rush of anger and tossed the bag of granola into the large black garbage bag. Finally, I felt satisfaction. Even though it was less than a ten-minute walk to the Dominion on College—a bright, inviting, clean and predictable grocery store—Sam had always insisted that we shop at Fiesta Farms, a large green box of a grocery store that took more than thirty minutes to walk to, and even longer on the way back since heavy groceries required frequent rest stops. There was nothing exactly wrong with Fiesta Farms, except that they tended to carry more of the organic and health foods so beloved by Sam. It was there that I was forced to stock up on spelt pasta, wilted but pesticide-free kale and soy milk I could barely manage to choke down. Living with Sam had forced me to develop some tricks. For a few months, I'd gotten away with transferring Sealtest 1% milk into one of his soy containers and sticking it at the back of the fridge, hidden behind juice containers. But after finding a couple of open soy milk containers in the fridge one too many times, he finally tasted their contents for freshness and caught on.

I opened the fridge and tossed the soy milk into the garbage bag, and then pulled out the Tofurkey slices and Not Dogs from the meat drawer.

An hour later, the kitchen was Sam-free, although there wasn't much food left. Thankfully, I had been successful in repackaging my cereal—Shreddies, Rice Krispies and Corn Flakes—to pass for Sam's "healthy" alternatives (how unhealthy could my mainstream cereals be?), by putting them in Tupperware containers at the back of the cupboard. Now, I had milk in the fridge, three types of brand-name cereal, raisins and an unopened bag of Oreos I'd forgotten about.

I slumped down on the cat-hair-coated blue carpet, and looked at the mess of tapes, papers, comics and posters around me. Then I opened the bag of Oreos and turned on the TV (disregarding the snow-filled screen that comes with cable-less TV in a basement) to catch a fuzzy edition of *eTalk* that was just beginning. Pumpernickel kneaded my socked feet and flopped over onto them.

Halfway through a segment on celebrities and their diet secrets that was threatening to crush the joy of my cookie-eating binge, I heard a tapping on my bedroom window, a few feet away. The window was slightly below ground level, and I was contemplating crawling toward the bathroom to hide out, when I heard a familiar voice call "Helloooooo". Pumpernickel scampered away, and my urge to follow him was even greater now that I knew who was on the other side of the window. I wondered if I was really keeping up my promise to Bradford not to become a hermit.

I walked into the bedroom to face the all-too-familiar ruby-red leather shoes at the window. My sister, who was bent over to peer into my place, waved and grinned, holding up a package wrapped in bright yellow tissue paper and cellophane, with a string attached that led to a matching yellow helium balloon.

"I thought maybe you weren't home!" she shouted, and I thought, *I wish I wasn't*. I pointed her around to the door of my apartment, then went up the stairs to the front entrance.

I watched from the front steps as Victoria, carrying Cookie's Cookie Bouquets, walked gingerly across the lawn in red kitten heels, a matching red sweater set and black linen pants, with Versace sunglasses perched on top of her head. As she flipped a piece of her freshly cut perfect black bob behind her ears, she pursed her lips—the exact shade of red to match her outfit—and looked at me with what I could only assume was pity. But then I was distracted by the set of Louis Vuitton monogrammed canvas luggage on the front walk. She'd bought the entire set for herself last year on a girls' weekend shopping jaunt to Paris, to get her out of what she claimed was a pre-Christmas winter slump. The full set wasn't in sight, but a good portion of it was sitting there, including one traditional suitcase, one soft-sided overnight bag, a smaller carryall and a beauty case.

For a moment I wondered whether there was any possibility that she was giving me her luggage, or had bought me my own set. But I knew there wasn't.

"I've come to stay with you!" Victoria announced brightly, confirming what I dreaded.

She handed over the cookie bouquet, then grabbed two of the bags and danced around me in the doorway so she could get down the stairs. My mother had used my "Loss of Boyfriend" situation as a call to action. Apparently, my being dumped had warranted a special trip to drop the cookies off at Victoria's house. But why couldn't she have brought them to me herself, rather than passing them off to an unwanted houseguest?

I knew the answer. While my mother would drive in to visit my sister, she would never come directly into the city to visit me, despite it being only a few exits and less than a half-hour's drive farther east along the highway. My mother couldn't acclimatize to Toronto traffic, so she refused to visit me. She would visit my sister because she lived twenty minutes closer to Niagara-on-the-Lake, in the west end of the city, just ahead of the spot where the apparent "traffic" took hold of my parents' van and swallowed it whole.

I stuck the cookies under my arm and maneuvered my sister's remaining two pieces of luggage into my apartment.

"This place is a disaster!" Victoria said, looking around. She appeared afraid to breathe, as though there might be lingering traces of SARS she could catch. I explained to her that I had been cleaning. Obviously. Victoria was already eyeing the bag of Oreos on top of the roaster box.

"Did I interrupt your *dinner?*" she asked, her voice full of sarcasm. She then pulled a bright orange envelope from the side pocket of her Louis Vuitton handbag and handed it to me. "I forgot—here's the card."

I ignored the dinner comment and opened the envelope to remove a matching orange card that read: *Sorry for the loss of the love of your life. But just remember, when life hands you lemons, use a bit of zest to make lemon shortbread!*

I pulled the ribbon and balloon off the cellophane and let the balloon rise to the ceiling while I peeked at the bouquet. At the end of each green plastic "stem" was a lemon shortbread cookie, cut into a lemon yellow—colored sun, complete with pointy rays my mother had iced in a darker shade of yellow.

How cheery.

I maneuvered a cookie from its stem and held out the package to my sister. She shook her head, typically, since a "treat" to her was a glass of water with a lime wedge. I decided not to prolong the pain and asked Victoria why (and for how long) she was visiting.

"As long as it takes," she replied, brushing past me, inspecting my place and, I assumed, implying as long as it took to *fix* me. As though I was broken. Which I wasn't. I'd merely been dumped, and I already had a plan for getting back on my feet (the OM list), and I'd already attempted to complete one task (Item Number 4: cleaning), which I was confident I would've completed if I hadn't been interrupted.

Victoria was oblivious to the possibility that I might want to have a say in whether I needed assistance in getting over Sam and on with my life. She was more concerned with how she was going to make my form of substandard living manageable.

"Obviously, I'm going to need to get some items out of storage," she said the next morning, while I mixed Shreddies, Rice Krispies and Corn Flakes into my favorite purple oversized mug, grabbed a handful of raisins and poured milk on top.

"Why? How long are you staying?"

She ignored me and rattled on as I walked back into the living room, which was once again clean, and opened the closet door to find that she'd stashed there everything I'd pulled out the night before.

"There are a bunch of items we just didn't want when we moved into our new house," she said, "but it's just so frowned upon to have a yard sale in our neighborhood, so we put them in storage. We probably should've just given everything to charity, but now it works out because I can give everything to you. Well, for as long as I'm staying with you, anyway," she added. Then she listed off items she would pull out to help make her stay more comfortable: a bed, a kitchen table, chairs, a coffee table and other so-called essentials (a full set of dishes, pans, a blender and a food mill—whatever that was) plus some art for the walls and a bunch of other mess-inducing knick-knacks that would only clutter my place when I was trying to purge. I could see she was already plotting to turn Mara Manor into the Grand Victorian Residence. "Am I forgetting any-thing?" she asked, and I thought, *my opinion*, while she added, "I'll send a mover to get those items today."

I tried to tell her I didn't need, want or have any space for her items, but she couldn't hear me over her mind-churning chatter, the water she was running to wash unseen dishes, and the honk and hiss of the traffic report on the all-news station that she'd tuned the clock radio in my bedroom to. While a bed would be a nice touch, I had to wonder if it was for her own benefit (while I roughed it on the futon) or whether she was attempting sisterly bonding and thought we'd sleep together as we had the previous night. I wasn't sure how all her things were going to fit, yet at the same time, if she had furniture to spare, I could certainly use a few extra chairs for the kitchen table she'd be supplying, since my dinner party guests would need to sit somewhere, and we could hardly carry on proper dinner-table conversation if we weren't all sitting at one.

"Could you bring nine chairs? And a floor lamp? And maybe a DVD player, since I don't have cable?"

"Nine chairs! Don't be ridiculous! Where would we put them?" Victoria scoffed.

I was being ridiculous? She was the one trying to redecorate my cell for her short stay.

"How long are you staying, anyway?" I asked.

"Mom and I talked, and we figured that the best thing we could do would be to lend you some big-sisterly support. So I'm here for you. Day and night. The boys are in school until the end of June, and their nanny makes their lunches and watches Serena, so it's not really an inconvenience for me to be here with you for a while. Besides, George is always working late, so not having me home to tuck them in will give the kids more time with their father. I'll go home on the weekends, and we'll all spend quality family time together then." She smiled, pleased that she, with just one spin-around, had become the Wonder Woman problem-solver in my life.

I nodded because it was all, at this point, I had the power to do, and told her I'd see her after I returned from work. She told me we could clean my house properly once I got home, and I thought, *Is this supposed to be compensation for getting dumped?*

"Why don't you just get Etta to come over here and clean my place?" I asked, wondering if I'd done enough cleaning myself last night to legitimately cross off Item Number 4 on the OM list, or, since I'd phrased the item as "Keep an immaculately clean living space," whether this was just a kick-start.

"Because Etta is paid to clean *my* house, not yours. Besides, before you can be a good boss, you have to know how to do the job yourself."

And so, I grabbed a cookie off the kitchen counter and went off to work to save women from growing old naturally, while Victoria took my cereal mug and spoon, apparently pleased to have something to wash in the sink.

They say bad things happen in threes, but Victoria's life had turned out perfectly in groups of three. Victoria had grown up dancing, and, just as she did with ballet, she made everything look effortless. Although she was even accepted to Juilliard, she gave it up to go into law at Queen's and came out with a husband (Big G, captain of the football team). Her starter home in Bloor West Village had three bathrooms, and they stayed there until Victoria became pregnant with Serena, quit her job for good and began her life as a society wife.

I have always loved my sister, as any good girl would, but we had never really gotten along very well, with the exception, perhaps, of the two years after I was born, before I was able to realize that I didn't enjoy being bossed around by someone three times my height and double my weight. As I grew up, I realized that not only did I have a mom, but I had a mini-mom in Victoria, who apparently thought dolls were too inanimate for her meddlesome abilities. It started out innocently, with her telling me to put my toys away, an order I obviously ignored, not even knowing what the word "toys" meant. But as I began to understand her, and she gained the power of knowing that I understood her, she developed into a controlling, judgmental monster, asking me how much of my allowance I had spent or how many math questions I had gotten wrong at school. When I was still young, I hated the way she acted and the way my mother let her treat me. But by the time I became a teenager, I started to hate her less and myself more when I was around her.

When I got to work, the phone on the reception desk was lit up like a veritable Pocket Simon game. I lunged for line one and fell into my seat, kicking off my flip-flops and reaching down under my desk to search for my office-protocol black slingbacks. I didn't have to wear slingbacks or black shoes, but I was not allowed to wear any shoes with laces or rubber soles or shoes that flipped and flopped when I walked.

"My husband said yes!" Rhonda Stephenson screeched into the phone. I knew instantly that it was her, not by her voice but because her baby, Ronin, was always screaming in the background of her phone calls. Rhonda was a perpetual lip-plumping addict and had tried it all— from collagen to hyaluronic acid—to keep her lips luscious. But I knew that what she was referring to was her campaign for a boob job and lipo session that had been ongoing for the nine months leading up to and the year since Ronin's birth. Her girl-friends had informed her that the perkiness in her breasts and the size 8 jeans she wore would be a mere memory once she was a mom. Rhonda's husband, however, had been refus-ing to pay. He wanted her to breastfeed the weight off—and considering that Rhonda's favorite food was ice cream, it wasn't the perfect equation to drop the forty pounds she'd gained during the pregnancy.

"He's come to terms with you and size 8?"

"Hardly. His mother just got lipo. She's raving about it, and said she'd pay for me to get it, too. So then he said if I was going to get one thing done, I might as well get it all at once."

"Excellent news for you," I said.

"He wants to know if I get a discount for getting two pro-cedures at once."

"Not likely. You know what Marjorie's like," I said, just as Marjorie walked through the door. I looked at my computer clock to confirm that she was right on time, and I hadn't even started making the coffee yet. Which she was well aware of, as she looked into the kitchen, looked back at me with a glare and then huffed into her office.

"I thought I'd ask. Oh, and thanks for e-mailing me the info about that eye cream with vitamin K. I swear, I had dark circles last week and this week already, they're gone. Considering that Ronin is now teething, I hardly think it's due to increased sleep. Now I just need a stretch mark balm recommendation, since I'm guessing the lipo isn't going to get rid of them."

I told Rhonda I'd look for a solution for stretch marks, since there were few treatments that worked, booked her in for her breast lift and lipo session and then logged onto my e-mail. I was fairly certain I'd found one of Marjorie's other clients a stretch mark balm that did the trick.

It wasn't in my job description to look for other body blunder solutions, and in reality Marjorie would probably fire me if she knew I did it, since it showed initiative—something not highly commended at the slavery clinic, where all I was expected to do was file, make coffee, get lunch, book appointments and make sure she got to her personal appointments, such as massages and dog-grooming, on time. Also, Marjorie wouldn't make money if her clients decided to use a product instead of a procedure. But helping her clients made me feel appreciated—something that didn't happen often with Marjorie, unless I lucked out on a lunch choice for her. Besides, I had a roster of only about four women who relied on me to keep them up to date on such cosmeceuticals.

I hung up, leaving the other blinking lights to their own devices, and hurried into the kitchen to start the coffee as

Esther Bartos, a statuesque but slightly overweight Czech woman, clacked through the door in leopard-print faux fur stilettos, carrying her purse-sized pooch under her arm. I looked at the schedule (she wasn't slotted in) and prayed I hadn't made a mistake. The last time I forgot to slot in a patient, Marjorie "forgot" to give me my paycheck for three days— illegal, but not unheard of at the slavery clinic.

Then I saw Mrs. Bartos's eyebrows. They were hanging over her eyes, indicating an obvious emergency. She puffed air at them to get a reaction, which, of course, she got out of me.

I knew the background: Mrs. Bartos had had an eyebrow transplant two weeks ago to rectify the over-tweezing obsession she'd picked up in her teenage years and had stuck with well into her fifties. Although the transplant was quite a successful treatment, the hair used was from the back of the head so you needed to trim your brows regularly since the hair grew out of control.

"This is ridiculous!" she exclaimed furiously, yanking on the micro-mini black leather skirt she should've stopped wearing twenty years ago. "I want to get laser hair removal."

"On your eyebrows?" I asked, perplexed.

"*Obviously.* I need to reduce the rate at which this hair is growing! I mean, I knew my hair grew fast, but this is ridiculous," she reiterated.

"You just need to trim it," I reminded her. "If you get laser, you'll be back at square one—with no eyebrows. If you want, I can trim them for you."

"Where's Dr. Wickham? You don't know anything. You're just a silly secretary."

It's always nice to have people walk in off the street and remind you that your life is meaningless. I told her to sit

down, and then I dialed Marjorie's extension to ask if she'd
see her.

"Does she have an appointment?" Marjorie barked.

"Well, no, but her eyebrows are inching toward her nose
by the minute—and your first appointment isn't until—"

"I don't care." Marjorie hung up on me, and I looked at the
clock. Only two hours to go until lunchtime. I kept my eye on
Esther and pulled out a Twizzler. Esther had now taken a seat
and was starting to flip listlessly through a copy of *Vogue*, while
her chihuahua was chewing on a corner of the area rug under-
foot. I hit line two and dialed Bradford's number to complain.

"I told you, you need to get out of there," he said.
Something was clicking in the background.

"Are you typing while you talk to me?"

"I'm using my calculator," he said curtly, "because I already
got out of Marjorie's claws and got a job I actually like and
would like to keep, which means that I don't have time to listen to you bitch to me all morning while you look at the clock
and count down to lunch."

I huffed and clicked on the Tetris icon inside the
"Accounting" folder I'd set up as a foil. If he could multi-task,
so could I. Did talking and playing Tetris count as completing
Item Number 6—multi-tasking—on my OM list?

"Listen, I don't mean to be harsh, but that job was supposed to be temporary, remember? So instead of playing Tetris,
which really doesn't do a thing for your social or career skills,
why don't you look for a job?"

I clicked off Tetris.

"Or, at the very least, call this number." Bradford rattled
off a number, which I hastily scribbled on a Post-it, and then

told me to ask for Sofi at Mok, a moksha yoga studio on the Danforth.

Before I could ask what moksha was, Esther started to wail and I had to hang up the phone to assess what was going on. I couldn't see Esther's eyes through the combination of her bangs and eyebrows, but her head was bobbing up and down in a way that suggested either she had suddenly noticed the elevator-music rendition of *The Cosby Show* theme song playing in the clinic or she was crying.

I went into Treatment Room A, grabbed a pair of scissors from one of the drawers, then returned. Ten minutes later, Esther Bartos was hugging me, perfectly pleased with her trimmed brows. Maybe I had a hidden talent, after all, I thought, as she handed me a twenty-dollar bill and left, pup in hand.

Just as I was beginning to feel better about myself, the phone rang. It was Victoria. She couldn't seem to find where I had put all the food in the house. "I've looked everywhere: your cupboards, your fridge..." If I hadn't known her for twenty-eight years, I'd have thought she was a senile grandmother. "Is there somewhere I'm forgetting to look?"

"The grocery store?" I replied.

"I don't understand," she said, intentionally feigning naïveté, so that I had to explain that I didn't (aside from the freak shopping-splurge-as-novelty event) stock the fridge. And that, in my cleaning spree, I had tossed all of Sam's supplies since I never liked eating his organic, vegetarian provisions anyway, and now I didn't have to. To which Victoria replied, "But where is *your* food?"

I reminded her that I had eaten a well-balanced meal of cereal, milk and raisins just this morning, and that was as well stocked as it got. Besides, despite my complaints that there was nothing to eat in the neighborhood near work, I much preferred taking a half-hour trip in my flip-flops to find interesting food over spending my spare time shopping for, preparing, and packing a lunch and then using up my lunch hour eating a soggy, too warm or too cold meal in the tiny kitchenette at work. So, aside from my cereal stash, I told her, which I planned to really cultivate now that I had the space and freedom to do so, there wasn't much else—gastronomically speaking—that I needed to live as a single woman.

"You mean like a student," she said. "There's absolutely no reason why you should be eating takeout when all you need to cook a healthy meal is a little imagination and a pot. Which I also noticed you don't seem to own."

I hadn't actually gotten around to cleaning out the cooking utensil drawers, so I had to take her word for it. Apparently Sam had taken the kitchen gear with him. I tried to explain to her that I didn't need a pot, since I didn't actually cook (and never really had, even with Sam, since he always ate dinner at work before coming home at nine o'clock), but she was too busy grumbling about the grime under the sink.

"I'm just trying to help you, Mara. You could be a little more cooperative."

I told her I needed to get back to work, which was true as Marjorie had dumped a month's worth of patient files on top of my *Allure* magazine, in which I'd been reading about a new anti-wrinkle hand cream.

Then my mother called, making it two calls at work in two days—totally uncharacteristic, which could mean only one thing: she was worried about me. But first, she wanted to know whether the people on the cover of her Harlequin Blaze romance had gone under the knife, and if I'd ever met a Harlequin model at the clinic.

"They haven't gone under the knife, Mom. They've gone under the airbrush."

"Oh, no, I believe you're mistaken," she insisted. "What about Fabio? He's real, and I know those muscles are, too. I've seen him on TV."

We agreed to disagree, and then she moved on, asking how I liked the cookies and my sister's surprise visit. I told her that one of the two was palatable, and that it was a good thing she'd sent them because, until Victoria arrived, I apparently didn't know how to fend for myself and often went for days without eating. This was meant to be a compliment to my mother's baking and a complaint that perhaps I had gotten along just fine before Victoria arrived, but my mother, ever the problem-solver, said: "You should ask Victoria to teach you how to cook. She's a great chef. She can help you make stew with your leftovers. You know, 'Leftovers in their less visible form are called memories. Stored in the refrigerator of the mind and the cupboard of the heart.'"

"Who said that?"

"Oh some British churchman."

Ironic, considering that my parents subscribed to the Church of Cable TV. Every Sunday morning at nine when I was growing up, my father turned on the service for shut-ins while my mother turned on the coffee maker. Then they made peameal bacon and chocolate chip pancakes side by side, while I colored the apostle scenes in my paint-by-number Sunday missal and Victoria painted her nails or pretended not to feel well so she could talk to her boyfriend-of-the-moment on the telephone in the bathroom. One hour later, we were better people for it, and sat down to a lovely Sunday brunch.

"What does that even mean?"

"That you should ask your sister how to help you use up your leftovers so they don't go to waste. It's like scrapbooking for the appetite."

Apparently my mother was also delusional about my cooking habits—she thought I was cooking so much that I accumulated leftovers. Even if I had had more than leftover pizza or deep-fried chicken balls to contribute to a stew, I really hated stew. I told my mom I would take her suggestion under advisement, then hung up the phone and began deconstructing the pile of patient file folders on my desk. Each contained at least one appointment that needed to be entered into the computer, after which I had to create an invoice for the client, check whether they'd prepaid, paid on service or billed their account, and send out the invoice accordingly. Not brain surgery, just brain numbingly boring work.

Seven hours and twenty-three files later, I arrived home to find an envelope addressed to me, in Sam's handwriting.

The explanation note. I sat down on the front steps and prepared myself. What would he have to say? That he was sorry? That he had made a mistake? Or just what I did to make him leave? I slid my finger through the space at the top, ripped open the envelope—ungracefully—and pulled out the single sheet of paper. A check fell to the ground, and I picked it up to see he'd sent the rent money, as promised.

I unfolded the unlined white sheet of paper and read:

M,

The movers packed the bed by mistake—but since I'm paying
for a month's rent I'm not using, let's call it even?
Best,
Sam

Best? I lived with him for six months and that's all I got? Besides which, if he really wanted what was best for me, he wouldn't have left without a discussion. Without a word. Without me.

I folded the note and put it, the envelope and the check into my bag. Feeling alone and unwanted, I started to cry.

"You're home!" Victoria said in a slightly accusatory tone. I sniffed and turned around to see her in the doorway. "We've got lots to do, come on in," she said, as though she were inviting me into her own home. I stood up reluctantly and followed her inside.

My apartment was filled. Aside from the general layout and the location (still on Clinton, still below ground), very little looked the same. Sam's futon was now in the living room where his couch had formerly sat, but instead of the stained green cloth, it had been draped with a creamy beige slipcover adorned with blue and yellow embroidered flowers.

"It's Laura Ashley," Victoria informed me, wiping her wet hands on the floral-print apron she was wearing. I wondered whether she was referring just to the slipcover or to everything she'd brought into my place (including her apron, the ribbon she had tied to keep her hair off her face and her slippers, which all followed the floral theme). I nodded and smiled, then looked into the bedroom, where there was now a large, lovely-looking bed covered by a duvet in a flower print similar to the one on the futon. I was already feeling a bit woozy about all the florals in the living room, but I was looking forward to going to sleep that night in a real bed, even if it wasn't my bed. I wanted to crawl under the covers and digest everything that had happened in the ten minutes since I'd arrived home from work. Although I had to wonder whether the bed was for my sister or me.

I followed Victoria into the kitchen, which now had an oblong oak table with four chairs, complete with blue dupioni silk seat covers with ties that made bows around the spindles, and matching silk placemats. Four more chairs, identical to the others, were stacked in the corner (I'd be one short for the party, but that was better than being short nine). Under the TV was a small table where the phone books had been; on top of the TV, Victoria had placed a silver DVD player.

Victoria had decided that, instead of waiting for me to get home, she would clean the apartment herself, using new cleaning supplies she'd purchased, since she didn't approve of any of the supplies I'd selected the previous day. Hers were apparently much better for the floors, walls, countertops and especially the environment, a key factor for any Bloor West Villager, where it was very important to use biodegradable products—not because you actually believed in the environment but simply because your neighbors were not beyond snooping in recycling bins.

"I would've vacuumed, but I couldn't find a vacuum *any-where*." She looked at me expectantly.

"I have a DustBuster."

Victoria shook her head. "No wonder it's so filthy in here. Honestly, Mara, there's enough cat fur to make a stole. And it's really hard on my allergies. I can hardly breathe. I had to put the animal outside. I hope you don't mind."

I marched to the back door and opened it to let Pumpernickel in. I wanted to tell her that I wasn't forcing her to stay with me, that she could return to her uncontaminated mini mansion at any time, but she had already moved on to other matters.

"I thought it would be more useful for you to learn how to cook," my sister explained, and I realized then that she and my mother had planned the intervention long before Sam had even broken up with me.

Victoria had already purchased and stocked the pantry and fridge with supplies suitable for a holiday party for a hundred. She told me to put on my apron. Which, of course, I didn't own.

"No apron? How do you keep your clothes clean?" she said in shock and then quickly undid her own apron and slipped it over my head, turning me around so she could tie it behind my waist. Then she began fumbling through the drawers for tea towels, which she fastened together with a few chip clips. She then used the ribbon that had encircled her head to hold the tea towels in place around her waist.

"There," she said, satisfied with her makeshift apron.

I expected her to teach me how to cook lasagna or tuna casserole or some other easy one-dish meal I could make once and eat for days, but Victoria had other plans.

"I really had to stock your cupboards," she announced. "You didn't even have garlic or lemon juice or *basil*."

It wasn't that I didn't enjoy a good home-cooked meal. I just liked someone else to do the cooking before I took the meal home. This wasn't a result of laziness or lack of riches; it was a well-thought-out process that made complete sense, given my skill set. Cooking for myself had always seemed arduous and gave me no real sense of accomplishment or appreciation. My mother, on the other hand, seemed to think cooking was similar to scrapbooking. At least with arts and crafts there was a display factor that could make others ooh and ahh. Not so much with my version of chicken à la king.

"How much did you spend?" I asked, opening the fridge. Knowing Victoria, I was well aware that she might want me to reimburse her for the groceries. I now not only had twice the rent to pay each month, but a houseguest with high standards.

The fridge was stocked with barely edible items: red cabbage and green beans, asparagus and avocados, bean sprouts, Balkan-style yogurt, a jar of no-sugar peanut butter and a whole fish with head intact. Still, the contents were free of any reminders of Sam, and for that I was grateful.

Victoria waved her hand in the air dramatically and told me I could consider it a big-sister gift.

"I also noticed you had some no-name knives, so I brought my one-man Henckels out of storage, as well as a box of pots and pans we keep just for camping. I'll leave them here until we need them, and if you decide you want to keep them, you can just pay me for them," she said.

Victoria had a way of passing off condescension as a charitable impulse.

"You can start by separating the eggs," she said, handing me a bowl filled with brown and white eggs. "We need twelve whites."

It sounded like a make-work project.

"Those are organic eggs I bought at the St. Lawrence Market," Victoria said. Of course they were. "I hand-picked them, and they've been sitting out for an hour. When you're going to be cooking with them, it's best to bring them to room temperature first."

If Victoria hadn't sounded so full of herself, I might've acted impressed. But I didn't want to give her that satisfaction, so I simply began plucking the brown eggs out of the bowl and setting them on the counter, while Victoria grabbed a shallow frying pan and placed it on the stove.

"So, is it weird for you to be here?" I asked her.

"What do you mean?" She flipped her hair behind her right ear. It was a nervous habit she seemed to have developed with this new haircut. Or maybe it was just a bad cut.

"I mean, being away from George and Stanny and Aidan and Serena."

"Please don't call him Stanny. It makes him sound like a geriatric."

I obviously couldn't even live up to my sister's exacting standards for nicknames.

"Anyway, of course it's difficult for me, but sometimes we make sacrifices," Victoria continued. "You need me, and I'm being a good sister. The kids will be fine. They have Francie. She's not me, but she'll do," Victoria added smugly.

I wondered if Victoria trusted the nanny over her husband when it came to child care.

"George must like having more time to spend alone with them, too," I prompted as she placed a pat of butter in the pan.

"I'm sure. Hand me the whites."

I felt like Victoria was dancing around all my personal questions. "What are we making?"

"Frittata. It's a healthy quiche."

I thought quiche was already healthy. "Is there cheese involved?"

"No. Hand me the whites," she said again, "before this butter burns."

I handed her the bowl of white eggs. She stared at them and then at me. Then she began cracking the eggs open one by one, flipping each half back and forth in her hand like a Slinky until the egg whites fell into a bowl on the stove. She dumped the yolks into a glass measuring cup.

I sat down on one of the kitchen chairs while she rattled on about poaching. Aside from illegal hunting (which wasn't common in downtown Toronto), the only poaching I knew about had to do with eggs, but judging from the way my sister was whipping the egg whites around in the frying pan, it seemed more like scrambled, not poached, eggs she was making. Then she grabbed the yolks and dumped them into the pan, so apparently, even if I'd gotten the separating task right, it was still a make-work project as I'd suspected.

"Mom said to tell you to teach me to make stew." I intended it as a joke, but Victoria was taking her chef session quite seriously.

"Stew?" She shook her head. "Surely you know how to make stew. You cut up a bunch of vegetables and beef and throw them in a pot." She pointed to some vegetables—red and green pepper, tomato, onion and zucchini—and told me to chop them. When I had completed the task (successfully, I might add), she threw them into the pan.

"Now, typically you'd just throw a lid on this and stick it in the oven for an hour, but we're going to scoop it into mini muffin pans," she continued.

I wondered if she thought that would give me the incentive to pack the frittata for lunch. Which, of course, it would not.

"Easy, right?"

Not as easy as scrambled eggs with vegetables thrown in, which is exactly what it looked like, and which I already knew how to make.

"Plus, it's perfect for your guests without teeth," she said, and laughed at her own joke—if it was supposed to be a joke. My sister may have been talented at many things, but making jokes was not one of them. Maybe she just assumed that my next boyfriend would be so old (or so white trash) that he wouldn't have teeth. I wasn't sure, but apparently she was keeping my options open. So was my mother, who at that moment called to ask me what I thought about Charles.

"Charles who?"

"Charles, Auntie Carol's son. You know, he's quite handsome and very well established at the law firm in Georgetown. Quite a catch."

"For *who?*" Had my mother suddenly gone senile in the past forty-eight hours?

"For you, silly dilly!"

"Charles is my cousin," I reminded my mother.

"Not technically. Auntie Carol had Charles before she married your father's brother. So there's no blood relation at all. So don't give me that. I could arrange a little meeting. Or . . . I could send him a little cookie bouquet from a certain secret admirer." Her voice tinkled.

"That won't be necessary. I've learned to make frittata. I think I can set my standards higher." Teeth or no teeth, anyone was better for a date than a relative. Besides which, I wasn't looking to date, given that I hadn't included it on my OM list as a priority. Of course, neither my mom nor my sister was aware of that fact.

Thankfully, the frittata seemed to throw my mother off track. "Frittata!" The tinkling became more of a fireworks explosion of excitement. "I remember when your sister made that last Easter. It was just perfect for George's grandfather and Stansmith, who was losing three baby teeth and missing at least another four. All he could eat was ice cream and eggs."

After a minute of rave reviews of my sister as an all-around fabulous mother, daughter and chef, and an update on my father, who was taking a Build Your Own Website course at the community college so that she could offer "Cookies on the Go" for people "driving on the information superhighway," I was able to get off the phone.

I decided to try a different tactic with my sister. Perhaps her idea and my idea of what I needed to know how to cook were completely different.

"It's not that I don't think the frittata is interesting," I began, "it's just that I'd really like to know how to cook items for dinner—"

"You can have frittata any time of day. It's a lot better to eat at dinner, in fact, than pasta or rice dishes, since they're just laden with carbs."

"Eggs for dinner?"

"Excuse me, I didn't realize that you were so set on pigeon-holing your food. Weren't you just eating a cookie for breakfast this morning, or was that my imagination?"

Somehow my sister had managed to make me feel like I was twelve again.

"I was going to teach you to poach salmon, too," she said.

I wasn't really fond of fish, unless it was in sushi, and even then I tended to get the vegetarian rolls rather than the sashimi. Victoria handed me the mother of all Martha Stewart cookbooks and, since the cover bragged about the 1,200 recipes inside, I decided to be honest with my sister about my general dislike for fish. Surely there were at least a thousand recipes that didn't contain fish.

Victoria glared at me, told me not to generalize and then conceded that she wasn't about to waste her time trying to help me learn to cook if I was going to be so ungrateful.

"I thought you'd teach me something I'd actually want to make," I told her. Surely the best thing was to be honest. "I want to have a dinner party, and I just don't see myself cooking mini egg muffins or a slab of fish."

"What do you think poached salmon is?" she snapped.

I wasn't sure if that was a rhetorical question, because as far as I knew salmon—poached, grilled, baked or otherwise—was fish. And I really didn't enjoy fish, particularly salmon, given the number of bones and, in this case, the very large head, eyeballs and teeth that were slapped on the counter in front of me. Victoria flipped the cookbook over to the back and pointed to the picture. Smack dab on the back was a photo of what appeared to be the poached salmon.

Well, if it was good enough for the back cover of *The Martha Stewart Living Cookbook,* it was good enough for a dinner party, I supposed.

Two hours later, I was starting to see why Martha Stewart had ruled her own empire for so long without any competition. Women everywhere were apparently purchasing her

:cipe books merely as status symbols. Surely there was no way
that any woman could know if all her recipes actually worked.
If this one cookbook alone had 1,200 recipes, multiplying that
by her dozen other cookbooks took you up to 14,400 recipes.
Even if someone (someone crazy, obviously) attempted one
recipe a night, it could take somewhere in the vicinity of
thirty-nine years to test all her recipes. And I was already
twenty-eight years behind.

Perhaps Whole Poached Salmon 101 was easy, but in my
books, easy was not defined by a recipe that took three
columns and ten steps to explain in font so tiny it gave me eye
strain. Each step contained nearly one hundred words and
included things such as Court Bouillon, for which there was an
entirely different recipe on a separate page, and fennel fronds
for garnish.

Then there were the items not even listed until you got to
the instructions, such as cheesecloth (apparently anyone using
a Martha Stewart cookbook would possess such an item,
which Victoria had helpfully brought along) and a poaching
rack (in this case, she said, we would just be using cookie
sheets instead). In terms of the instructions, step 4, for example, instructed me to slide a wooden spoon through the handle
of the poaching rack, lift out the rack and elevate it by prop-
ping spoons on the edges of the poacher, then maneuver one
of the spoons to angle the poacher so that the head of the fish
was higher than the tail. Finally, I had to insert a thermometer
into the wide part of the back of the fish where the fin used to
be. Right.

The phone rang just as we were completing step 7, which
included preparing an ice-water bath—really just a bunch of

ice cubes with water in a bowl, Victoria explained. I longed for my own bath.

It was George, who skipped the pleasantries and asked for Victoria.

I handed her the cordless phone. She took it and told me to continue with step 8, since this was the crucial part and we couldn't let the salmon stay too warm. Unfortunately, step 8 instructed me to examine the head and tail and, if both looked presentable, to leave them on for decoration.

They were still attached, and I did not want to leave them on for decoration. Pumpernickel rubbed against my leg and looked up at the fish.

The next step explained *how* to remove the unwanted body parts, by snipping the tail with kitchen scissors and pulling off the head with my hands. Then I was supposed to flip the fish over, peel off the skin with a paring knife, again flip the fish onto a serving platter, remove the rest of the skin and scrape off any brown fat. *Disgusting.*

I could hear Victoria's hushed, angry voice coming from my bedroom, and I tried to convince myself that I didn't want to listen, though of course I really wanted to. So I flipped the fish off the rack into the cheesecloth and carried it over to the kitchen table, where I could overhear better. Unfortunately, Pumpernickel chose that same moment to move into the exact spot where my right foot was headed. I stepped on his tail, and he yowled and spun around, causing me to stumble. Instinctively, I reached for a chair to steady myself and let go of the fish. The next thing I knew, it had landed on the linoleum, and Pumpernickel, who had possibly planned the whole thing, scurried over to delve into the landlocked salmon.

Holy mackerel. I quickly assessed the situation. I could salvage the fish and pretend nothing had happened; trash it and explain the situation to Victoria; or leave it for Pumpernickel, which would still involve 'fessing up to my sister.

"What's going on out there?" Victoria called. I scooped the fish off the floor (the bones would make Pumpernickel sick anyway) and slapped it onto a tray on the table.

"Nothing," I mumbled.

I wondered if I'd learned enough to cross Item Number 3—become a fabulous chef with my own unique dossier of recipes—off my list.

Chapter Four

MOKSHA: TO SET FREE.

This liberation of all bonds is achieved through realization of the self.

$\mathcal{M}$ok—the moksha yoga studio—was located on the Danforth in the Carrot Common, a hangout for environmentalist, herbalist, homeopathic and naturopathic types. It was my destination on Saturday afternoon after bidding a fond farewell to Victoria (although she promised she'd be back by Sunday night), as she put a Tupperware lid with a handle over a mini-muffin pan of frittata, turning it into a sort of flat suitcase. She was bringing the tray to Stansmith's Scouts meeting, since it was her turn to bring a healthy snack, proving that she actually had an ulterior motive for "teaching" me how to make the egg dish two days earlier. I wondered if the salmon had had a destination too before it ended up on the floor, but I'd never know. She did tell me that she had baked flaxseed-spelt muffins with pumpkin seeds and made fresh-squeezed prune juice that morning, and left them in the fridge for me. In comparison, the frittata actually looked delicious.

The studio's mandate, posted on the street-level entrance, involved a commitment to ethical, compassionate and environmentally conscious living, which seemed to work well with the surrounding stores—a natural supplements store to the left and a raw-materials clothing store to the right. The studio was up a flight of stairs on the second story, and when I entered, an unpleasant rush of tea tree oil hit me. The smell of tea tree oil made me uneasy. People don't use tea tree oil unless they're confident about their lifestyle, which means they recycle and compost and buy brown rice (never white) and eat whole-grain bread, not twelve-grain, because they know that's just a gimmick, and they would certainly never fall prey to a French baguette. Ever. Simply put, that wasn't me.

However, in an attempt to be optimistic, I hoped that I would grow accustomed to the tea tree oil and that it would cleanse my system, remove my toxins and result in a loss of five pounds. Or ten. As Sofi had explained on the phone, moksha was a form of hot yoga, a series of twenty-six poses performed in a sweltering 100-degree-Fahrenheit room, which would loosen my body so that it was more flexible, cause me to sweat out any impurities and prevent me from being hungry afterward.

The dark-skinned woman behind the reception desk was wearing a beige Rawganique organic cotton Zen top (this I knew because the sign behind her head said so), and her coarse black hair was piled in twists on top of her head. She smiled instantly and asked me if I was new. I wondered if it was that obvious that I didn't belong. Then she stood up, and

I saw that her belly was about to burst. I realized that she must be Sofi's girlfriend, and mother of the baby that was scientifically Bradford's but spiritually his niece or nephew.

I explained who I was and the situation.

"Oh, great!" Libby said. "Sofi told me you'd be coming in. Why don't you try the first class for free, see how you like it, and then we can discuss the receptionist position."

She handed me a clipboard with a form and a pen.

"Did you bring appropriate clothing?" she asked, and I wondered if she meant yoga clothes in general or some sort of organic, all-natural, handmade garment of local design. But I assumed the former and did a mental check.

Mat. Check.

Water. Check.

Shorts. Check.

Shirt. Check.

Shirts were optional for men, which I thought could be quite distracting, but far better than being optional for women.

Bathing suit. Again, optional, and an option I did not exercise given that I was looking to perfect my Fish Pose and not the beached whale position.

Towel. Check.

I was sensing a beach theme, and I was looking forward to it. I couldn't really imagine any other sport besides swimming that recommended bringing a bathing suit and a towel, and considering that the classes were ninety minutes long, it seemed plausible that there would be some relaxation time— some lazy-hazy-lying-on-my-back-in-*savasana*-pondering-life time. Surely there was no way we'd actually be expected to physically exert ourselves for the whole ninety minutes. As I signed the waiver, which explicitly stated that the studio wasn't responsible for any injuries I incurred while doing non-supervised poses, other students began trickling in and I became less worried. Although I might've been a size 10, there were definitely size 12s and even 14s, and I wondered why I'd been so intimidated by these authentic studios for so long.

I wasn't sure that ninety minutes of anything (especially exercise) was within my range of capabilities. I mean, I could barely stay focused on movies for that long without popcorn and jujubes to keep me occupied. I certainly couldn't file invoices at work for ninety minutes. I couldn't even clean for ninety minutes. Actually, I couldn't think of one single activity I could do for ninety minutes, or which I'd even tried to do. I imagined some people would find it simple. Professors, perhaps, who taught two-hour lectures; or truck drivers, who drove for eighteen hours straight; or lawyers, who were in court for much longer than ninety minutes. But not me.

I was determined to attempt the class. After all, it seemed very structured. Moksha was a standard series of twenty-six poses. So I'd know how far along we were and, more importantly, when it was over.

The door to the studio had a sign requesting that yogis unroll their mats before entering and observe total silence once inside. Instead of feeling intimidated, I felt a calming sensation wash away the feeling of anxiousness caused by the tea tree oil. No one would be *allowed* to talk, which meant I wouldn't have to worry that I didn't fit in. I could never tell if people already talking—at a party or fitness class alike—had just met or had been longtime friends, which meant I never knew whether to try to join the conversation (and risk ostracization) or keep to

myself (and look like a too-good-for-everyone bitch). I somehow couldn't seem to assess situations properly.

All this agonizing analysis meant I was forever trying to
time things right so that I could sneak in just as the class was
starting. This often meant annoying someone as I put my step
or mat beside them, making them move over to make space
and shifting them, perhaps, from the ideal spot they had
picked out when they had arrived *early* to the class for just
that reason.

But with this no-talking rule, it was like a social ban had been
placed on the room and I felt relieved, knowing that if I ever
returned, I could actually arrive early, and I too could select my
ideal spot without fear of being shunned or stereotyped.

I pushed the door open, and the heat slapped me in the
face.

The room was long and narrow, and about a dozen men
and women were already inside, all lying down on their backs
in Corpse Pose, their towels on top of their mats and their toes
pointed toward the back of the room.

I tiptoed across the cork floor and laid my mat down in a
corner near the back, away from the mirror. The narrowness
of the room meant that only two mats could fit depthwise
from the mirror, so even though I was in the back I was still
close enough to actually see my own body. I spread my Dylan
McKay towel out and lay down on top of his body. I stared up
at the ceiling and waited. I could feel drops of sweat forming
under my arms and at the back of my neck.

A few minutes later, Libby came through the door, greeted
us and walked to the empty mat at the front of the class. She—
in her state—was about to do yoga with us?

"Let's begin," she said calmly, and then put her hands together in prayer position in front of her chest and instructed us to stand and take six deep breaths.

Surely, this wasn't a workout? Breathing?

But I followed along through six sets of inhales and exhales, which seemed to take nearly five minutes. Then Libby and the rest of the class, who all seemed to know the routine, continued to breathe deeply but started a series of moves in which they raised their arms above their heads and then lowered them in front of their chests. I followed along. Libby reminded us that we should be pushing the air completely out of the space between our flat palms, our thumbs should be against our chests to feel our hearts beating and our elbows should point out to opposite walls. Well, that got a bit tough to focus on all at once. And I was just standing in one place—I hadn't even tried to do a pose yet.

We moved into Mountain Pose, and I thought things were going well until Libby pulled out of her own Mountain Pose and came over to me.

"Mara, stretch up through your fingertips," she said, adjusting my left arm, which I thought was reaching as far toward the ceiling as it could. "Feel the stretch right through your ribs, to your waist, to your hips, thighs, calves, down to your toes and into the ground." That was a lot of stretching, but I tried not to feel intimidated or singled out. In fact, I felt a sense of belonging because Libby had remembered my name—and she seemed to know everyone else's name, too.

And then it only got harder. We were attempting Tree Pose, but unlike at Miss Fit, where we'd hold Tree Pose for a few seconds, we were holding each position for a full minute. And then, after taking a break, for another thirty seconds. A minute and a half of holding each position was a lot harder than it sounded, even if your right foot was just balancing on your left thigh.

"Now, if you're balanced in Tree Pose, move down into Toe Stand," Libby instructed. She somehow folded herself over her bulging belly and was reaching down to the ground.

Toe Stand? I watched as half the class bent their body over to touch the floor and then bent their leg until they were sitting on their left heel, balancing on the toes of their left foot. I wobbled in Tree Pose and put my right arm out to steady myself before moving my hands back together into prayer. The sweat was pouring off my forehead and down my face. Even my legs were starting to sweat, which caused my foot to keep sliding down my thigh.

"Remember to take long, deep breaths to really maximize your experience," Libby reminded us, bringing her hands into prayer position.

I struggled to keep my foot fixed to my leg, while breathing really heavily in short, quick breaths. Forget deep breaths, I just wanted to stand on one foot without falling over.

Finally, we lay down in Corpse Pose. I collapsed to the ground.

Wow, I thought. *I made it.* I wasn't perfect, and I fell over a few times—in *garurasana* to be exact—but I'd never done Eagle Pose before and, really, unless you have twig legs, it's impossible to wrap one around the other and then squat, resting your weight on just one leg, as though it was comfortable. And Dancer's Pose is really something only a dancer could be expected to perfect. I wobbled in a few others, too, but it was okay. I'd completed the class. I'd made it through ninety minutes, and I hadn't even noticed anyone else around me most of the time. I couldn't believe it.

And then Libby started to speak.

"We'll now move on to the floor exercises," she said.

Was this another class? Was it like when you took the step class and then they tacked on a fifteen-minute optional ab class at the end for the hard-core students? But no one was leaving. And I couldn't ask because of the silence rule. And then it hit me. Maybe the Corpse Pose was like halftime. Maybe there was still forty-five minutes to go.

I guess I should've been able to figure it out since there were supposed to be twenty-six poses, but it sure seemed as if there had been a lot more than that already. It seemed more like forty-eight. Or eighty-two. Maybe some poses were just extensions of others?

I rolled over onto my stomach and caught sight of my tank top, which was white. Because my sweat had saturated it, it was completely see-through. I quickly dropped my chest down to the towel, mortified, and let my head sink down into Dylan McKay's soggy chest. I wanted to cry.

But instead, I relaxed my jaw and took a deep breath.

I could do this.

Forty-five minutes later, we lay down in Corpse Pose again and, this time, the class was over. Because Libby said so. And then she added breathlessly, "Have a beautiful evening" and "*Namaste*." And everyone said "*Namaste*" in response, and I felt myself cringe slightly. It seemed forced. Contrived. It wasn't as though we were on a mountaintop in Nepal. I felt embarrassed in the same way I was embarrassed whenever anyone did karaoke.

In the change room, there were only two showers. I peeled off my clothes, wrapped my sweat-soaked towel around me and queued up. Women brushed past me, most of them naked, unaware of skin touching skin, even if their bodies were squishy and saggy in places. Unlike at Miss Fit, where most of the women had perfect bodies but covered them up, the yoginis here danced around me with the confidence of Victoria's Secret models. I considered the possibility that this might be refreshing if I ever came back, but the overwhelming stench of tea tree oil getting stronger as the minutes passed was too distracting.

Inside the stall, the smell was even more overpowering. On a wire shelf in the corner was a clear ketchup bottle with murky green liquid inside. The handwritten label taped on top read "Body and Hair shampoo for you. *Namaste*." It was biodegradable and good for the environment and looked disgusting, and when I pushed down on the pump the murky, watery substance squirted past my hand right to my chest. I tried to rub it into my body but the "shampoo" had already run down my stomach. I tried again for another squirt, but by that time the stench was making me feel nauseated and I decided it was better to be sweaty than to smell tea tree oil seeping from my skin for days.

Emerging from the shower, I realized I was ravenous. Sofi, while explaining the principles of moksha, had mentioned that I might not be hungry afterward, that hot yoga could diminish my appetite for hours, and I had anticipated the pounds dropping off. As I dried myself with my damp towel, I realized that was not going to be the case. I got changed as quickly as I could (I was already sweating again) and headed to the front door to grab my shoes. Libby asked if we were going to discuss the position, and when I shook my head she called after me, reminding me to drink plenty of fluids to rehydrate.

Fluids? All I could think about was meat as I eyed the yellow-canopied hot dog stand on the corner outside the Baskin-Robbins. But before I succumbed, I saw a sign, right beside the yoga studio entrance, for Suck It Up, a smoothie shop. Not only were smoothies healthy, but surely they counted as fluids, too.

Maybe I would lose weight, after all.

And so I ordered a Raspberry Razz smoothie, saying no to the sprouted flax, whey protein, spirulina, hemp and maca. There was still a difference between healthy and just plain crazy.

~

The following week, I made a date with Olivia to tackle Item Number 5 on my list: Unleash inner decor diva on apartment. My plan was to meet Olivia Friday after work to get her to help me choose a color for my walls, and then have her and Mitz over on Saturday and Sunday to paint my place a nice, warm crème caramel. This way, I could bond with my two best friends while Victoria was back with her family. By Sunday night I'd have made my place my own. I figured it would be one of the last steps I needed to prove to Victoria that I didn't need her help and that she could go back to her home full-time, knowing I was doing fine, while still letting her think she'd played a role in my recovery by teaching me how to cook and clean. I secretly hoped that she would leave her bed for me, but

I wasn't optimistic since I'd had to threaten to take back my key just to get her to let me sleep in her bed—in my bedroom— while she took the futon.

Olivia's office was on the nineteenth floor of the tower above the Bay's flagship store on Queen Street, and her window looked out over Lake Ontario and Centre Island. I wondered what it would be like to have a view of the island that Torontonians escaped to in the summer for picnics, parties, bike rides and bocce ball tournaments. The only view from my desk at the clinic was the gray walls of the reception area, since only Marjorie's office and the treatment rooms had windows, and even they looked only out onto the Subway sandwich shop across the street.

"Shut the door," Olivia said as soon as I entered her office after work. She pulled down her pants and turned around so her back (and butt) was facing me. "Seriously, can you notice a difference?"

I shut the door and took a seat in her leather office chair, trying to avoid staring at her butt, taking a sip of the Blackberry Green Tea Frappuccino Blended Crème I'd picked up at the Starbucks on the corner of Bay and Queen before heading into her building. The green tea made it sound healthy, and since I hadn't actually done a yoga class that day, I figured having green tea was the next best thing to keeping me on the road to achieving a perfect body.

"In what?" I asked.

"My butt and thighs," she said, as I kicked off to spin around in the chair. "I just got my first cellulite treatment."

I put my feet on the ground to stop my second 360. Why wouldn't Olivia ask me for advice before getting a cellulite treatment? If I had any sort of expertise in anything at all, it was cosmetic enhancement.

"Where did you go?" I asked.

"Dr. Ellie, of course. Everyone knows she's the best." She pulled up her pants and fastened the ribbon-tie at her hips.

As far as cosmetic surgeons went, Dr. Eleanor Overholt had a high profile not just in Toronto but in L.A., where she split her time between two boyfriends and was a regular on *Venice Beach Vanity*, a reality series about cosmetic surgeons. Dr. Overholt was fondly known on TV and radio as simply Dr. Ellie, though her critics called her the Overhaul for her ability to transform her clients into new people.

"Do you know what machine?" I asked.

Only a handful of doctors had Smooth Operator, the latest— and best—piece of equipment on the market for combating cellulite, and I was pretty sure Dr. Overholt wasn't one of them.

"Ender something . . ."

"Endermologie? I can't believe she did that treatment on you. It doesn't work. There's no suction. It's all heat. You might as well stick your ass in the microwave."

"So you're saying I still have cellulite."

I wanted to tell her that everyone has cellulite, even models, but I didn't think that would go over very well.

"I'm meeting with a real estate agent in half an hour, so I picked out the color for you," Olivia said, handing me a paint chip labeled "Mocha Steamer."

I couldn't believe she was blowing me off. It was hardly the supportive shopping trip I had hoped for.

"I thought you were going to *help* me pick out the paint," I complained.

"I thought this was helpful. I just saved you an hour," she said with a dismissive wave of her hand.

"You're still going to come over with Mitz tomorrow to help me paint, though, right?" I asked her.

"This weekend? I can't. How about . . ." She flipped through the day planner on her desk. "The first weekend in July?"

"I'll just do it myself." I wasn't going to wait three weeks to paint my walls.

"Why don't you get your sister to help you now that she's staying with you? It could be good bonding time." She picked up a stack of paint chips and handed them to me. They were an assortment of browns. "Now, remember, you need to block off the walls in sections using painter's tape, so there are white bands to break up the solid color. You don't want it to look like a chocolate bar."

I wasn't sure how any shade of brown—in sections or not—was going to highlight my dark basement, but I trusted that Olivia knew best. I had to. Otherwise, my OM list was a sham.

"You know, painting's fine, but it's not everything," she continued. "You should think about getting a coffee table. Refurbished-looking coffee tables are huge right now. Here, I'll show you," she said, and led me out of her office and down the elevator to the sample room. She showed me a coffee table that looked like it should have been in a junk shop, not on the floor of the Bay's home decor section.

"It looks like you've taken a framed mirror, banged out the mirror, put glass in and then added legs to make it into a table. Except, you haven't," Olivia explained.

"Wouldn't it be cheaper—and more authentic—to actually do it yourself?" I wondered aloud.

Olivia looked at me and laughed.

"Ick. If there's one thing I can't stand, it's other people's used junk," she said. "Why do all that yourself when you can just buy it new? You know, none of these will fit in your place, but there's this great little shop out by my place that makes furniture specifically for people with teeny-tiny condos. Why don't you paint this weekend, and we can make a date to head out there in a few weekends when I'm free?"

I shook my head.

"I think I'll just stick to the painting for now," I told her.

Besides not having any money to buy furniture, I had this romantic notion that I would buy real furniture when I had a real husband.

"I can hear what you're thinking. That you wish you had a man to make these decisions with, like it's romantic. It's not. Think about it. If it was, then why did Sam go and buy a couch—that you hate—without even consulting you? How do you think I'd get anything done if I just waited for Johnnie to propose? I'd still be living in a basement apartment. No offence," she added.

It wasn't the same for me as it was for Olivia. Olivia chose to be a feminist and to make all the decisions, and I didn't think it was fair that she was making me feel bad for feeling the way I did.

"Sam's not the boss of you anymore," she said, grabbing my hand. "Tell me, who's the boss of you now?"

"Me," I said feebly.

"Wrong. I'm the boss of you now," Olivia informed me, as she guided me back to the elevator. "So listen to me. Some girls think they need a psychologist to analyze their emotions, fix what's going on inside them. You don't need that rubbish. You need a psychologist for your home. It all starts with your surroundings. I'm the Dr. Phil for your home. Trust me."

"It's just paint. How hard can it be? Besides, Mitz will be with me for a second opinion." I didn't think Olivia was being very supportive. If she thought I needed help, then why couldn't she be a friend and help me?

Olivia laughed. "Mitz is not going to help you! When was the last time you heard her mention painting? I bet she doesn't know a straight brush from a sash brush."

I didn't know a straight brush from a sash brush.

"Anytime she needs a room painted, she just calls her relatives. At least three of her cousins are professional painters. Okay, tell me which shade you're going to pick." She took a tube of M.A.C Lipglass from her orange leather Tod's handbag and applied a bit to her pinky, then dabbed it onto her lips.

"Actually," I said, sifting through the paint chips, "does it have to be brown? My place is so dark already. I thought maybe something brighter. Or prettier."

Or less brown.

She shook her head and pulled out an ornate little notebook and a pen from her handbag, scribbled down a number and then ripped the pink piece of paper out and handed it to me.

"Go see Bylon at West Side Couleur," Olivia said, as we took the elevator back to her office. "It's just north of Eglinton, off Bayview, on a tiny street, first one after the lights. It's couture."

"There's nowhere closer?" *Or on the way home? Or on a subway line?* I thought miserably. All I wanted was Benjamin Moore or Debbie Travis paint, not some ridiculous couture brand nine subway stops and a twenty-minute walk away.

"God, no. West Side is so chic. So's Bylon. I buy all my paint from him. I told him you're coming. He'll set you up with the right paint. Call me if you need anything else!" she said cheerfully, giving me a quick squeeze. "Oh, listen," she added, as we entered her office. "I was cleaning my closets and I have all this stuff to get rid of." She reached behind her desk and lifted up a black garbage bag large enough to hold a very large, dead animal. She dumped it at my feet. "Would you mind dropping it off at the Goodwill on your way to work? I double-bagged it," she added, "since I know you walk to work. Wouldn't it be funny if it burst open on the sidewalk?"

Hilarious, I thought, and picked up the bag.

"Hey," I turned around in her doorway. "Did you get the invite to my party?"

Olivia looked up from her BlackBerry, her forehead wrinkled. "Oh, yes. What's the occasion? What are you celebrating?"

I tried to be nonchalant, shrugging, which wasn't easy, given the heavy load in my right hand. My shrug was more of a wobble. "Not working."

She gave me a look.

"You know, civic holiday?" I felt dumb, so I added, "Good friends." *Or being civil,* I thought.

"Who else is coming?" she asked, as though she didn't know all of my friends. Who did she *think* was coming?

"Mitz and Amir, Victoria and George, and Bradford and Tob—"

"Of course," she said abruptly.

I wasn't sure how to take that. Was she testing me to see if I had any other friends and then just brushing me off because, of course, it was the usual suspects? Or was she just respond- ing that way because she didn't like Bradford? I considered telling her that if she couldn't get along with Bradford she didn't have to come, but I knew better. She was so stubborn she might just hold me to it, and the whole point of the party was to show Mitz and Olivia that I was as talented as they were. So I needed her there. Plus, I needed all my friends; otherwise, it could hardly be a dinner party. It would just be dinner.

"You know, that's eight guests, plus you. Anything over eight and you should really have it catered. Do you want some names?" She pressed some buttons on her BlackBerry, I assumed to pull up a roster.

Of course I didn't want names of caterers. For one, I couldn't afford a caterer, but more importantly, that wasn't the point. The point was to showcase my cooking skills, not some- one else's.

"I can get you chairs, too. I mean, I can just bring one or two of mine. I'm going to turn my dining-room table into a gift wrapping center in the basement of my new house when we move, so I don't mind if the chairs get beat up."

After convincing her I didn't need her chairs, I made my way to the basement of the building, through the underground passage toward the subway and the long trek to the paint store, lugging the homeless bag behind me. I thought about what had just happened—that Olivia hadn't asked me for advice before getting a cellulite treatment, but that she felt fine giving me all her advice, about everything from chairs to caterers to paint. And the thing was, I would never even consider buying paint without consulting Olivia. She was, after all, a skilled interior designer, and a *buyer* for a *home-decor* section in a department store. And she had owned three condos, rented four apartments or condos before that, and decorated every one of them with a coherent theme throughout: calm, cheerful, retro, traditional, modern, nostalgic. So why didn't she think that I could possibly do the equivalent for her? I knew Marjorie's competition, and I could've sent her to someone else if she preferred. But she never even gave me the chance.

⌒

Quite possibly, I shouldn't have strayed from the plan. When I finally got to the paint store an hour later, Bylon, the paint guy, was standing behind the counter, bobbing his shaggy-haired head to either the Beastie Boys song escaping his paint-spattered boom box or the paint-shaking machine that was on full speed—I wasn't sure. He grinned at me, and I handed him the paint chip Olivia had given me.

"Mocha Steamer, eh? So you like brown?"

I didn't like or want brown. How would brown be inspiring? Brown stood for all the things I hated about myself: my blah-brown hair, my brown freckles, my brown eyes. The brown chair at the brown desk that I sat in every day at Face Value. I hated everything brown in my life—except Pumpernickel.

"I'd like that brand and finish"—I pointed at the chip in his hand—"but in yellow."

Yellow seemed inspiring, happy and refreshing. Just what I needed.

Who knew you could go so wrong choosing a shade of yellow in a lineup? But somehow, I'd managed to choose wrong, and now I wished I'd just gone with Mocha Steamer. At least if the wall was too brown, I could just say, "Doesn't it remind you of a mocha steamer?" It would be calming, inviting, warming. Instead, my shade of yellow—Canary Yellow—was a little invasive, to put it mildly. In fact, it ended up sort of looking like a flock of canaries had, indeed, smashed into my wall.

And painting wasn't that easy, especially when I didn't have a stepladder and I did have a cat who was quite interested in a phenomenon he'd never witnessed before. As I was reaching for the high parts of the wall behind the futon, Pumpernickel kept jumping up on the futon while I tried to keep my balance on a mattress that had little stability. In hindsight, I probably should've moved it out of the way and stood on a kitchen chair instead (which would've cleaned up more easily when I splattered paint), but my place was so tiny, that would have entailed moving the futon into the kitchen and, let's be honest, it was just too much work. Anyway, the yellow paint splatters sort of blended in with the Laura Ashley floral pattern. At least, that's what I told myself.

"You're just painting, you're not plastering the wall. It's just like Mountain Pose," Olivia said when she called on Saturday afternoon to see how it was going, and I complained that my arms hurt from holding them over my head for so long. I mean, Mountain Pose lasts, like, sixty seconds (at most) and you don't need to hold a paint roller (which is surprisingly heavy, especially when it's full of paint). Apparently, my arm muscles just weren't that strong.

But that wasn't the real problem, I realized an hour later, when I got down to the bottom half of the wall and saw I'd forgotten to block off sections with tape, as instructed, so I'd ended up painting the entire width and height of it. As I stepped back to look at it four hours later, when I was finally done, it didn't look good. At all. It looked like a giant Post-it Note.

I dumped my painting supplies in the kitchen sink and grabbed the last three cookies out of the bag in the cupboard, then lay down on the floor, angled so I could look at the ceiling and keep the yellow wall out of my vision. Maybe I really was destined to die alone, in a Post-it-Note-themed, Post-it-Note-sized apartment, fat, with only my cat and a bag of Oreos. At least I'd completed Item Number 5 on my OM list. Or, it was as completed as it was going to get.

⌒

"It looks like a Post-it Note," Victoria said when I walked into my apartment Monday after work. She was sitting on the couch, reading a book, which she quickly slapped shut and stuck under her thigh since there was no seat cushion on the futon to hide her literature under. She handed me an olive-and-cream scalloped envelope, which I took from her after dropping my khaki canvas Gap bag on the floor and kicking off my flip-flops.

"It's an accent wall," I rebutted.

"Accent walls went out of style five years ago," she informed me.

I ignored her and turned the envelope over, then opened the flap, which was held in place with a gold sticker embossed with the letters OC.

Stuck in Downward Dog

You're invited to an
Engagement Enhancement Party
In honor of Mitsuko Moretti's upcoming nuptials
Please choose one of the following:
I, _____,
will be attending and would like the following treatment:
❏ *Botox* ❏ *Injectable lips*
❏ *Injectable—wrinkles* ❏ *Cellulite treatment*

Sunday, July 16
ForeverYoung Medi-Spa, Dr. Eleanor Overholt
555 Hazelton Avenue
RSVP to Olivia Closson, Maid of Honor
Envelope enclosed

Olivia had been named maid of honor? When had that happened, and why hadn't Mitz called me? And what had happened to afternoon tea or pedicure parties to celebrate getting engaged? Was I seriously being invited to relive my work week on a Sunday?

"What is it?" Victoria asked, peering over my shoulder.

"Mitz's engagement party."

"Fun! Did you plan that?"

"No. Olivia did." I was slightly offended that my sister would think I would plan something so superficial. Weren't we supposed to be celebrating a blushing bride who'd be gorgeous no matter what? She was in love. Besides, she was already so much more attractive than the rest of us who didn't even have boyfriends. Then again, if anyone *was* to throw an Engagement Enhancement Party, *shouldn't* it be me? Shouldn't *I* know best?

Did being surrounded by lip plumpers, fat suckers, tummy tamers and thigh thinners forty hours a week not count for anything? Apparently not.

Olivia called at that moment, and I threw down the invitation to pick up the phone.

"So what are you going to fix?" Olivia asked.

Surely Emily Post wouldn't approve of Olivia's etiquette blunder: insinuating that all the guests had physical flaws that needed fixing.

"Nothing. I'm adding an option," I responded.

"You can't do that."

But if Olivia could make party guests feel bad about their appearances, I could add my own line to an RSVP. I was sure I could find an etiquette expert to back me up.

I changed the subject to the real problem that was bothering me. "When did Mitz choose her bridal party?" I asked. I felt a slight sense of anticipation at the prospect that perhaps I would be an attendant, too. Maybe Mitz just hadn't called yet to tell me. Maybe it was protocol that you chose the maid of honor first and then the bridesmaids. Maybe—

"Ooooh..." Olivia said as though she were slowly burning herself with a flat iron. "She didn't tell you? I told her she should really say something to you, but she thought she didn't need to say anything unless you *were* in the wedding party. Honestly, she felt really bad, and she wanted to make you a bridesmaid, it's just that, well... she has four sisters and she couldn't exactly not make them part of the wedding, and five is such a good number. It's all about the dozen. Her and Amir, the four sisters on her side, her brother and Amir's three brothers on the groom's side, plus Johnnie and me—"

"Johnnie's in the wedding party?" Olivia's boyfriend had beat me, Mitz's best friend of sixteen years, into the wedding party?

"Well, it just makes sense. I mean, Amir and Johnnie are good friends, and this way there are five girls and five guys, plus Mitz and Amir makes a dozen, which is just so much easier for buying things for the whole wedding party. Honestly, it's a job, Mara. You're not missing anything. And you know me, I'm so anal about everything that it's really just like a business contract. You know, she's just hiring me to do the work. And I'm sure her sisters will be totally useless. They're so wrapped up in their own lives and living all over the globe that they won't have time to help. Don't think of it as not being asked, think of it as me being the only non-family member to be included."

I wasn't sure how that was supposed to make me feel better. Olivia should've just stopped speaking right then.

"And if she asked you," Olivia continued, "well, then they would be short a guy."

So I was being penalized for being single.

"Anyway, like I said, it's not even about friendship. Being a bridesmaid is a job, you know," she said, sliding into Marsha Brady mode. I imagined she was giving her long blonde hair a flip for effect. "It's about having the best girls for the job. Most of the work gets delegated and done on each girl's own time. It's not like we've suddenly formed the Mitz Wedding Club. Nothing about our friendship will change."

But it already had. Mitz was getting married. Olivia had already moved in with Johnnie. And I lived in a basement apartment.

"Honestly, I *wish* it were you, not me," she continued, apparently unaware that her soliloquy had gone on long enough. "With the house and—did I tell you we found the perfect place in Port Credit?"

She hadn't.

"Isn't that where the bikers go on Friday the thirteenth?" I asked, skeptically. It didn't seem like the right environment for Olivia. "You don't even like fish," I added, since that was the only other feature the small lakeside town was known for.

"Port Credit, not Port Dover. It's off the QEW."

"You mean Mississauga?" I wasn't sure why she hadn't just said so. "So when are you moving?"

"In the fall."

I sat back on the couch and tried to understand. Weren't things supposed to happen one at a time and not all at once? Everyone else was moving, getting things done, and I was just standing still. Stuck. I had nothing to offer. Which was, perhaps, why I wasn't a bridesmaid. I had to think that it was more than the fact that I didn't have a boyfriend. If Mitz really thought I was special, she would've made me part of the bridal party. I was unbalanced and unfocused. That had to be the reason. I was useless. Even in *natarajasana*, Balancing Pose, in yoga, I usually wobbled or had to use my hand to keep my leg up. And all it required was holding one leg in the air while the other was rooted on the ground. How hard could it really be?

"So, how did the painting go?" Olivia interrupted.

I decided to avoid the obvious and ask the pressing question. "Are accent walls still trendy?"

"Not at all." She paused, and I sensed she was multi-tasking while talking to me. "Why? What did you do?"

"Nothing." I hung up and then grabbed the invite and a pen.

You're invited to an
Engagement Enhancement Party
In honor of Mitsuko Moretti's upcoming nuptials
Please choose one of the following:
I, <u>Mara Brennan</u>,
will be attending and would like the following treatment:
❑ *Botox* ❑ *Injectable—lips*
❑ *Injectable—wrinkles* ❑ *Cellulite treatment*
☑ **Attend without treatment**

Sunday, July 16
Forever Young Medi-Spa, Dr. Eleanor Overholt
555 Hazelton Avenue
RSVP *to Olivia Closson, Maid of Honor*
Envelope enclosed

I was fairly certain Emily Post wouldn't approve of adding such a line to an RSVP note. But while I didn't want to set myself further back on the path to completing Item Number 7 on my OM list, become an etiquette expert, I just couldn't succumb to cosmetic enhancement. For one thing, that wasn't on the OM list, and besides I had bigger, more important issues to attend to, such as the fact that I didn't appear to be well balanced (in other words, busy). This showed a clear failure in terms of Item Number 6 on the OM list: Improve my time-management and multi-tasking skills to appear busier to others and create an air of importance.

I was clearly not projecting that air of importance, or I

would've been deemed worthy to be a bridesmaid. I had to do something about it. And given that I wouldn't need to save my Friday nights for bridesmaid duties, I picked up the phone and called Sofi at Mok.

"Are you still looking for a receptionist to work Friday nights?"

Chapter Five

DAURMANASYA: DEJECTION AND DESPAIR.
When such a mental state manifests, one should survive the mood, not succumb.

On the last Friday in June, I finally remembered to haul Olivia's old clothes to the Goodwill on the way to work (it was surprising how easy a task it was to forget, given that I'd had to walk over the bag daily just to get in and out of the apartment). Dropping off Olivia's garments was quite the feat, given that I also needed to carry another bag with a yoga outfit to change into that night, since nothing more than my shoebox-sized wallet and a huge jangle of keys—three just to get into my apartment and four for Face Value—fit into my handbag.

I wasn't going to actually do yoga, but I needed to dress the part for my first shift. Sofi said I could come after I was done working at the clinic and she'd show me what to do. Then, if I liked it, we could work out payment in classes. If I didn't, she'd pay me for the shift and we'd go our separate ways. However, given my recent discovery of the Suck It Up shop next door to the studio, I felt I had a vested interest in making the original plan work. After all, it was completely out of my way to get a smoothie without doing yoga, and although I believed substituting smoothies for meals would help my figure, only by doing yoga would I become better than Olivia and Mitz at it.

At the Goodwill, I lugged the black garbage bag up to the cash, where the cashier (a tiny woman with frizzy orange hair twice the size of her head) took the bag from me and handed me a pink slip.

"This is a voucher you can use to get $5 off anything in the store," she told me.

"Oh, I—" I wanted to say I was just dropping the clothes off for a friend and that she would, of course, never shop there (she couldn't even be bothered to drop off her own donation) when I saw the sign: New Arrivals *HOURLY*. There was also a Designer Labels collection at the back of the store. Could the Goodwill be a hidden gem?

Maybe I would have to return. After all, I walked right by it every day. It wasn't like I'd be going out of my way to shop second-hand. Besides, weren't these clothes just vintage waiting to happen?

That afternoon at the slavery clinic (after a morning full of faxing out press releases to magazines and newspapers announcing Marjorie's new wrinkle-reducing machine, then making follow-up calls, all the while wondering why Didi Sky wasn't doing this), Marjorie reminded me that my work was not done just because it was Friday afternoon. At nearly three o'clock she came out of Treatment Room A with Joey Turturro, who had been getting his pubic hair lasered off.

"You should see me now!" he said, slapping down his credit

card, which was the same thing he had said the last time he was in for an appointment. Seeing Joey's privates sounded like a better option than the alternative, which Marjorie delivered at that moment.

She handed me a pile of brochures just as I was swiping Joey's card and said, "So you're going to set up the booth now, *right*." Because it wasn't really a question, though I had one of my own.

Booth? And then I remembered. The cosmetic surgery trade show this weekend at the International Center. By the airport. Far, far away.

I hated cosmetic surgery shows.

I hadn't always hated these kinds of things. In fact, I recalled a time when I willingly traipsed along behind Olivia and Mitz to the seasonal One of a Kind craft shows. While they found shabby-chic watering cans and wrought-iron mailboxes to decorate their homes, I honed my condiment proficiency at the jam and jelly stands, spreading Maude's Magnificent Marmalade on broken pieces of Premium Plus crackers and washing it all down with mini samplers of fizzy fruit juices.

Until I had to work a show. Every few months, Marjorie bought a booth at the latest cosmetic enhancement fair, then gave me the details and expected me to be there. What angered me most was that Marjorie's publicist, not me, should have been standing at the booth, promoting Marjorie and microdermabrasion. The reason she wasn't, of course, was because Marjorie had to pay Didi Sky for her services on a per-project basis. It was much cheaper to pay me $15 an hour to hand out brochures about thread lifts and tummy tucks while the creepy liposuction distributor beside me asked if I wanted to check out his fat-sucking cannula. The only upside was that sometimes Marjorie would take pity on me and stand at the booth for an hour while I got to walk around, which is when I was able to check out new cellulite creams or at-home peels before they were available on the mass market. And if I was lucky, I'd get free samples.

The show that weekend was called The Path to Perfection, and its organizers were heavily promoting an appearance by *Survivor*'s Sue Hawk, the former trucker who, after she *didn't* win the million bucks, won a free face and body makeover, courtesy of *Extra!* She had been doing the women's show circuit to showcase her new look ever since.

While she was always entertaining (I'd seen her spiel twice before), she was only a half-hour distraction from the weekend-long torture. I was supposed to be perky and pleasant, but I felt like a damsel in distress. Even worse, I now had to trek out to the airport to set up the booth and then get back to the city in time for my very first shift as a yoga receptionist. The humor, I must admit, wasn't lost on me.

While I was setting up the booth at the fair, Mitz called to tell me that she and Olivia had planned an impromptu jaunt to Niagara-on-the-Lake for the weekend, with the boys, to go wine tasting and choose wines for the wedding.

Mitz's parents, like many wealthy families in the late '90s, had moved from their pleasant bungalow to an acre plot of land and started to grow grapes that they then sold to local wine producers. Though they didn't own their own winery, they owned shares in several in the area.

"Do you want to come with us?" Mitz asked. "We only have one guest room, but you could sleep on one of the couches or even stay at your mom and dad's."

I told her that I had to work the show. Then she launched into an explanation about the bridesmaids.

"Listen, I was going to have only my sisters, but then Olivia kept quizzing me on what my sisters' qualifications were, and I got to thinking about how Eiko's going to college in the fall and Juri's leaving for an exchange in Italy next year and Sachie just had her baby and Naomi's . . . well, Naomi is fourteen and only cares about dancing around to *High School Musical* in her Abercrombie sweats, so all in all they just wouldn't be that helpful, and you know how Olivia's a taskmaster."

"It's fine." I knew Mitz was just being honest, true to her nature.

The thing was, I wasn't sure if I really was fine. I felt left out.

～

I made it to Mok just before 8 p.m., with enough time to make a smoothie stop at Suck It Up before my first shift at the studio started. Technically, it was my dinner, but how much healthier could a dinner get than a blend of berries, yogurt and juice?

"Aren't those addictive?" Sofi asked, greeting me as I entered the reception area. I nodded, my lips attached to the straw. "Especially if you load up on enhancers. I usually get so greedy, I add five or six supplements to mine," she said.

Five or six supplements? It seemed like a way to ruin an excellent smoothie.

Two hours into my shift at Mok, I realized that working reception at a yoga studio was a lot like working reception at Face Value, which made it easy to do, but not terribly exciting.

Friday nights at Mok were like a busy day at Face Value. There was only fifteen minutes between the end of one class and the start of the next. During that time, I had to mop up the damp floor, replace the tea lights along the windowsill and remove any sweaty rags, mats, towels, water bottles and Gaiam yoga bricks students used during class but didn't put away afterward. I had never used a yoga brick myself, mostly because they were intended to help if you were too inflexible to do a position, and I was not going to admit to *that*. The point was to get more flexible, more lithe and much, much skinnier. Not to just get by with assistance. Really, it was like using a cane or the remote control. And I was not that lazy.

Then it was back down to the reception desk to make sure members signed in, paid for their class or got their cards stamped.

"It's so important to get them to sign in," Sofi explained to me. "Not only so that we don't exceed the capacity in the room, but also because we really want members to feel welcome. And it's important that you hand the class form to the instructor before each class so that they can review all the names."

So *that* was how Libby remembered everybody by name.

While the class was in progress, I had to clean the change rooms, sopping up more pools of water and refilling the tea-tree oil shampoo containers from a large vat of organic tea tree oil shampoo. Given that I was accustomed to cleaning treatment rooms, filing payment slips and handing papers to people who asked for them, after a fifteen-minute walk-through of what I had to do, Sofi left me to go to it while she taught a class. Which is how, when I was tidying up the change room, I found out the truth.

Inside one of the shower stalls was a gleaming purple bottle of very commercial shampoo and conditioner in all its evil, inorganic, unnatural goodness. I picked it up and looked it over, thinking it was perhaps just a prettied-up all-natural shampoo, like Burt's Bees and Kiss My Face. But it wasn't. It was full of chemical loveliness in the form of Green 3, Yellow 10 and methylchloroisothiazolinone. I longed to fill the studio's containers with this volumizing shampoo and permanently extinguish any remaining fumes of tea tree oil from the change room, but I knew it wasn't my place. Instead, I took it out of the shower and was about to throw it in the trash when I spotted a tube of Cell-U-Gone beside the sink.

If I knew anything, it was cellulite creams. Marjorie's most popular procedure was liposuction, and more than half the women who came in for a procedure were trying to cure cellulite. Liposuction could actually make cellulite appear worse if you removed too much fat, which is exactly what I told Audra, the wild-haired woman who came rushing back into the change room just as I was deciding what to do with the Cell-U-Gone.

"Caught me," she said with a half laugh, half skeptical look, as though she was fully prepared to deny the cream was hers. "I guess I should just accept my cellulite—or ante up for liposuction," she added, then introduced herself.

"No!" I said, surprising myself with the force of my interjection. I lowered my voice and added, "I work at a cosmetic surgery clinic. Liposuction just makes cellulite worse."

"Really?" she said with the same disbelief that everyone had when I told them this. "So, would you happen to know if this cream is any good, then, or if I just wasted my money?"

I did know, and I also knew that she had wasted her money. But instead of being blunt, I explained to her that if she wanted to try a cream that did work, she should order Avon's Cellu-Sculpt. "It has caffeine in it, and it honestly works." I'd seen Tonie Gruber's legs post-lipo and after she'd used four bottles of it, so I knew.

"*Avon?*" she said skeptically. I couldn't blame her, but I assured her the cream was legit.

For the rest of my shift I felt sort of dirty, as though I needed a tea tree oil shower to cleanse myself and make me pure again after helping Audra fix her cellulite problem. Sure, I knew that nothing really cured cellulite, but I felt bad betraying my new position as an all-natural and chemical-free yoga receptionist, even if I could only be accountable as such for six hours. Until I found out that members were allowed to bring their own shampoo.

"You can just put that in the Lost and Found," Sofi said when she saw the bottle of shampoo in my cleaning bucket. The Lost and Found container was filled with various brands of shampoos, conditioners, deodorant, curling irons and all sorts of hairsprays, none of which appeared to be hemp-happy, one-with-the-earth-type brands.

"Morning yoginis and Friday night members are famous for primping," Sofi told me with a laugh. "I suppose as much as we want yoga to make us naturally beautiful, we've all got our favorite products that we rely on. We try to encourage a natural way of life, but we can't stop members from using drugstore deodorant if they want to."

"So you can bring any products you want," I complained to Bradford when I got home, "and use them. And leave them behind, and we won't even throw them out."

"Is there a climax to this complaint?" Bradford said sleepily. "Because it's nearly 1 a.m. and I'm tired and I just want to go to sleep."

"It's just that I thought yoga was supposed to be the complete opposite of the world I have to work in every single day at the clinic. People obsessed with their looks, doing anything to make themselves look better."

"That's not the world you work in, Mara. That's the world we all live in. It's not a cosmetic surgery thing, it's called life. Get used to it. Besides, now you can stop complaining about smelling like tea tree oil and use all your favorite John Frieda products like I know you want to."

He had a point.

Three hours and five insults disguised as humorous comments about my being too young and too inexperienced and, well, not a doctor, to know anything about cosmetic enhancement later, Air, my former yoga instructor from Miss Fit, showed up at The Path to Perfection show.

"Mary, isn't it?"

"Mara," I corrected her.

How was it that I had gone to her class for years and she still didn't know my name? I'd managed to learn her new name after she'd changed it.

"Right. Where are your friends—Olivia and Mitz?"

Of course she hadn't forgotten their names. But she didn't wait for an answer.

"Do you work for a cosmetic surgeon?" she asked, eying

the brochures and the backdrop behind me, which said Face Value Cosmetic Surgery Clinic. She was as bright as a freshly peeled face.

I nodded.

"So that's the reason you haven't renewed your membership!" she laughed and then adjusted her surfer shorts around her hips. "Don't need to work out if you can just suck out the fat, right?"

I wanted to tell her that several of her "students" had been sucked and point out that she herself was at the show, but she rambled on. "You know, nothing replaces flexibility. And lack of it is what really shows your age."

"Thanks."

Air lost interest in me soon after, but not before she took a flyer.

An hour later, Victoria appeared. She handed me a Diet Coke, which I took and then told her to hang on. When I got back from my very first bathroom break of the day, since Marjorie insisted I not leave the booth unattended, Victoria was watching a cheek implant surgery on the television a few booths over. When she saw me, she came back over to the booth.

"How long were you away from the booth?" I asked her.

I checked the consultation box to make sure that no one had tampered with the lid, since it wasn't uncommon to hear that surgeons (or their assistants, more likely) were trying to steal consultation forms from other doctors so they could then steal potential clients when they got back to their offices.

Victoria ignored my question and pointed to the lip plumper I'd picked up at a booth four rows over on my way back.

"What's that?" she asked.

"It's for these," I said, pursing my lips together to show Victoria the tiny lines above my upper lip. Then I opened the lid on the tube of Forever Young Lippity Split and squeezed out a bit. I'd gotten a preview sample at the last Enhancement Expo, a trade show for doctors and distributors that took place several times a year, and was addicted. Most lip products plumped your lips but forgot all about those lines above them.

"I have those, too," Victoria said.

I couldn't see any visible lines, but I handed her the bottle anyway.

"Take this one," I said. "I'll get another tomorrow. But it's really dehydration and drinking through a straw that causes those wrinkles, you know."

I would know, and was actually thinking that my lip lines were likely getting worse, given my new affection for Suck It Up smoothies.

"I thought it was just from smoking," she said cynically, testing me, but I felt confident.

"Well, you don't smoke, do you?"

She saw my point.

"Where's Marjorie?" she asked, looking around.

I wasn't sure why she was asking—or why she cared.

"She rarely shows up unless she's doing a seminar onstage, which she's not."

I handed the woman in front of me a consultation form and a pen.

"I feel like I don't belong here," Victoria said, looking around her, not so much self-consciously, but in a judging way, as though she was too perfect to belong. But she did belong. Most of the women who came to these shows had never had any type of work done but were intrigued by it. Most were too scared but knew that looking was okay, and a show was the safest way to find out more without acting interested. It was like going to a car show—you might not be able to afford the Porsche Cayenne, but your next-door neighbors would never know if you were considering it or the Honda suv. The women who got work done didn't bother with the shows; they already had a plastic surgeon who gave them collagen and a Christmas card every year. No, Victoria was exactly like these women, most of whom would also leave with a lip plumper, an eye cream or a hand cream that helped reduce the appearance of veins.

"Does Marjorie sell this?" she asked.

"What, and take away from her injectable business?"

I doubted that Marjorie would ever consider anything I suggested. When I had first started, I'd shown her an anti-wrinkle vitamin I'd discovered at the first show I worked at, but she just laughed.

"If I went around telling my clients to take vitamins instead of getting procedures, I'd be out of a job. Obviously, Business 101 did not agree with you."

After that, I'd decided that Marjorie was a one-woman show.

"Why are you being such a cynical bitch?" Victoria said bluntly.

I was sure Emily Post would hardly approve of her candor.

"Because *I'm* stuck indoors, working this booth, instead of her PR rep."

"Looks like an opportunity for advancement if I ever saw one."

Then she wandered off to look at the rhinoplasty forceps at the next booth.

Was Victoria right? Could I show Marjorie that I could be her PR rep and do a better job than Didi? Maybe Victoria's unexpected visit was just the inspiration I needed to get started on Item Number 2 on my OM list: Get a promotion or a real job.

Impressing Marjorie with my fabulous promotional abilities didn't go exactly as planned, particularly because as I lugged all the show items back to the office Monday morning (thankfully, I was able to convince Victoria not only to pick me up at the show Sunday night and help me tear down the booth, but to drive me to work Monday morning so I wouldn't have to pay for a cab or carry everything on foot), I realized that I was missing the box of consultation forms. The ones that I'd had women fill out all weekend at the show. The forms that Marjorie used to get new clients in for consultations and then to play off their insecurities to convince them of procedures they needed to make their lives more fulfilling. The forms that were the payback for the price Marjorie paid to have a booth at the show. I was doomed.

"She's going to freaking kill me!" I screamed as I tore through the other boxes for the fifth time as Victoria drove up Clinton to Bloor and turned right. "Don't go this way! We're going to be late. Bloor is a nightmare!" I yelled, tossing a tape dispenser into the back of Victoria's pretentious minivan, which just happened to be a Porsche Cayenne.

"Do you want a ride or not, Mara?" Victoria snapped back.

"Turn around. We've got to go back home."

"We're not going back. You didn't leave anything in the house. We didn't take anything out of the car, so if you left it anywhere, it's at the show, and we're not driving back out there."

"Go back to the house!" I screamed.

I didn't feel myself at all, I was so stressed out. Between trying to paint and clean and cook and get a promotion, it was all too much.

Victoria made a right at the next light, turning up the classical music and not saying a word to me.

When I returned from the house five minutes after we arrived, Victoria looked at me.

"Didn't I tell you so? Honestly, Mara. If you just organized yourself a little better, these things wouldn't happen. And freaking out is not helping at all. Look, it's already almost ten o'clock. I thought you needed to be at the office at nine thirty."

"This isn't my fault," I said. "Marjorie is going to kill me."

"She's not going to kill you. Buck up, buttercup, and deal with it."

Buck *up*? What did Victoria know about dealing with a crazy boss? She hadn't worked in years, and even when she had, she probably had a boss who loved her.

We parked behind Face Value, and I grabbed two of the boxes and prepared to face the wrath of Wickham. Victoria grabbed the signage box and followed me in. Marjorie came out of her office with a young, gorgeous woman with jet black hair, full lips and lashes that framed her dark eyes. She was tiny and wore a sheer white sundress with a pink polka-dot lace camisole underneath. I couldn't imagine what she could want done.

I dropped the boxes on my desk and looked at Marjorie.

"Um, sorry I'm late."

Marjorie looked from me to Victoria and back to me, and then to my flip-flops.

"I was bringing everything from the show and there was traffic and—"

"It's my fault," Victoria interjected. "I offered Mara a ride, and I didn't get my butt moving fast enough and she had to wait for me."

Victoria put the box she was carrying on my desk and then walked over to Marjorie.

"You must be Dr. Wickham," Victoria said and held out her hand. "I'm Mara's *older* sister," she said as though it would be completely inconceivable that she could be older than me. "I've heard so much about you. And, of course, seen you all over the television." She was outright lying. I could count on one finger the number of times Marjorie had been on TV in the past year. "But you look so much younger in person. You know, while I'm here . . ."

Marjorie snapped her face into fake smile mode and eyed Victoria's all-too-authentic Louis Vuitton handbag.

"What can I do for you?" she asked.

"Well, you know, I've had three kids, and my thighs used to be so trim . . ."

"I understand," she said and grabbed Victoria by the arm. "I have some time before my next appointment. Why don't you come into my office, love, and we can talk."

Victoria threw me a winning smile and jauntily followed Marjorie, who turned to me and said, "Mara, book Catherine in for breast augmentation at my next available time and order her implants. Cohesive gel, 300cc."

I turned away to face Catherine and flipped open the appointment book. I started to write her name in a morning slot two weeks from now. I wanted to believe that Victoria was somehow scamming Marjorie so that I wouldn't lose my wages, but I wasn't sure. I couldn't believe she'd sacrifice her thighs for a few hundred dollars in my pocket.

Suddenly it all made sense. I was furious. Victoria hadn't driven me to work to help me out, she'd come to take care of herself.

"That's Catherine with a C," Catherine with a C corrected me. As though it made a difference. I wrote C on top of her name.

An hour later, Victoria left and I told Marjorie about the consult forms. "I should dock you all the wages from the weekend, since what you're telling me is that you are, in fact, useless. That's what you're saying, correct?"

"There weren't *that* many forms."

"So even before you lost them, you weren't doing your job?"

I took a deep breath.

"I should fire you, but I won't. And I won't dock you any wages, but that's only because I'm getting $3,000 out of your sister for liposuction, so I suppose I can afford the $200 you earned at the show. And at the next show, you can make sure you bring in at least a hundred consult forms to make up for it. Now smile, say thank you and go get me a chicken club wrap from that little deli on Church Street."

I grabbed my bag just as she added, "Did you put in the order for Catherine's implants?"

Of course I hadn't. And now I couldn't remember what size I was supposed to order, but there was no way I was going to ask Marjorie, not now, when I was on the verge of being disbarred from my receptionist duties. So I nodded and then ducked out, taking a pen out of my bag and writing 400cc on my left palm to remind me to place the implant order when I got back.

I tried to focus on the beautiful, hot day and let myself get a bit of a tan, but I couldn't. I was too focused on two words: Victoria. Liposuction.

The nerve. If Victoria thought I was going to get roped in to taking care of her while she recovered from a procedure to make her look like a Barbie doll, then she was more delusional than Tara Reid thinking her lopsided foobies were anything close to fabulous—or natural-looking. I needed to take action and get Victoria out of my apartment and my life before she became a needy little pseudo-celebrity—and *I* had to take care of *her*. It was July 3rd, which meant I had almost exactly one month to complete the rest of the items on my OM list, and I couldn't afford distractions.

Once at home, I made the mistake of saying "I need to talk to you" as I walked through the door instead of "You need to leave." Because I only got the chance to say one line before my eyes focused on the scene in front of me.

Victoria, standing at the counter, turned around toward me and held out a bright pink box of cereal.

"I made your favorite: cereal with milk," she said, laughing, and I couldn't tell if she was mocking me or actually being nice. I eyed the counter, where she'd set up a bowl and a new carton of milk, and then focused in on her hands, in which she held a box of Frankenberry cereal.

"Frankenberry?"

And that was it. There was no chance to tell her to get out. The sight of my favorite childhood cereal was too distracting.

"Wow. They still make this?" I said, grabbing the box.

"Texas is the home state of retro cereals. I picked up a few boxes last time George was there on business."

Victoria liked to accompany George to Texas for the diamond shopping and the outlet malls. She poured the cereal into a bowl, added milk and a spoon, and handed it to me.

"Oh, and I wanted to tell you that I spoke to George, and he said it was only fair that if I was staying with you, we should help cover the rent. So how about I pay half?"

I was doomed. How could I say no to half the rent?

"So, you're going to get lipo then?" I said between mouthfuls of Berry goodness.

Victoria closed the top of the cereal box without looking at me. "Would it be okay with you if I was sort of cooped up on your couch for a few weeks?"

I shrugged. "Actually, wouldn't it be easier if you were home? I mean, you have a housekeeper and a cook and a nanny. Surely one of them will be there at all times to get you anything you need. I'll be at work. I won't be able to fetch you anything."

"I won't be broken, just a little bruised."

"But what about seeing the kids?"

She waved a hand. "Oh, I'll manage."

And then it hit me (Frankenberry *was* good for your mind). "You're keeping this a secret from George, aren't you?"

Victoria started wiping the counter. "You know, I just want to do this for myself. I thought I could trust you. I'm even supporting your career by going to your boss."

"This isn't about me. This isn't about my job. It doesn't affect me one way or another where you go, because working there is not my career. It's a temporary *job*."

"Oh, so what's your career?" she asked lightly. "Working at the yoga studio?"

Very slowly I took a long yoga inhale and then even more slowly I let it out, counting to ten. Then, in a quiet but firm voice, I said, "Get out."

Chapter Six

SIVANANDA: FISH POSE.
This position counters the plow position and stretches the chest.

 $\mathcal{V}$ ictoria refused to leave, but instead, three days later, she apologized by way of buying me a pair of Lululemon yoga capris—in a size 12, which I figured was her way of being spiteful despite her generosity. Part of me wanted to inform her that I wasn't into yoga because it was trendy and I didn't want her trendy pants, but once I tried them on (surprisingly, they fit perfectly, though I assumed that was just because they were stretch and even a size or two smaller would've fit just as well), I couldn't give them back. They were so comfortable, and so flattering that they made me feel and look (I was sure of it) like a size 6. At least. So I accepted them and decided to forgive her, but mostly because she had also gone ahead with the lipo, and now had leg ooze. I felt that it was my chance to be the bigger person (morally, of course—Victoria's presence ensured that I was always the bigger person physically).

At least when she was lying on the couch she couldn't tell me what to do or pretend she was better than me. And she actually acted like she needed me. The leg ooze was freaking her out, and she wanted me to tell her that it was totally normal, which I did. In fact, most people got oozing when they got liposuction. Of course, it was technically called tumescent fluid leakage and, to be honest, it was disgusting, but I didn't say that. Instead, I told her that it would go away soon and she would be lovely once again. I gave her a container of Caramel Cone Explosion ice cream, since she had stocked the fridge with spelt bread, sprouts, carrot juice and flaxseed oil, which hardly seemed like comfort food. I even gave her the bed, though during the day she moved out to the futon couch so she could, I presumed, watch me come and go.

Having her lying on the couch was good motivation to get me out of the house, because as much as I thought her being helpless would give me the upper hand, she was more demanding and judgmental when she didn't have the ability to do anything else.

What was worse, she didn't leave the following weekend, claiming she didn't want the kids to see her in her "condition," and although I felt there was another deeper underlying reason, I didn't say anything because perhaps she had a point. It certainly wasn't in her best interest as a mother to get their sympathy (or to scare them) with her self-inflicted surgery.

"Where are you going?" she asked, as I left the house for my second yoga class of the day on Saturday. "I haven't had a cooked meal in days. Could you please make me something before you go? Anything. Some soup or maybe an omelet?"

I handed her a pizza flyer and the phone. Maybe I wasn't being the best caregiver, but she hadn't asked if she could stay on my couch, and if she really wanted someone to take care of her, she could've gone home to her husband, for whom, presumably, she had gotten liposuction, or her cook, whose job it was to make omelets and soup. Besides, I had to focus on my own dinner party.

"You're going to be better in time for my dinner party, right?" I asked her. "Because you haven't mentioned it, and you haven't RSVP'd."

She looked up from the copy of *Flare* I'd brought home from the office. "Dinner party?"

"I mailed your invite over a month ago."

I thought she turned a little pale, as though I'd told her I'd sent her an invoice for sleeping in my bed, even though it was technically her bed.

"Oh, it must've just gotten lost in the shuffle since I'm not taking in the mail myself every day. When is it?"

I told her, and she immediately said it would be just her, since George would be in New York on business that week.

It seemed suspicious that she knew his schedule so well and yet she had no qualms about coming anyway, given that she hadn't even checked to make sure the nanny could watch the kids. But what did I know about being a mom? I shrugged my shoulders, grabbed my yoga bag and headed out.

~

Like any good PR rep, Didi Sky tested the services she touted—a lip injection before holiday mistletoe action, a chemical peel at the end of the summer and an upper eyelid lift to stop her brows from sagging even farther down her face.

Now Didi wanted a little facial rejuvenation.

"I want the fat from my butt," she said, slapping her butt cheeks with both hands, "sucked out and put right here." She pinched her face cheeks. I grimaced.

What she wanted, in technical terms, was liposculpture. Didi did have a rather big bottom, but it matched her thick thighs, large arms, profound breasts and inflated ego. The thought of getting butt fat put into your face seemed particularly revolting, but Didi didn't think so.

In addition to working for Marjorie, Didi had recently signed Dr. Ellie as a client, since Dr. Ellie had just divorced her husband, who had been doing her press. Typically, Marjorie didn't like the arrangement. But when Didi came in to visit Marjorie in the middle of June, Marjorie saw how the relationship could work in her favor. Dr. Ellie was set to go to L.A. to do a taping for *Venice Beach Vanity* and couldn't make an appearance on *eTalk* the following week. Didi agreed to get Marjorie on instead if she gave her the liposculpture and eyelid lift she wanted for free. Marjorie told me to slot Didi in for her surgery as soon as possible, and suddenly I could feel my potential foray into public relations becoming that much more real. Didi would need to be off work recovering for at least two weeks, which meant that I could really prove myself to Marjorie and take over as her publicist myself. I wasn't exactly sure how, given that I had no connections to the media, but I figured that at least I could offer to field any media calls that came to Didi regarding Marjorie. The key to getting the job that I wanted was to befriend the one woman who already had it.

And so I offered to make myself indispensable to Didi. Unfortunately, she didn't really go for it. She said she was sure there wouldn't be a ton of work to do for Marjorie while she was off, but that if she did set up an interview or appointment, I could assist if she wasn't in any shape to attend.

I tried not to get discouraged.

But then, it was as if good kismet finally kissed my butt (which happened to look amazing in my new yoga capris, currently paired with a long top so Marjorie wouldn't notice I was wearing sweats to work). Or rather, kismet kissed Didi's. She got an allergic reaction to the anesthetic in her bottom, which made her butt cheeks inflate like helium balloons. So she couldn't attend the *eTalk* appearance, and Marjorie agreed that I could go with her instead, and get her water and hold her handbag while she was on the air.

And then, a few days after that, I got a call. It was just a PR student at one of the local community colleges, but she was writing a story about real-life PR reps. I couldn't believe it. Had my own appearance feigning to be Marjorie's PR rep actually gotten me noticed?

"Sure, I've got a few minutes," I told the girl on the phone.

She laughed. "Oh, I actually was calling to talk to Marjorie."

"You realize Marjorie's not a PR rep?"

"Of course. I wanted to get a quote from her about her own PR rep, Didi Sky, right?"

I couldn't believe it. My one shot at fame, gone. I decided to make it hard on the PR-rep-in-training.

"Well, you actually have to go through Didi to get an interview with Marjorie," I told her.

"Well, I would, but I heard she had some sort of accident...she's friends with my best friend's mom. Something about her butt being swollen?"

I laughed, because even though I was sure Didi was in pain, it was sort of funny that she had a balloon butt.

"I guess you could say that."

"Well, that's the premise of my article, that PR reps have high risks."

"I wouldn't know about that. It was sort of self-induced. She just had an allergic reaction during a procedure. Sort of a hazard of the perks of PR—and goes with the territory if you're a PR rep for a cosmetic surgeon. But she'll be fine. Besides, it was free, right?" I said. "Listen, I can tell you Marjorie's not going to do a student interview."

"That's okay, I've got what I need," the girl said and hung up without so much as a thank you.

Things went further awry when Catherine, the petite woman who had wanted B cups, got C cups instead. Because apparently she hadn't wanted jugs. But Marjorie had given her jugs. Actually, I'd given her jugs, because instead of ordering 300cc, I had ordered 400cc, the most common implant size, which will take a woman with an A cup up to a C cup. Even if she didn't want a C cup. Which Catherine didn't.

Catherine didn't really know at first. She thought she was just swollen because that's what Marjorie had told her before sending her home. But a few days later, when Catherine's swelling had gone down and she'd removed the bandages for good, it was confirmed that Catherine had bocce balls where she'd wanted tennis balls. Which is when Marjorie compared Catherine's consultation form to the implant invoice and realized the mistake.

I was dead.

"I'm going to call the company and tell them that they obviously sent the wrong implants," Marjorie said to me. "Because that's the only answer, isn't it?"

And I realized what Marjorie was doing. She was covering for me, because in doing so, she was covering herself to avoid being sued.

And although I felt horrible, I was secretly relieved. The trouble was, even though I had caused the whole mistake, I just didn't care. Sure, I felt bad for Catherine, especially because her tiny chest had just been stretched to fit the C cups, and now there was a risk that her skin would be a bit saggy with the smaller implants and she might need further surgery to fix that. And I felt bad that I had been so careless. But otherwise, I just didn't care about anything that happened at the clinic.

And that was the real problem.

~

"Don't do anything I wouldn't do," Victoria called after me as I left for Mitz's Engagement Enhancement party the following Sunday, but given that she'd gotten liposuction when she was already skinny, I wasn't sure what type of procedure she *wouldn't* get.

I was the first one of Mitz's friends to arrive at the Forever Young Medi-Spa in my new Lululemons (which I couldn't stop wearing because they made me look so good, but also because everything else in my closet seemed constricting in comparison) and with a trio of gravy boats in tow. Olivia had insisted Mitz wanted them and they'd make a perfect shower gift, but I wasn't sure why anyone needed three gravy boats.

Mitz's mom—Mrs. Ami Moretti—and Mitz's four sisters (Eiko, Sachie, Naomi and Juri), as well as a group of fifty- and sixty-something ladies who, I assumed, based on age and their brightly colored warm-up suits, were her mom's friends, were chittering like baby birds waiting for worms. I felt slightly out of place and wished that Olivia had invited me to come with her and Mitz, but the party's theme was supposed to be a surprise, and she figured the more people she involved, the more suspicious Mitz would be.

"Mara! We've been waiting for you!" Mrs. Moretti said, rushing forward, arms extended to hug me. She was normally quite reserved, but had become more affectionate since we'd moved away from home years ago.

"We want to see how it's all done," one of her lime-green-clad friends cooed, coming up behind her. Once Mrs. Moretti untangled herself from me, the lime-green woman linked her velour-jacketed arm through mine. I wasn't sure I could trust a sixty-year-old woman wearing velour.

"Oh, I'm just going to watch," I said to both of them. "I didn't check any services off."

"Nonsense, nonsense. I'm paying for it all, and we want you to show us the way. You're the expert, after all, right?" she said loudly, so everyone could hear.

As much as I wanted to be flattered that someone thought I knew a thing or two about cosmetic enhancement, I felt as though I were twelve years old again and had just been told my Rice Krispies squares were the best dessert at a neighborhood Christmas party.

"Shouldn't we wait until Mitz gets here?" I asked, hoping to stall for time or deflect the attention away from me.

"Well, we could be waiting all day, couldn't we?" she said, still smiling but obviously annoyed. "*Olivia* was supposed to have her here before everyone arrived, and they're off somewhere without their cell phones on. Those girls." She shook her head and led me over to the chair.

It seemed odd that Olivia, who had planned the whole thing, wasn't being her usual controlling self and overseeing every aspect. Mrs. Moretti told me to sit in the chair, and with her getting antsy, I was worried she was going to instruct Clare, the esthetician who was assisting Dr. Ellie with the treatments, before I could. So I did the best thing I could think to do without looking like an ungrateful guest: I instructed Clare to simply inject a quarter of a vial of hyaluronic acid into each lip, knowing that tiny amount wouldn't make a huge difference and would dissipate within a few weeks.

I wasn't sure who to be upset with: Mitz's mom for pressuring me, Mitz for not even being at her own party, or myself for being so spineless I deserved to look like a fish.

It was okay, I told myself as Clare cleaned my lip with a cotton puff. It was just temporary. It wouldn't last long, and it would be barely noticeable. All it would mean was that my lip-plumping lipstick would last longer. I kept telling myself this as Clare stuck the vial in my top and then my bottom lip.

Then, she pulled out another vial.

"Wait! Wazzat?" I sat up as straight as was possible in the reclining chair.

She patted my shoulder and told me not to worry, that she had just given me the anesthetic.

"No anesthetic! No anesthetic!" I said and batted her hand away. But it was too late. My lips were frozen.

I got up from the chair and whipped off the bib.

"What's wrong?"

"I'm going to react to the anesthetic. Everyone does!"

"That's not true," she said unconvincingly.

She was right—it wasn't true. I was overreacting, but since the anesthetic was a synthetic, there was a higher risk of reaction. I'd seen dozens of women at the slavery clinic come in looking for a subtle plump in their lips, only to get a reaction to the anesthetic that left them with fish lips for three days before the swelling went down, leaving only the "subtle" effects they were looking for from the plumper. I just hoped I wouldn't swell—because without the actual hyaluronic acid it would all be for nothing, even if I didn't want plumped-up lips. It was my own fault for being so weak. I didn't want a treatment, and I should've just said so.

It was too late. My lips were numb, and when I looked in the mirror they were already swelling. Just my luck to have a reaction to the anesthetic and not even get the filler, so I'd having nothing to show for it. I could feel tears welling up in my eyes, and I grabbed my bag and my coat and headed for the door just as Mitz came through with Olivia, who looked very pale and a little bloated in her loose sundress.

"Where are you going?" Olivia asked, grabbing my arm. She tilted her head to the side, her gesture of disapproval and disappointment.

"Home," I said. I could feel my lips swelling by the second. I longed to say something spiteful to put her in her place, but my lips wouldn't cooperate.

—

My trout pout didn't go over well with Marjorie, who was not impressed that I had gone to another clinic. Looking back, it wasn't the best thing to have done, given that I was vying to be her publicist.

"But it's bad publicity, don't you see?" I had a point. "And I got it for free. I didn't even *want* it. And this is just a reaction to the anesthetic. I didn't even get the injectable."

"Well, you certainly could've used it. You're lucky. You realize you signed a non-competition clause, don't you?"

Of course I had no idea. Once Marjorie went back into her office, I called Bradford.

"She's just bullshitting you," he said bluntly. "But it was still a really dumb thing for you to do."

"Thanks." I wasn't sure whether he was referring to the act of attempting to plump my lips or the act of supporting the competition. Either way, Bradford was disappointed in me.

I just hoped the swelling would go down soon.

When I got home from work, Victoria was puttering around the kitchen. She was healing quite well from her liposuction now that the oozing had dissipated, and within a week she was up and walking around—still in my apartment. She probably thought that buying me the Frankenberry cereal entitled her to ignore my ordering her to get out. (And come to think of it, I must have thought so too, because I hadn't followed through and made her leave.) So I told her again that it was time for her to go. For good. I no longer needed her around, even during the week. If I had any hope of completing the om list and throwing the dinner party on schedule (it was only two weeks away), I needed total focus and solitude. Or, at least, no one standing around, watching me screw up.

She threatened to take her plates, cutlery, table, chairs and bed with her, but after I promised to give them back as long as I could keep them for the dinner party, she agreed to leave them.

"You'd think you'd appreciate having me around, especially when you're trying to throw a dinner party," she said with spite, but I refused to let her get the best of me. I had more important things to think about.

I had finally reached the best part of the OM list—and all signs were leading to the dinner party and the debut of the new, fabulous me. I'd been working out so much, I was sure I'd lost weight. Even my Lululemon capris were feeling loose. It's true I'd had them on for days on end without washing them (which might have accounted for some of their bagginess, but the last time I'd gone to Wash 'n Wait I'd been *wearing* the pants, making it difficult to wash them without waiting in my underwear). But I couldn't help wearing them so much. Besides making my butt look smaller, they made my hips look sexier and my stomach look almost flat. Almost. I hated to admit that maybe that was part of the reason people spent so much money on designer yoga wear. Maybe there was more to it than just a brand name.

To reward myself for sticking with yoga while completing everything on the OM list (which was surely multi-tasking at its finest), I wanted a memorable outfit. Something fabulous. And then it hit me. I had the five-dollar discount for the Goodwill, and if Olivia gave her designer clothes to the chain, maybe others did, too. No one would ever guess that was where I'd found my fabulous outfit. At least I could give it a shot. If nothing fit, I could always hit the mall.

After work, I headed deep into the store to the women's dress section. After nixing a floral acrylic dress with matching belt and a pilled royal-blue knit sweater dress, I saw it. An authentic black and white polka-dot Chanel cocktail dress in a size 6, which wasn't really my size, but given all the yoga I'd been doing, I was confident I could squeeze into it. Besides, I had just read an article about how cheap clothing fits smaller because they minimize the amount of cloth. So given that I was buying quality cloth, surely I could go down a size or two—at least.

But when I went to the fitting room to try the dress on, only the bottom half of my legs wanted to squeeze into it. It was like a tree skirt, hugging my knees. How was this possible? Was it really a size 0, and I had misread the label? I twisted the dress around on me and looked at it. No, it was a 6 all right. It just didn't fit. Maybe I'd gained more muscle than I thought. That was probably it.

I took the dress off, got back into my Lululemon capris and returned the dress to the rack. Holly, a red-frocked girl with purple hair and red name tag, looked at me.

"Didn't fit," I told her.

"Oh, you might need to go up a size or two to get the actual size if you're going to go vintage," she informed me. "Vanity sizing has screwed with all of us. You know, we think we're a 4, but we're really an 8."

Up TWO sizes? I needed to wear a size 14? That would make me Rosie O'Donnell without the wit.

And then I remembered how much Olivia despised vintage clothing, or anything used. If I was trying to impress her, I might as well stop subjecting myself to clothes whose sizing was ridiculously condescending. And I was not about to admit that I was two sizes larger than my tags suggested.

"Maybe I want something more modern, after all," I told the salesgirl.

She nodded and stepped out of the way, and I gave the dresses one more look before heading to the separates section. I went straight to my size (I didn't mind vanity sizing), grabbed a couple of floaty tunics and some long shorts, capris and a pair of satiny pants that I was fairly certain were only considered fancy in the late '90s and hadn't made a comeback. But I couldn't resist, and took them into the change room.

Nothing fit.

Buttons were pulling, and everything was too tight, even on my arms and my stomach, leading me to believe that perhaps I hadn't gained any muscle after all, since there were no apparent abs showing when I looked at myself in the mirror. Had I gained fat?

And then a rush of gorgeous purple and pink silk appeared over the door to my change room. I touched it. It was soft and felt like warm butter between my fingertips.

"This Diane von Furstenberg came in just the other day. I can't believe no one's snatched it up," Holly said from the other side.

I couldn't see what size it was—the tags had been ripped out at the neckline—but the fabric content tag, assuring me it was authentic Diane von Furstenberg, was still attached to the inside right seam of the shirt. I *had* to fit into the top, no matter what. Diane von Furstenberg was one of Olivia's favorite designers. She would be so impressed. And unless Diane herself became one of Marjorie's clients and started paying in garments, this would be my only shot at wearing designer any-thing. I eyed it dubiously, willing it to fit.

"It's a wrap," Holly said, as though she could hear my thoughts through the door. "So it's practically adjustable."

I pulled my yoga capris back on and then gave the shirt a shot. As I pulled the top on, it felt a little snug in the shoulders, the arms were a bit tight, it didn't quite close over my heaving cleavage (at least there was one positive), and it sort of gripped my hips, but it was surprisingly loose in the mid-section. Maybe I was just disproportionate. Still, I couldn't *not* get it—it was a Diane! And it was only $7! It even looked great with my yoga capris. The result was very chic. And so unlike me, but I'd take it. I'd buy a pair of thin black capris (*not* from the Gap) and a pair of flats (also *not* from the Gap), and my ensemble would be complete. Olivia would be so impressed with my newfound fashion sense.

As I slipped out of the top, I noticed the one tiny snag—metaphorically and physically—with the fabulous frock. There was a hole at the back of the neckline where the Diane von Furstenberg label and size tag had been ripped out. The hole wasn't big, but it ran vertically from the neckline, splitting the silk for about an inch and a half. Still, I wasn't worried. I could sew it up at home, and no one would be the wiser. It was just too bad that being skillful at sewing wasn't one of the goals on my OM list.

I pulled on my T-shirt and flip-flops, and took one last look at myself in the mirror. I *really was* getting skinnier, which, come to think of it, was amazing. I mean, I hadn't actually changed my eating habits, except for the daily smoothies, which I'd been having on top of my regular meals. But I'd been

doing yoga, and obviously I'd been burning many, many calories, which explained the incessant hunger and need for the
smoothies. Except for the days when I didn't actually *do* yoga.

But never mind. My one-stop shopping excursion had
resulted in the successful completion of Item Number 9 on my
OM list: Stop dressing in Gap and create my own signature
style—even if my signature style was somewhat similar to
Olivia's. Still, Olivia had never worn this particular DVF wrap
shirt, which looked amazing on me. Whatever size it was, it
was surely smaller than anything I'd ever worn before, since I
was certain no designer (especially Diane von Furstenberg)
created garments in size 14. Or even a vanity-size 10.

The next OM list task to complete as I prepared for the party
was Number 8: Be well read and knowledgeable in order to
engage in enlightening conversations. So the following weekend, I headed to the Yorkville Library to get coffee-table books
for my dinner party, which was now only a week away.

The Yorkville Library wasn't the largest one in the city, but
it was my favorite, old and traditional with immense iron doors
at the top of a set of seven steps. My research (mostly on
eHow.com's dinner party guidelines) had said the key to a successful dinner party was to make polite conversation using
references such as current events, history and literature. And
then to use opening lines that would lead to discussions: "What
do you think of [*enter famous author here*]'s latest work?" or
"What do you think about [*enter political writer*]'s view of [*enter
topic here*]?" Since the news changed daily and I didn't have time

to start reading back issues of the newspaper to catch up on the years I'd missed, I figured my best bet would be to top my makeshift coffee table (I was going to concoct one using the very large box Marjorie's new sun-damage-removing laser machine had arrived in) with big, important books (whose inside flaps I'd have read to get a basic idea of the contents). Then I would ask open-ended questions of my guests, and, because I'd be the one asking the questions, my guests would go about proving their own knowledge on the topics, all the while thinking that I, of course, was an expert.

After some research on Amazon.com, I found "Amy's Books to Look Smart" list, in which she listed Franz Kafka, apparently a notable writer of the early 1900s, thus covering two of my planned topics: literature and history. Amy had also written a little summary about Kafka, which I printed off.

Kafka was a neurotic introvert. He spent the majority of his life feeling insecure. Always filled with a sense of inadequacy, Kafka wrote in an attempt to find personal fulfillment and understanding. He published very little in his lifetime and insisted that his manuscripts be burned upon his death. Sympathetic readers understand the feeling of powerlessness Kafka's heroes experience.

Now all I needed to do was memorize the paragraph and I'd sound brilliant.

Unfortunately, when I got to the library I realized I'd forgotten to bring the sheet, and I couldn't remember my neurotic introvert's name. It started with a K, but that was no help at all, so I decided to let it come to me while I picked up a copy of *Moby Dick*, which was at least impressively thick and which I didn't need to read since everyone knew it was a story about Ishmael and the whale.

Then I moved on to the history section, picking up a few other interesting-looking titles—notably *Paris 1919*, which according to the inside flap had to do with historical and political details surrounding the Peace Conference, and *Gulag: A History*, simply because I thought that Gulag was an interesting word, the author had won a Pulitzer, and it was about a whole slew of concentration camps. And those, considering I'd read Judy Blume's *Starring Sally J. Freedman as Herself* when I was eight, I knew a thing or two about. I added a book about President Bush to the mix and was heading to the checkout desk when I spotted a very large book on the trolley, waiting to be reshelved. It had a bold, striking cover and struck me as very coffee-table-appropriate.

I picked it up and turned it over to look at the author: Yousef Karsh. Karsh—that was it. What luck, I thought, that the very same book I'd selected by cover alone was by the author I'd just researched. I stuck the book under my arm and moved on.

When I got home, I laid my new coffee-table books on the kitchen table and pulled out the masking tape I should've used to block sections in my wall (but hadn't) and a pair of scissors. Then, carefully, I cut strips of tape just big enough to cover the Dewey Decimal–like coding on the book, and took my Crayola markers and colored the tape to match the rest of the spine: black for *Paris 1919*, orange for Bush, green for *Moby Dick*, yellow for *Gulag* and red for the pièce de résistance: *Karsh*. An hour later I admired my newish books.

I was brilliant. I was well on my way to accomplishing Item Number 8 on my OM list—and I couldn't wait to see the impressed reactions of my dinner guests.

Chapter Seven

SATSANG: TRUTH GATHERING.
The intention is to inspire one another to express the truth, free
from judgment.

*E*mily Post insisted that I not try out a new dish at a dinner
party, but my question for her was this: if I'd never had a dinner party, never prepared a proper meal and the only menu
item I'd made from the Martha cookbook was a headed salmon
gone wrong, how was I supposed to use a dish I'd already prepared for a previous party? It seemed incomprehensible and
unreasonable, and besides, wasn't the point of a dinner party to
try out new culinary trends? And since the cookbook was a
tenth-anniversary collection published in 2000, some of those
recipes (I had no doubt the salmon was one of them) could be
at least fifteen years old by now.

Since Victoria was going to be no help in this department,
I called Mitz to ask her advice.

"CulinaryConnoisseur.com," she said. "It has all the best
recipes from *Gourmand* and *Palate* magazines. I'm surprised you

don't know it," she added, just as I was thinking she was being so helpful.

I wanted to say, *I'm surprised you don't know I've never cooked a meal,* but I thought better of it.

"You can even type in a theme, and it'll come up with great recipes. Like Summer, for instance," Mitz continued, and I had to admit, she was near-psychic. How perfect would it be to get a themed menu for my event, just like that? "And don't get bogged down if there's an ingredient you don't like. They're very adaptable recipes, so you can just improvise to make them your own."

I liked the sound of that, especially since Emily Post also advised: "Your imagination is the only limit to the menu, although be aware of your guest's dietary restrictions." I hadn't actually asked any of my guests about their dietary restrictions, but it wasn't as though I planned to serve Iron-Chef-esque dishes like bone marrow or sea urchin. Besides, I felt I was clearly ahead in the etiquette race (not that this was a competition or anything). After all, Olivia had sent out invites to Mitz's Engagement Enhancement party only three weeks before the event, and I'd yet to receive an RSVP in the mail from any of my dinner guests. Anyway, I knew none of my guests had allergies—I'd eaten meals with all of them, even Amir and Johnnie, on enough occasions to know that. So all that was left were their dislikes. I could take care of those details with a quick e-mail to each of them, which would not only display my sense of compassion but also impeccable etiquette savvy. Clearly I was managing Item Number 7 on the OM list and would have no problem checking off etiquette as a mastered skill.

And so the next afternoon at work, after composing my e-mail to my dinner guests, I clicked over to Culinary Connoisseur.com and typed "Summer" into the search bar. A summer-themed menu appeared on screen, and the first recipe that came up was Summer Vegetable Frittata. I was torn. I hated eggs, but I *knew* how to make this dish. Or at least something quite similar, thanks to Victoria, and Emily Post had said you should make a dish that you'd already tested. And Mitz had said that this was the website to use if you wanted to impress. And the recipe had "Summer" right in the title.

I clicked on the frittata recipe. I planned to serve several courses, and this would be just one of the appetizers I would circulate while guests were arriving. That way, if they, like I, didn't enjoy eggs, they didn't have to eat it, but they would at least be impressed, and I would be off to a good start with an item I couldn't mess up.

An hour later (having been distracted by Marjorie, who wanted me to clean up Treatment Room A), I printed off the summer-themed menu:

- *Summer Vegetable Frittata*
- *Summer Platter of Shellfish with a Trio of Sauces*
- *Grilled Polenta and Summer Thai Salad*
- *Summer Strawberry Gazpacho*
- *Summer Melon with Basil-Mint Granita*
- *Crown Roast with Asiago-Stuffed Summer Squash Blossoms, Shaved Sweet Potato and Toasted Pumpkin Seeds*
- *Vanilla Port Poached Summer Figs with Honey Crème*

Then I printed off each recipe.

"What are you printing?" Marjorie yelled from her office.

"Invoices."

"You'd better send them out today, because the mail doesn't go out Monday," she called. "But you know we're staying open, right?"

"On the holiday?"

"Of course—we're booked solid," she said, and I flipped the appointment book to Monday, August 7. She had filled it—writing straight across the line I'd run vertically through the day to indicate a holiday   with appointments. I couldn't believe it. I had a feeling it was illegal to deny a worker a statutory holiday, but after the fiasco of the consultation forms, I was worried about losing my job and decided I'd better not challenge Marjorie.

Anyway, I didn't have time to think about how I was missing out on a three-day weekend. I quickly hit Print on the perfect palate cleanser: Summer Melon with Basil-Mint Granita. If anything, I knew that was going to wow my dinner guests. It just didn't get much more Nigella Lawson than that. I might not have her breasts or her accent, but I would serve a meal that would impress even her.

My plan was to hit the St. Lawrence Market on the morning of my party. An indoor market that took up more than a city block, filled with fresh fruit, vegetables, cheese, bread and flowers, it was the perfect place to do my shopping, because everyone knows that if you're going to be a fabulous chef, then you shop for all your items fresh on the day of the dinner party. And, of course, you let the market atmosphere inspire your menu.

I intended to do just that, so instead of bringing each recipe with me, I'd made a list with the ingredients I needed. In hindsight, I probably should've brought the recipes, since I'd forgotten to write the quantity required for each item. I was going to have to guesstimate the amounts that would satiate my seven dinner guests. And now, it also appeared that my list was somewhat vague. The platter of shellfish was open to interpretation since I'd failed to write which types of shellfish were in the recipe—but that would just force me to be inspired. Which was what I was going to have to do with the summer melon, too, as it became clear to me that a fruit called "summer melon" didn't actually exist, according to the vendor at the first fruit stand I happened upon.

"You could get honeydew or cantaloupe. They're both quite nice. It's your personal preference."

How could I have a personal preference when I hadn't made the recipe before and didn't actually know which would taste better? I opted for one of each, thinking that perhaps the title of the recipe was a generalization, meaning a selection of summer melon. And I figured I liked both types of melon, so why not have both together?

I also hadn't organized my list into fruits, vegetables and meat, so once I left the produce stand, where I bought one honeydew, two cantaloupes, a quart of strawberries and the vegetables for the frittata (which turned out to just be zucchini and Swiss chard leaves), I realized I hadn't picked up the summer squash blossoms or the sweet potatoes.

But since I didn't want to fight the crowd to go back to the big veggie stand, I settled for a smaller booth, and the man there told me that summer squash was merely a fancy term for zucchini, and that the blossoms were the flowers on the end of the zucchini. I looked in my bag, and the zucchini I'd just bought didn't have blossoms, so I was forced to buy another selection of zucchini with blossoms. I got so frazzled that, instead of buying sweet potatoes, I ended up buying plain old baking potatoes.

And then I saw George. Which was weird, because I could've sworn Victoria had said she couldn't bring George to my dinner party because he would be out of town (the reason I was planning for only seven dinner guests). Maybe he was *going* out of town. But surely, if you were going out of town that afternoon, you wouldn't be buying a baguette, cheese, a quart of tomatoes and a bag of green beans. Why wouldn't Victoria be doing the shopping? Wasn't that the job of a full-time housewife and mother? Or the housekeeper?

I waved, and I was sure George saw me, but he purposely looked away. He also put on his sunglasses, and since we were still inside and his last name was *not* Michael or Bush, it was sort of weird. Then the moment passed and he got lost in the crowd, so I dismissed the incident.

I needed to focus on the rest of my menu.

I couldn't even begin to worry about my discovery that there were two types of crown roast, pork and lamb, and I had failed to write down which the recipe called for. I chose the pork because I figured pig was safer than lamb when it came to potential dislikes (a question my guests had all failed miserably to reply to), and besides, the butcher said the roast was already prepared, which was perfect because it was one less thing I had to worry about. All I had to do was put the little crowns on top of the posts (er, bones), before serving, he said. *Hosting a dinner party is a cinch,* I thought, though I had no intention of telling my guests that I'd bought a prepared roast.

The first fishmonger I found was hawking mussels, oysters and shrimp, and I decided that particular combination would go just fine with my trio of sauces.

"Jumbo black tiger or pink shrimp?" the fishmonger asked me.

Black tiger sounded decadent. Plus, they cost an extra dollar a pound, so I went with those.

"Don't forget to shell the shrimp first, split the oyster shells open and serve them on ice, and the mussels should open when you cook them," the fishmonger said, looking at me doubtfully.

"Right," I assured him confidently, nodding. Surely my recipes explained those details.

The final thing, which I couldn't seem to find, was polenta. After asking at three different stands, since I wasn't sure whether it was a cheese, a fruit or a vegetable that would go in my summer salad, a lady who was pressing the ends of a cantaloupe (something I hadn't done when I bought mine) said to me, "Most people make polenta. You could buy it pre-made, but I'm not sure if you'll find it here."

Sure enough, when I got home, I realized that I hadn't printed out the recipe for polenta, which must have been another recipe on its own. I called Mitz, who was in a florist's shop, on her cell phone.

"Do you think tapas are going to be totally out of style by the time I get married?" she asked. Who knew one trip to the market could make me exude culinary expertise over the phone?

Of course, I had no idea tapas were even trendy right now. Maybe I'd have to serve the frittata in the mini-muffin pans after all. I didn't want to let on my ignorance to Mitz, so I just answered her question with a question. "Have you noticed a lot of restaurants doing tapas instead of mains?"

"See? I knew it. It's going to be just like Thai," she sighed.

Thai was out? Maybe I'd have to eliminate the Thai influences from my Thai salad.

"Do you have a recipe for polenta?" I asked her, since it was time to get down to business.

"Polenta? It's just cornmeal mush. You mix cornmeal, water, olive oil and maybe a dash of salt. Easy."

Easy for who? Still, I was glad I'd called her.

Except, of course, polenta wasn't the only recipe I was missing. The trio of sauces for my platter wasn't actually on the recipe I'd printed out. For that I needed to print out three other recipes: one for the Saffron Mayonnaise, one for Roasted Grape Tomato Relish and one for Lemongrass Glaze, which all in all sounded much more complicated than appetizing.

I wondered if regular mayo, sun-dried tomato salad dressing and some lemon wedges would do the trick. They'd have to. I didn't have a computer at home, and at that moment I had more important culinary concerns to deal with.

Also, I realized now that the Summer Platter of Shellfish recipe had suggested scallops, king crab legs and clams to match the trio of sauces—*not* mussels, oysters and black tiger shrimp, as I'd purchased. But I was fine with my seafood selection and my ability to be inspired by the freshness of the market. I wasn't worried. The fishmonger had told me that the oysters just needed to be opened and placed on ice, the black tiger shrimp needed to be shelled, and the mussel shells had to open on their own once I cooked them. Since I had a recipe for clams, I'd just follow it to cook the mussels.

The real trouble with cooking was that nothing was what it seemed. Who knew that summer melon didn't exist and that summer squash was really zucchini and that I couldn't just buy polenta? I was thinking about this as I unwrapped the crown roast to warm it up, since the butcher had said it was *prepared* and all I'd have to do was add the crowns. But that was apparently not what he had meant. At all.

Of course, I didn't figure this out until less than half an hour before my dinner guests were set to arrive. Because that's when I was unwrapping the roast. Which is when I realized that the lovely roast was raw. *Raw*. With blood oozing out.

When the butcher had told me it was prepared and turned away to wrap it, I thought he meant he was *getting* me a prepared—cooked—roast from the back. Not wrapping up the raw one.

All I could do was hope for the best, so I slipped the paper crowns on the bones just as the phone rang.

"Can I bring anything?" Victoria asked.

"Actually, yes." I cradled the phone between my ear and my shoulder and shoved the roast in the oven. "I can't find the mini-muffin pans," I told her. "Do you have them at your place? Can you bring them with you?"

"I—I've already left."

Great, I thought. "Well, can you go back and get them?"

But Victoria said it wasn't convenient for her to go back, and I wondered why she'd called, or offered to bring anything, in the first place. It was probably just a case of etiquette, which, really, was a bunch of bullshit if you asked me.

I hung up the phone and shoved the frittata (still in its pan) in the oven. Maybe I could just scoop the frittata into bowls once it came out of the oven?

As I was changing into my Diane von Furstenberg shirt, I realized I'd forgotten to buy flats. I'd also failed to buy black capris (you'd think they'd be a dime a dozen in a twenty-eight-year-old woman's wardrobe, but the pair I had were faded and too tight, no doubt from too many washes and the occasional dryer mishap). Anyway, it hardly seemed sensible to spend fifty dollars on a pair of capris just to wear with my shirt. My full-length black pants, which I wore to work several times a week, were also so tight nowadays that they felt just like stretch pants, which were neither fashionable nor formal. Besides, my dinner party was meant to be special—and that meant *not* wearing clothes I wore to the slavery clinic. And jeans didn't seem fancy enough, which is how I came to pull on my Lululemon capris (at least they were fashionable, if not formal). Then I grabbed a pair of slippers from my closet and checked my reflection in the dresser mirror. Not bad. I'd wanted to pull my hair back in a loose bun (which would keep my hair out of the food while looking chic), but I couldn't since I needed to conceal the fix-job I'd done on the hole at the back of the shirt. It was a bit bunchy where I'd had to gather the fabric, but as long as I wore my hair down to cover it, I was sure I'd be fine. My hair was a bit greasy since I hadn't washed it in two days, but I sprinkled a bit of my Cake Beauty Satin Sugar hair powder on my roots and rubbed it in. Then I brushed my hair, smoothed a dab of Dermaglow eye cream on the frizzedout ends and headed back to the kitchen, stopping to adjust Victoria's flowery tablecloth, which I'd put on top of the laser-machine-box-turned-coffee-table. Satisfied that the cardboard wasn't peeking out at the base, I realigned the library-books-turned-coffee-table-books and continued on to the kitchen.

It was time for the polenta. Mitz had said to mix cornmeal with olive oil and water, but I wasn't really sure how much of each to add. I thought perhaps I'd start to blend them together, sort of like cookie batter, until it seemed like the right consistency. The thing was, the mixture was really quite chunky, and even though I kept adding more and more cornmeal, it just didn't seem to be creating a lot in the bowl. I finally added the entire box and mixed it with water and oil into a lumpy sort of couscous concoction.

Victoria arrived first, and it seemed to me she could've had time to go home, but I was thankful that she showed up just as I was preparing the salad. The salad was a cinch, since nothing needed to be cooked, and I was glad that she was seeing this part of the preparations.

I placed the arugula on each plate, and topped the greens with button mushrooms, mango, zucchini and bamboo shoots. The bamboo shoots were kind of odd looking, so I took the green onions, which I was supposed to chop finely, and instead used them like strings to tie the shoots into bundles, which looked much cuter and was, as Emily Post recommended, much more original. Then I added the polenta to each plate and turned the stove on to heat up the strawberry gazpacho, which I had already pureed. It tasted sweet and summery, and I felt confident that it would be a hit.

Bradford arrived and handed me a bottle of Pinot Noir.

"I know, I know. I swore off Pinot for more than a year after that damn movie came out, but I was thinking that a sufficient amount of time has passed that it's now so uncool it's cool again," he said.

I took the bottle of wine. Alcohol was alcohol, *Sideways* or straight up.

Tobias came through the door, handing me his keys. I took them, admiring his smooth cuticles. They were second only to his smooth elbows, which were the reasons why Tobias was a body double on *Color Therapy*, a show that helped couples repair their marriages by renovating their homes. It was a concept I found ridiculous. Had the producers never been to an IKEA store, where half of all marriages end? I couldn't debate this point with Tobias since he wasn't actually a psychologist; he just doubled for the real one who analyzed the couples' problems and then recommended paint. Although Tobias's brush strokes might have ripples (and the actual painters had to repaint the wall between scenes), so did his deltoid muscles, which were exactly what television viewers wanted to see in the background.

He looked at me, then pointed at my shirt. "Diane?"

"At least your boyfriend knows designer when he sees it," I said to Bradford.

"Yes, well, you and Diane have got yellow bits all over yourselves," Bradford said, pointing at my shirt.

I looked down at the random pieces of polenta sticking to my sleeves and chest.

"Didn't you wear an apron?" Bradford asked.

Of course I wore Victoria's apron. But it was an apron, not a muumuu, and it didn't cover *everything*.

I shrugged.

"Let's get you out of those yoga pants, girly," Tobias said, grabbing my hand and pulling me to the bedroom.

I looked down at my Lululemons. Maybe they didn't have quite the same effect as *actual* capris, after all.

When it was clear there were no pants that would fit, Tobias pulled out a black A-line skirt.

"It's simple and lovely—just like you," Tobias said, guiding me back to the living room.

Just then, Johnnie opened the door slightly and poked his head in.

"Fire department!" he joked, entering the living room. Olivia slapped him on the shoulder with her free hand— slightly harder than what might be described as affectionate— then came into the kitchen and passed me a voluminous red paper bag. I looked inside at the large stainless steel bucket. I wasn't sure if it was a trash can or perhaps a pot for plants.

"For your bubbly," she said. I wondered if she assumed we'd be having champagne tonight, or whether she thought I drank Veuve on a daily basis. I'd get more use out of bubble bath. She tilted her head and looked me up and down. There was an expression on her face I couldn't quite read. "Fancy outfit," she said, and I said thank you because I couldn't say the same back. She was wearing her favorite Rock & Republic jeans, a white billowy tunic and a pair of gold gladiator sandals—and while she looked great (I knew jeans were trendy and seemingly appropriate for any occasion), I felt insulted that she didn't think my party was special enough to wear something nicer.

I placed the bucket on top of the fridge and then went to the cupboard to retrieve my jug of mint julep, which I poured into six glasses.

Emily Post had said I should take dietary restrictions into account, but had mentioned nothing about tastes. Truthfully, I hadn't really considered my own tastes. If I had, I'd have remembered that I didn't even like mint. Not mint gum or candied mints (I preferred Lifesavers and cinnamon gum) or mint tea. And the mint julep was very strong.

"It's very minty," Olivia said with a smile. I wondered if she disliked mint too, but was just too polite to say anything. "I'm driving, so maybe I could just have a glass of lemonade or something?" She handed the glass back to me.

Of course, any good host would have made lemonade, or *something*. I had the wine Bradford had brought. But no lemonade. I'd been too busy with the mint julep to think about anything else. Thankfully, I did have a box of Crystal Light, which I mixed with water while Johnnie joined Tobias at the Post-it wall.

"It's really excellent," Johnnie said.

I couldn't tell if he was being sarcastic.

"It's a little like being on the set of a Yellow Pages commercial," Tobias added.

I handed Olivia the strawberry-banana drink and she smiled, then turned to Victoria.

"So, where's George?" she asked. Knowing the answer, I thought *New York* just as Victoria said "London." Then I remembered that I'd seen George just that morning, and suddenly both answers felt wrong. I had the urge to protect Victoria from Olivia, though, so I offered my sister a drink, hoping it would take us back into the kitchen. But Victoria shook her head and followed Johnnie, who had announced he was going outside to smoke.

"Did you tell me you decided to only paint one wall?" Olivia asked me, and suddenly I had to defend myself. I shrugged, since it didn't matter what my answer was, really. I looked over my shoulder at Victoria. She was on the back stoop with Johnnie, who was lighting her cigarette.

"I didn't know Victoria smoked," Olivia said, thankfully distracted.

Neither did I, I thought, though I wasn't sure it could be called smoking given the way she was puffing out smoke without actually inhaling it.

"So how's the rooftop yoga?" I asked Olivia, pulling my top closed in the front where it was falling open.

I wanted to get a sense of how often she'd been going to yoga. Although I felt fairly confident about my own yoga skills, I wanted to make sure I was up to par when we chose a new studio in the fall.

"Yoga?" she said as if it were the first she'd heard of the activity. "Oh, didn't I tell you? I never joined," she said. "Why? You're not going, are you?"

"Of course she is," Bradford piped up, as Johnnie and Victoria came back inside.

Olivia obviously decided she didn't want to be one-upped in the who-knows-Mara-better game, so she took a sip of her drink and looked around as though we were in an art gallery.

"Yoga's so vintage, don't you think?" she asked of no one in particular.

I wasn't sure what she meant, but given Olivia's distaste for used clothing, I couldn't imagine it was a good thing. Then she looked at Bradford.

"*Sorry*," she said, straining her jaw to make a fake smile. "Doesn't Tobias's sister own a yoga studio?"

"Don't worry. They're doing well," Bradford responded.

"Oh, that's great. I guess that *community* isn't really concerned with trends, anyway. And they're so accepting. Isn't your sister having your baby?"

"Tobias's sister. And it's their baby. My sperm."

"Right. How are you with that?" Olivia said to Tobias.

"Happy. We think it's a great opportunity for their little girl," Tobias responded coolly.

"It *is*. Just think, she'll be able to relate to all types of people: her moms are lesbians, her uncles are gay, her uncle's her *dad*—she'll even understand her little trailer park friends better," Olivia said, smiling.

"Olivia, don't be a bitch," Johnnie said, emerging from the kitchen carrying two tall glasses filled with Crystal Light. He handed me one of the tumblers. "Spiked—is that okay?" he asked, and I nodded, thankful for the interruption and (as I took a gulp) the shot of Absolut he'd obviously found in my cupboard. Johnnie grabbed Olivia's hand, and she allowed it, though lightly, in the same way that you bring a handbag to a party but really wish you could set it down somewhere, or that you had just left it at home.

"Great party, Mara. It's super retro. Totally my style," Johnnie said.

I smiled unsurely and nodded, then looked at Olivia.

"So you don't want to do yoga again—even in the fall?" I asked her.

Olivia shrugged. "I don't know. I'm over it. I was thinking about something more innovative. Maybe fusion. Or hooping. Or ballet."

Hooping? Ballet? I couldn't believe that the one thing I was getting good at was the one thing Olivia didn't want to do anymore. How was I going to be better at it than she or Mitz if they never went to yoga again?

Just then, Mitz and Amir arrived. Amir flashed his shiny white teeth and a bottle of red wine, and Mitz handed me a cheese board and knife, wrapped with a brown taffeta bow.

"No cooking required," she said. Any other time I would've laughed, but given that I was hosting a dinner party for which I'd actually cooked, I felt insulted.

"Did you know Olivia doesn't want to do yoga in the fall?" I asked Mitz.

"Oh good," Mitz said, kissing Olivia on the cheek. "Me neither. We're saving our money for the wedding. Right, honey?" She looked at Amir.

"How does Vegas fit into that?" Johnnie joked, coming over and slapping Amir on the back.

"Vegas?" Mitz looked at Amir.

"Sure. I'm getting married, so I gotta have a bachelor party, right?"

Mitz grabbed Olivia's drink and took a gulp, made a face, then handed it back to her.

"Do you have anything stronger? And without aspartame?" she asked me.

"Mint julep?"

"Maybe I'll just have a glass of merlot," she said, and before I could wonder whether she meant *her* merlot or just assumed that any reasonable dinner host had a bottle of merlot to offer, Amir interrupted her, reminding her that he'd just whitened her teeth and the red wine would stain them.

I thought about suggesting that he have a glass to dull his own teeth, but instead I headed into the kitchen and decided to start serving up the appetizers, hoping that would take the edge off what seemed like a very tense dinner party so far. I could hear Mitz informing Amir that he would not be going to Vegas.

"Well, you don't want the strippers at the house, do you?" he joked, and there was more laughter, mainly from Johnnie.

I returned with the pan of frittata in one hand and a mint julep in the other for Mitz, which I handed to her. Then I offered the frittata to Amir, hoping it would occupy his mouth and thus ease the tension in the room. Victoria followed with spoons, plates and napkins.

"Is this scrambled eggs?" Amir asked. "Shouldn't you save this for tomorrow morning, once we all wake up?"

"We're not staying over, Amir," Mitz said, clearly annoyed. "We're not in college." She rolled her eyes, which actually seemed very college to me.

"It's frittata," I said, trying to sound chic.

Somehow, even though I knew how to make it, I was wishing I'd omitted it from the menu. I was basically offering my guests eggs. From a pan. For dinner. Everyone was polite and took a spoonful, trying to balance their spoonful of egg, drink, plate and napkin, which was when Olivia said, "Maybe I should move these books off the table."

She started to pick up my strategically arranged conversation-opener/impression-creating books off the table.

"No!" I said rather forcefully, lunging for the books.

She looked at me with surprise and dropped the books. Tobias picked one up and turned it over in his hand.

"Well, call me Ishmael. What are you doing with this?"

I felt offended. "*Moby Dick* is a classic. Have you read it?"

Tobias laughed. "God, no. In fact, I thought it might be an urban legend that anyone has read it. Is it Sam's?"

I realized that no one—not even my friends—had mentioned Sam, not for months, and I wanted to say something to redeem myself, that he'd called and wanted to get back together, or even that he hated it out west, but all I could think of was that I'd received a reminder in the mail a few weeks back from Holt Renfrew, giving him advance notice of an upcoming sale. It was the only source of mail for which he hadn't remembered to change his address and hardly a point of discussion, so I replied, simply, "No."

Since I had nothing to say about the outstanding quality of the whale book, I decided to change the subject to a book I felt more comfortable with so I could demonstrate my proficiency in Item Number 8, the one about being well read and engaging in enlightening conversations.

"I'm just going to go to the bathroom," Olivia said, moving out from behind the coffee table just as Johnnie sat down on its edge and the makeshift table began to crumple.

I leaped toward him and pulled his arm with my non-frittata-bound hand. He stood up, but not before the corner of the table collapsed.

"Sit on the couch," I said, hoping no one had noticed the coffee table's change in shape.

"Sink into the couch, don't you mean?" Johnnie laughed. He took a sip of his drink and nodded. "I like a girl with a well-used college bed."

I wanted to tell him that the futon was Sam's and that my

own college bed had never even had a guy sit on it, but I decided instead to change the subject.

"What do you think of Karsh?" I asked him, attempting to deflect everyone's attention from the misshapen coffee table. "I'm finding his work so interesting." I tried to act nonchalant, nodding and flipping my hair behind my shoulder with my free hand.

"Karsh?" Johnnie said. "Haven't given him a lot of thought. I'm not really into photography," he added. "Unless it's a photo shoot. You know, when me and the guys are getting our shots done for a magazine or something."

He made the devil's horns with his right hand, which seemed a little ridiculous considering he toured as a roadie with a boy band.

"Still," I said, feigning an air of intellectualism, "Karsh was one of the greatest writers of the twentieth century."

"Writers?" Amir said in what seemed to be a mystified tone, taking a swig of his spiked Crystal Light.

"Uh . . ." I tried to remember the line I'd memorized from Amazon.com, changing my *uh* to an *ah*. "He was neurotic . . . insecure and filled with . . ." It was coming back to me. "Always filled with a sense of inadequacy, he wrote in an attempt to find personal fulfillment and understanding. He published very little in his lifetime—*you know*," I added, to make my speech sound conversational and unrehearsed. "But now, he's really making a comeback. Sympathetic readers understand the feeling of powerlessness Karsh's heroes experience."

Amir threw back his cocktail. "Are you talking about *Kafka?*" he asked.

Kafka. That sounded familiar. I looked at the book on the table, but it clearly said Yousef Karsh. Kafka, Karsh. They were so similar. Had I picked up the wrong book at the library? And if so, who was Karsh?

"At least you didn't pay much for the book," Amir said, looking at the spine of *Gulag*. "Are these from a junk sale or something? They look like old library books." He picked at the yellow-colored tape on the book's spine.

I was mortified. I was a fake and they all knew it. Thankfully, Bradford took the frittata from me and asked for another mint julep, putting his hand on my back to lead me away.

"What's going on with you?" Bradford whispered, once we were in the kitchen. "Just be yourself."

But I couldn't be myself. I wasn't good enough. That was the whole point. I had to be the new Mara, the one who was interesting and accomplished and captivating.

I pulled the shellfish platter and trio of sauces out of the fridge. I'd had to put the sauces in Dixie cups since I needed the only eight bowls I had for the soup course. As I arranged the trio of Dixie cups on a tray, I thought, *a trio of gravy boats could've come in handy*.

Bradford poured himself another drink. Then he took the tray of sauces from me as I grabbed the shellfish plate from the fridge, where it was chilling.

"Summer shellfish?" I said, holding the plate out to Mitz and Amir.

"None of that, Mitz," Amir said, just as Mitz was about to dip a mussel into the sundried tomato dressing. "That red sauce will also stain your teeth."

Mitz sighed and put the mussel in her napkin.

"The shrimp is black!" Victoria hissed behind me, and Amir dropped the handful of mussels he was grabbing.

I was happy that she'd noticed, since the jumbo black tiger shrimp cost me almost double what pink shrimp would have. And I had to peel them and devein them myself.

"It's jumbo black tiger shrimp," I announced proudly.

"I don't think we should eat this," Victoria said, grabbing the platter out of my hand.

I looked at her, alarmed. She could be so rude.

"Victoria!" I followed her into the kitchen.

"Mara, it's not cooked. We'll all die of food poisoning."

"What?" What did she know? It wasn't supposed to be cooked.

"It's supposed to be pink," she said.

"No, it's supposed to be black," I said defensively, though I wondered now if I was right about that. The fishmonger had said to peel the shrimp. He hadn't said anything about cooking it. Although, the shrimp *were* kind of slimy-looking, compared to typical shrimp, but I thought that was just the way they were when you bought super-fresh shrimp from a fishmonger instead of from the supermarket.

"No, they *turn* pink. When you cook them," Victoria said, tossing the entire platter in the trash.

"Victoria!" I wanted to toss *her*. "So what if I made a mistake with the shrimp? I cooked the mussels and the oysters. They're perfectly good."

"Except that they were touching raw shrimp," Victoria whispered.

"You cooked the oysters?" Olivia called with interest from the living room.

"Can I get some more Kool-Aid?" Johnnie added.

"Let's just move on to the meal, okay?" Victoria said, rubbing my arm.

Since my only other option was to make round two with the egg pan, I agreed. I went back to the living room and asked everyone to come to the table, interrupting Tobias, who was explaining the concept of a new show he had pitched to the network.

"The whole premise is based around feng shui food," he announced and then explained that, apparently, you were only supposed to serve and eat food in your home that coordinated with your decor because it helped to keep your image unified. "For example," he continued, "if your house is modern, then you should serve sashimi and sake to your guests. Or, if your place is country chic, you should serve ratatouille and cornbread."

"So, given the Post-it, will we be having a brown-bagged lunch like we take to work?" Amir joked, and Mitz hit him.

"When was the last time you brown-bagged it?" Mitz said. I wondered if she was just trying to deflect criticism off me.

"Well, if you ever made me lunch and put it with love in a brown bag, maybe I would," Amir retorted.

I was too busy thinking about my menu to pay attention to Mitz's reply. Given the frittata and shellfish fiascos, I was beginning to wish that I *had* gone with a simple menu suitable for a brown bag—sandwiches and such. Still, I was more confident about the rest of the meal. I placed grilled polenta and summer salad in front of each person.

"Is this bamboo?" Olivia asked.

I nodded, smiling proudly at my edible decorations.

"So interesting," she said encouragingly.

Mitz looked at her plate as though she was spying. Actually, everyone seemed to be eyeing the plates with suspicion, and I realized why. The bamboo bundles looked pretty, but I wasn't sure how to eat them, and clearly neither was anyone else, judging from the skeptical looks on their faces. I wanted to set a good example for my guests and make them feel comfortable, so I picked up my knife and fork, first cutting through the green onion that was holding the bundles together. There. Then, I tackled the shoots. It felt like I was trying to cut through wood. Should I have put out steak knives? I didn't even own steak knives. Was I supposed to have cooked the bamboo shoots? I suddenly had no idea. But that wasn't the main concern. I pushed the shoots aside (avoiding eye contact with my guests) and ate a forkful of polenta, then tried not to make a face. I was starting to believe that perhaps it wasn't supposed to be served cold. It tasted sort of like the way sweaty gym socks smelled.

I looked at the others, who were busy chatting and drinking their wine.

And not eating.

I quickly stood up to clear the plates, and Victoria helped me. I handed her the set of bowls and followed her back to the table with the pot of steaming Summer Strawberry Gazpacho.

"Is this strawberry syrup?" Amir asked, looking down as I placed the bowls of gazpacho in front of everyone.

Mitz hit him.

"Don't eat it yet," Mitz said.

But of course they were supposed to eat it. Why wouldn't they?

"It's a sauce, right?" Mitz asked. "We're waiting for something else. The main course?" she said, trying to sound helpful, though I had to wonder if she just didn't expect that I'd have not one but two more courses to serve before the main.

"It's gazpacho. Strawberry gazpacho."

"Gazpacho is supposed to be cold," Bradford whispered to me. "That's what gazpacho means."

It did? Was I the only one who didn't know this fact? The recipe certainly hadn't said that. It hadn't even said to serve it chilled, or maybe it had and I just hadn't read to the end of the recipe. I stood up and cleared the bowls, taking them to the kitchen, and then pulled the recipe from the pile of papers in the corner. *Refrigerate until ready to serve.* Which I'd done, only I'd assumed the chilling process helped with the consistency and that when I *was* ready to serve it, I was to heat it up. Bradford put the bowls he'd cleared on the counter and his hand on my back.

"It's going to be okay," he said.

And I wanted to believe him, but my dinner party wasn't meant to be.

Things just got worse. Since no one had really eaten anything yet, save for a few spoonfuls of scrambled egg and syrup, it seemed a little ridiculous to have a palate cleanser, but I served it anyway. I placed the shot glasses of melon granita in front of everyone. I saw Mitz and Olivia ogling each other across the table.

The thing about mixing orange and green, I realized, is that it creates a shade of brown, which really isn't that attractive. And although it was supposed to be frozen, it wasn't, though I wondered if that had something to do with the vodka, which I'd added in a burst of creative improvisation. As a result, my granita was a kind of brown melon mush.

"Is this applesauce?" Johnnie asked.

For someone married to the queen of etiquette, he was hardly a king.

And then the oven started to smoke. I began to breathe very quickly, in a way that was definitely not the *pranayama* breathing I'd learned in yoga class.

Victoria yanked open the door to the oven. Flames were shooting from each paper crown on the roast. She grabbed the spray bottle she used for ironing from the top of the fridge and began putting out the flames.

"You were supposed to put these on *after* you cooked it," Victoria said. After she'd doused the flames, she stared at the roast. "It's still raw. When did you put this in?"

"The butcher told me it was prepared," I said defensively. "I thought that meant cooked. Ready to go. Whatever. I didn't realize it wasn't cooked until I opened the package to warm it up."

Victoria wrapped her arms around me. "Why don't we just have coffee and dessert?"

Coffee? I hadn't even thought of coffee. I didn't even know how to make coffee. Victoria went to the freezer and took out a bag of beans without saying a word. All I could do was hope that the dessert turned out okay.

I placed a Vanilla Port Poached Summer Figs with Honey Crème in front of each person.

"It's gorgeous," Bradford said reassuringly, and I took a deep, *pranayama* breath. Everything was going to be okay.

"Mmm—" Olivia said as she took a spoonful. A split second later she made a face. "What's in here? Garlic?"

"It said three cloves," I explained. "I only added three cloves. Is it too much?"

"Of *garlic?*" Mitz asked, sniffing her dish.

Of course *of garlic,* I thought. What other type of clove was there? And then I realized. I had added garlic to my port-poached figs. Instead of cloves. The spice. Sure, I had wondered about the garlic as I added it, but only for a nanosecond because I had so much else to do. And besides, I'd read somewhere that garlic got really mild when it was cooked, so I figured it was just one of those sophisticated haute cuisine things where the garlic would enhance the fig flavor or whatever.

Mitz laughed. "You're so cute, Mara," she said. And then she stopped smiling. "Wait a minute. What were we supposed to have for the main course?"

"Crown Roast with Asiago-Stuffed Summer Squash Blossoms, Shaved Sweet Potato and Toasted Pumpkin Seeds," I said. I'd memorized the course names perfectly (just not how to cook them).

"Strawberry gazpacho, the summer platter of shellfish, the crown roast..." She looked at me accusingly, and her face started to turn red. For a moment I thought maybe I'd poisoned her, or that she was allergic to something I'd served, just as Emily Post had warned. Although, how could I have poisoned her? She'd barely eaten a thing.

"Mara, this is my *wedding* reception menu!" she yelled. "You stole my reception menu!" She stood up, throwing down her napkin. "I can't believe your nerve. I *told* you this was my menu."

But, of course, she hadn't told me her wedding reception menu. Had she forgotten I wasn't a bridesmaid? I had no idea what she was talking about. Amir stood up, put his arm around Mitz and told her to sit down.

"No!" she snapped at him.

"Well, I think it's all for the best," Amir said. "I mean, if this is what you were planning to serve, better to find out now that it *sucks* than to try it out on our wedding guests." He laughed, though I think even he knew he wasn't being funny.

She glared at him.

"Of course, it wouldn't have tasted like this"—she waved a hand at the table—"because *I* would've been cooking it." She looked at me. "You got this entire menu off Culinary-Connoisseur.com, didn't you?"

I nodded, still confused. How did I steal her menu? All I'd done was follow her advice. She *told* me to look on CulinaryConnoisseur.com. What, did they only have seven recipes and I'd used them all?

"I told you I was doing the summer theme," she said. "Hello? My last name is going to be Summers. I can't believe you've just spoiled my entire menu."

"Why don't you consider it a trial run," Bradford offered, taking a sip of water. "Besides, I assume I won't be at your wedding, so now, it's like I was there. Drama and all."

Mitz glowered at him and then looked at Olivia. "Can you believe this?"

What I couldn't believe was that Mitz was going to cook her own meal—at her own wedding. I didn't know a lot about weddings, but I certainly didn't think that was customary. Apparently, it was news to Amir, too.

"You're not cooking a meal for three hundred guests," he informed her.

She looked at him as though he'd said he wasn't going to marry her. "Of course I am. What, I'm going to pay someone else to do what I can do better?"

"Well, it's news to me, but then what *isn't*, in the wedding planning," Amir said, throwing down his napkin. "So, go ahead. You cook the meal in your wedding gown. Maybe you can get splattered with cornmeal just like Mara did. Why don't you serve it, too? That'll really make us look classy. But you'd better get started if you're going to make the meal edible, because this menu needs a lot of work. Wait, I have an idea. Why don't you practice while I'm in *Vegas* having my *bachelor* party."

Then Amir stomped out the back door into the below-ground alcove outside the kitchen window and lit a cigarette, which infuriated Mitz, who looked like she was going to follow him, but instead turned left into the bathroom and shut the door.

I was wondering what a hostess should do when her guests are fighting—ask them to leave? Step in to solve the situation? I didn't think I could do either, so I stood up to clear the table.

At which point Olivia grabbed my arm and pulled herself up to face me.

"I wasn't going to say anything," she said, "but since we're on the subject of *stealing* . . ." She touched the sleeve of my shirt. "This looks so familiar." And then, in a high-pitched squeal, she added, "I believe you're wearing *my* clothes!"

I looked down at my outfit and then back at Olivia in her jeans and gladiator sandals. I was worried she was preparing for battle, though I wasn't sure what the battle was all about, since she clearly wasn't wearing anything that could compete with what I was wearing.

"What do you mean?" I asked. Was she staking a claim on all DVF garments? The entire line?

"I *have* this," she said. "No, no, I *had* it. It had a hole, right at the back of the neck, where I ripped the label out. I put it in that bag..." she spoke slowly, replaying the last few weeks in her mind, "...and I gave it to you to drop off at the *Goodwill*." She grabbed the collar of my shirt and twisted it to look at the bunched fabric where the hole used to be.

I felt sick. I had purchased a top that Olivia had given away. Because it was ruined.

"Did you go through my stuff?" Olivia shook her head. "I mean, if you really wanted something, couldn't you at least have asked?"

Johnnie came over. "This is yours? Didn't I bring it back for you from L.A.? You gave it to charity? You didn't even wear it!"

Olivia snapped her head to look at Johnnie. "Because I think it's a hideous pattern, okay?"

"Don't be a bitch just because it looks better on her than on you," he said.

Olivia picked up her handbag and headed for the door before I could say anything in response. Not that I had a response.

Then she turned around and looked at me, her eyes wide, which made her forehead smooth and emotionless.

"Oh, and by the way, it's a *dress*."

Chapter Eight

SAVASANA: CORPSE POSE.
This seemingly simple position requires stillness of the body but awareness of the mind.

$\mathcal{I}$ had a hangover right through Sunday until I awoke Monday, despite staying in bed for more than twenty-four hours straight. And I hadn't even had more than half a glass of spiked Crystal Light. It was more than a hangover, I realized. It was a blanket of gloom.

I hadn't just failed at the party, I'd failed at the entire OM list. I couldn't cook, couldn't clean, couldn't paint. I'd mistaken Karsh for Kafka. I knew nothing important and I felt fat, though I was secretly astounded that I owned—and could fit into—one of Olivia's hand-me-down dresses. I wanted to believe that meant that I, too, was a size 4, except that none of my other clothes—most of them size 10 or 12—were loose at all. Even my track pants, which I was forced to pull on because my yoga capris had polenta on them, felt tighter than usual. Was it possible that after all the yoga I'd done, I'd gained weight?

Stuck in Downward Dog

The worst part was that I couldn't complain to my friends about any of these problems—or my life hangover, because my friends hated me: Mitz for stealing her "Summers" dinner theme, and Olivia for stealing her dress. Victoria would probably tell my mother what a disaster I was, and they'd commiserate about how useless I was. I hadn't failed only at the OM list. I'd failed at my life.

If I'd at least gotten a promotion—or a new job—I could have taken solace in leaving my apartment and my disasters behind, immersing myself in my work. But I had the same misery-inducing job at the same motivation-crushing place. And in my state I just couldn't face it. I grabbed the phone from under the covers to call in sick at the clinic, and Pumpernickel hopped onto the bed and stood on my chest, purring. I coerced him into snuggling.

At noon, the pounding in my head was amplified by the pounding on the door. It was Bradford, with his Kerplunk game, a tub of Ben & Jerry's Karamel Sutra ice cream and a nondescript brown bag.

I looked at the game.

He shrugged. "You have to admit it's appropriate."

"You don't have to rub it in," I said, holding open the door so he could enter the hallway. "I know that my dinner party—and my whole life—is one big Kerplunk. Oh, and I'm already fat enough, so I don't need the ice cream."

"Stop feeling sorry for yourself," Bradford said. "It's bad for your complexion."

I made a face.

"What's that?" I asked, pointing at the brown paper bag in his hand.

"*Sixteen Candles.*"

"At least no one stole my underwear," I said sarcastically. "So I guess I have that to be thankful for?"

"Perfect. You're as doom and gloom as I'd hoped you'd be," he said, walking into my apartment. Pumpernickel rubbed up against his leg, and I sat down on the carpet in the middle of the floor. "I would've been disappointed if I'd wasted my day coming over here to find you happy as a hog. There's nothing like trying to cheer up someone who's already in a good mood. So here's my pep talk. It was just a dinner party. And the best dinner party, in my opinion, is one that gives people something to talk about."

"Well, that's just perfect, because it's not like anyone's going to be talking *to* me, so they might as well talk *about* me. I'm sure that the party will give them fodder for years. I mean, it's not like I just screwed up one thing. It's my whole life, and I put it all on display Saturday night."

"Your whole life?" Bradford asked. "Did I miss something?"

"No, you were here Saturday night. You saw what happened."

He sat down on the carpet beside me, opened the ice cream and then handed it to me with a plastic spoon. Pumpernickel climbed onto my legs and sniffed the side of the container. I took a scoop and handed it back to Bradford.

"Do you want to talk about what's going on?" he asked.

But there was too much to say. I wanted to trust Bradford, I just wasn't sure I could. The only thing good going on was that I had one day off from my useless job, which, of course, I'd also failed to get a promotion at. Or quit, for that matter.

"I'm supposed to be at work," I moaned.

"I figured as much, knowing Marjorie. I called you at work. Some girl answered. Tiffany?"

"Tiffany?"

Bradford took a spoonful of ice cream and shrugged.

I picked up the phone and dialed the clinic's number.

"Who's this?" I asked when a voice other than Marjorie's answered.

"Who's asking?" she replied, and I wasn't sure if I felt offended that I had to introduce myself at the place I'd worked for three years or intimidated by someone who clearly had more confidence than I ever exuded.

"I'm Marjorie's assistant, Mara. I work there. I've worked there for three years."

"Hmmm," she said, sounding bored. "Never heard of you. Anyway, I work here now. Actually, I'm more like Marjorie's PR rep. At least while Didi's laid up. I just got into town. I'm her niece," she explained. "I'm starting at Duke in January, majoring in communications. I'll be handling all of Marjorie's press events until then."

The one thing left on my OM list that I technically hadn't failed at yet—Item Number 2, get a promotion or a real job— was being handed to some college freshman who'd worked at the clinic for three hours.

"Well, I'm sick," I said. "I left a message that I'll be in tomorrow."

I could hear Tiffany talking to someone in the background.

"Oh, hang on," she said. "Marjorie wants to talk to you."

For a split second I felt I'd reached the turning point in my life. If this had been a movie, this would have been the part where the boss told the undervalued, underpaid main character that she really valued her and that she realized this fact on the one morning she'd stayed home sick and was promoting her to—

"Did you talk to someone at the *Post?*" Marjorie asked, abruptly interrupting the scene in my head. "Don't answer that—the writer's name came up on the call display history on your phone," she snapped. "You told this person"—I heard papers shuffling—"Natalie Germaine, that I gave Didi free surgery and that she had an allergic reaction?"

My head hurt. "I—It wasn't the *Post*. It was just a student doing a project about PR for school," I blurted out.

"It's all right here—in the *Post*. So obviously you were duped. Or the *student* realized the gem of a story she had and sold it to the newspaper. And now the College of Physicians is going to investigate my practice, and I'll probably get audited by the government who will find out that I've put through a lot more surgeries than I should have. And to top it off, Dr. Overholt is threatening to sue Didi for giving me the event she'd paid her to plan, which is a breach of contract, so guess what? Didi's suing me to get the money to pay my competition. I don't know what you've been doing all weekend, but this"—I could hear her slap the stack of papers—"pretty much sums up mine."

What? How had all this happened since a newspaper article came out a few days ago? I didn't know what to do, or say.

Marjorie did.

"This wasn't the first time you screwed up, but it's the last. You're fired," she said, adding that I should pick up my stuff and return my key the following day. Then she hung up on me.

I clicked the phone off and looked at Bradford. He looked back at me.

"I'm fired?" I said as though it was a question, as though maybe Bradford was behind all this. If he hadn't come over, he wouldn't have told me about Tiffany. I wouldn't have called. I'd still have a job. I started to cry.

While I'd been so busy thinking how useless my job was, Marjorie had apparently been thinking how useless I was. Had I really screwed up that much? I supposed, lately, I had made a few mistakes. I'd left the box of consult forms at the show, and I'd ordered the wrong size of implants for Catherine. But they weren't intentional mistakes, they were just a result of carelessness. Just like the interview—I hadn't intended to cause such a mess for Marjorie. And I hadn't forced Marjorie to illegally give Didi free liposculpture, or not to double-check her own chart to make sure the breast implants were the correct size before doing the procedure. That was her decision.

I said this to Bradford.

"I know you're trying to justify it, but it is your fault," he said.

I looked at him. He was blurry.

"I'm simply being honest with you," he said gently. "Someone has to. But the bigger question is why you made those mistakes."

I slammed my hand down on the carpet. It didn't give me the sound effect I'd hoped for, but my anger level was still high. Pumpernickel jumped off my lap and scampered into the bedroom.

"Because I just didn't care, okay?" I said loudly.

He looked at me calmly. "Exactly."

He had a point. I'd known this all along. I just didn't do anything about it. And now, I'd caused someone who did care about her business a lot of strife.

"So, what's really going on?" he finally asked.

I decided to show him the OM list. I went into my bedroom and retrieved the list from my sock drawer.

"What *is* this?" he asked, amazed.

"The list. Everything I wanted to achieve. Everything I failed to achieve."

"Become a fabulous chef?" He rattled off the items. "Become well read and knowledgeable so as to . . . what? Pretend to be someone you're not? Is this what that whole Kafka deal was all about?" He reached over to the coffee table to pull the library books onto the floor. "And all these books? I mean, *Paris 1919*? Do you even know what was going on in 1919?"

I shrugged. "No. See? Even when I try, I'm completely useless. I can't do anything right. I'm a total failure."

"What's the point of this list?" he asked incredulously.

I explained it to him, how I'd come up with the list to be more like Olivia and Mitz, who were both perfect.

"Oh, right," he said with sarcasm. "Has Mitz read *Paris 1919*?"

I didn't say anything. He wasn't getting the point.

"So, you want to be a chef or a department store buyer? That's the goal?" he continued. Of course it wasn't the goal.

"No. I don't want to *be* them, I just want . . ." I didn't even know what I wanted. But I knew that Bradford making fun of me wasn't helping.

"Listen, it's not as if you helped me," I said accusingly. "Because of you, I just got fired from a job I hated that I spent three years at, and I spend my Friday nights sopping up sweat for free so that I can get better at yoga. And for what? Olivia and Mitz don't even *do* yoga anymore. It was all a waste."

"Excuse me. I thought you liked yoga," he said.

I did, actually, but it didn't matter whether I liked it or not. It had made me fatter than ever before.

"Why do you think that Mitz is a good chef?" Bradford asked. "Because she likes to cook. And Olivia knows about interior decor—why? Because she studied it at school. She loves to decorate. That's her thing. The only way you're ever going to be good at something is if you enjoy it. And I got you that job at Face Value because you needed a job. I never told you to work there for three years. So don't put the blame on me. I just tried to help you, and you've never once thanked me. I offered you my apartment and a job and a way to continue doing yoga. If I had known the only reason you wanted to do yoga was to compete with your stupid friends, I never would've arranged it. You know, Sofi didn't even need someone for Friday nights. She always works it herself, but she agreed as a favor to me because I was trying to help you. I thought yoga would be good for you, that it would help you get your life in order. I guess I was wrong. You were too busy trying to show off with some ridiculous meal when you can't even scramble an egg, and by painting one wall when what you need to do is move into a place you can afford."

Pumpernickel re-emerged from the bedroom and walked back onto my crossed legs, turned in a circle once and then settled in.

"And these *friends* that you were trying to be just like don't seem so perfect to me. Mitz is outraged because you made some recipe she wants to make at her own wedding that she's planning to cater herself—which is the most ridiculous thing I've ever heard, and I'm not even a gay wedding planner—but more importantly, you are her *friend,* and there were only three people at your dinner who would be at her wedding, so why would it even matter? And what, Olivia's mad at you because you wore some dress she didn't even want and gave away." He shook his head. "She should feel *embarrassed* that she didn't offer her clothes to you. And where are these friends today? And where were they this whole time you were attempting to turn your life around and be like them? Were they helping you?"

"You just don't get it," I said weakly.

"You're right, I don't," he snapped. "Because I've been here for you this whole time, and I've tried to help you because that's what friends do. I just didn't know that it was so bad to be me. I guess because I'm gay, or a guy, or not gay enough or whatever, I'm not good enough. You know, you're so busy trying to be *like* your friends, you forgot how to *be* a friend."

I didn't say anything, and for a few minutes neither did Bradford.

"I'm sorry," I said finally.

"Getting help from your friends isn't a sign of weakness. It's a sign of friendship. I was just trying to be your friend. I'm sorry if that made you uncool." He stood up and walked to the door. "You know, you're so worried about trying to be like your friends, but all I see is a shallow, self-absorbed, self-centered version of a person I used to like. So if those are the aspects of Mitz and Olivia you're trying to emulate, well, then, you've got that down pat. Congratulations," he said and walked out.

Bradford was right. About everything. I wasn't sure why I had been so ungrateful to him. Without him, I wouldn't have had a job, and it wasn't like I'd been trying so hard to get another one over the past three years. And I did like yoga, and now I got to do it for free, thanks to him. And every time I'd screwed up or something hadn't gone my way, I'd complained to Bradford, and he'd listened. He'd been my true friend. And today, Mitz and Olivia hadn't even called me to apologize for their behavior. It wasn't about bad etiquette—I didn't care that they'd laughed at my lack of cooking skills or flair for decorating. But I was upset that they'd been so wrapped up in their own lives that they'd been rude dinner guests and left my party without even saying goodbye.

I picked myself up off the floor and grabbed my yoga bag. It was funny: the one thing I hadn't included on the OM list was the one thing I actually liked doing, and thought I was getting better at. When I was at yoga, I felt calm and focused and, for those ninety minutes, I forgot all about comparing myself with my friends.

As I was locking the door, Mr. Rubinstein, my landlord, came up the front walk. He looked at me grimly and said he didn't have good news.

"You have to move."

"What?!"

My rent hadn't been late. I had taken out the garbage (at least once a month). I certainly wasn't having sex too loudly for my above-ground neighbors. I could already feel myself starting to get tight-chested, which could only mean tears were a moment away. Wasn't it bad enough that I had been fired? Surely I couldn't be jobless and homeless in a day.

"Silly girl," Mr. Rubinstein said, patting the top of my head as if I were a dog. "It's not you. They're tearing down the house, gonna build a row of townhouses because the lot is nice and deep."

"How long do I have?" I moaned. It was a bit dramatic, but losing my home and my job called for a little drama.

"First of September." That was just three and a half weeks away.

I plopped down on the front steps of a place where I would soon no longer live and let it sink in. I had no job and no home. And since I had exactly $237.82 in the bank, it was barely an exaggeration to say I had no money. I wasn't sure what to do first, find a place to live (would anyone take a jobless, penniless girl as a tenant?) or try to find a job (when I had no fixed address).

How had this all happened?

I went back inside and sat on the floor. The OM list was on the carpet beside me where Bradford had left it. I picked it up and ripped it into tiny pieces. I realized that the list had never been more accurate than it was at that moment—in Sanskrit, *om* meant contemplation of the ultimate reality.

I had to face my reality. Bradford had once said that before things could get better they had to hit rock bottom. And I had hit rock bottom.

Chapter Nine

VINYASA: A SERIES OF POSES.
This breath-synchronized movement is a transition between postures, and allows the yogi to set an intention, then take the necessary steps toward reaching that goal.

Y ou know this is a Level 2 class, right?" Libby asked me as I was about to duck into an afternoon class the next day. With everything that had happened, yoga seemed like the only escape.

Of course I knew that, I told her. *Now,* I didn't add. I hadn't looked at the schedule, and I certainly hadn't done Level 2 before, but there was no time to sneak out. Libby shut the door, signaling the start of the class.

I'd forgotten there were sporadic Level 2 classes in the schedule, though I'd remembered reading their description when I'd first joined. Only now I couldn't remember what it said, because at the time, all the Level 2 classes had been at times I couldn't attend anyway—during the day, when I would've been at work.

I took a deep breath. I could handle this. After all, I could handle Level 1. In fact, in some poses, such as Tree, I was even steady. Sort of.

Except that I was totally picturing the class going into Headstand. And there was no way I could do that. I'd tried a headstand once, during a yoga video at Olivia's place the year before. I couldn't even get both my feet off the floor and balance with my knees on my elbows without falling over, while the yogis on the video shot their legs straight in the air without wobbling one bit.

The room was half-empty, which should've been consoling but felt worse because there was a higher chance that I would be the only one flailing around and falling down.

As we started to breathe deeply, I took a sneak peek and noticed that some of the people looked to be in worse physical shape than those in some of the Level 1 classes. There were also more men—with paunches. If they could do Level 2, surely I could. Not that it mattered what they looked like. But still.

And then the class started, and Libby instructed everyone to turn and face the back wall, away from the mirrors.

"By facing the wall, we bring our awareness inward," Libby said as we began our breathing exercise. "There are no distractions, and there's no confirmation that your body is aligned as it should be. Instead of seeing yourself and correcting based on appearance, you have to *feel* what's right and correct based on your intuition."

Then we began. At first, the class was difficult, but I could manage. Until the third pose, which was not, as it was in Level 1, Eagle. Instead, we did a balancing pose, lifting our leg in front of us, holding our big toe and then moving our leg out to the side.

"By changing the order of the poses, we take ourselves out of our comfort zone and challenge ourselves," Libby continued in a soothing voice.

I slowly lifted my leg in front of me, trying to convince myself that I could do this pose. I could go at my own pace and reach my own limits.

"Focus all your energy inward," she reminded us.

I had no idea whether I was the worst yogi in the class or not. There was no way to view myself or anyone else, since the only thing I could see was the wall in front of me.

But judging from the sound of stillness, I realized that everyone else in the class was able to do the poses, too. Not having mirrors reinforced the fact that I really couldn't judge based on appearances, that I had doubted the ability of some of the other people in the class because of their body types, just as I'd doubted myself. Appearances, I had come to realize, had never been more deceiving.

After class, I saw Audra pull out her Avon cellulite cream.

"I took your advice," she said. "I *love* this cream."

"Told you," I said affectionately.

"And I have another question. My sister's having a baby, and I know that stretch marks are natural and a sign that you carried that baby around for nine months, but . . ."

"You don't need to give me that line," I whispered with a smile. "No one likes stretch marks. You can tell her to call me if she wants," I added.

As I put on my shoes in the reception area, Libby said to me: "You're doing really well."

I smiled. "Thanks." I didn't know if she told everyone that, but it was nice to hear.

"If I don't see you for a while, keep it up, okay?"

I suddenly felt disheartened. Was I being fired from the desk, too? I couldn't believe my un-luck.

She patted her belly. "I'm due in three days," she said.

Of course. I wished her luck and then descended the stairs to the street, taking deep breaths and feeling good. And then someone tapped me on the shoulder.

I turned around to see Rhonda Stephenson, one of my favorite surgery-addicts from Face Value.

"Where have you *been?*"

Not at the clinic, obviously. I told her I'd been fired.

"I've been calling all week, trying to get your replacement—who by the way is an idiot—to give me your home phone number. I ran out of that shea butter you gave me months ago, and my scalp has been flaking ever since. And I couldn't remember where you said to get it. I tried asking Marjorie, but she just told me to use Head & Shoulders."

I tilted her head and looked at her scalp. It *was* a bit flaky. I tried to remember when I'd given her the shea butter.

"Did you keep the bottle?" She shook her head. "Did I pick you up something at one of the shows?" I thought aloud. And then I remembered which show I'd gotten the cream at. I couldn't remember the brand, but I was sure I could find an equally good product. "I'm on it."

"Really?"

"Really," I told her. I was glad of the task. Suddenly, I felt a sense of purpose. I jotted her number on the back of my hand and told her I'd call her.

"You're the best," Rhonda said, giving me a quick hug. "Listen, you find the product and I'll pay you back, plus service charge." She winked.

I felt useful, and a bit excited. I liked finding products for people who didn't know or didn't have the time to figure things out themselves. If only there was a job that required that as a skill. Even though the OM list had been a sham, I *did* need a new job, since it was unlikely the yoga studio was going to promote me to instructor anytime soon.

What Rhonda needed was an all-natural shea butter, and I could think of no more appropriate place to start looking than in the Carrot Common, where all-natural was more common than carrots.

~

"I know you don't want help, but if you can't find a place to live, you can live at my place," Bradford said the next week when I called him to apologize for being a very bad friend.

This was after I'd called my mother to tell her that I had lost my job, lost my apartment, and that, yes, I would be fine. She didn't believe me, but I successfully distracted her by convincing her to send Bradford a cookie bouquet on my behalf as an apology for not appreciating him. She wanted to send a bouquet of mini car-shaped gingerbread cookies.

"Gingerbread feels too festive, and it's still four months until Christmas," I told her.

"But gingerbread is *brown*, Mara. And the cars will look just like Fords!"

I wondered when Ford had started making all their cars look alike—or like gingerbread.

"And I'll put brown icing on them and they'll be *brown Fords*. A brown Ford for Bradford. Get it?"

I didn't, really. "Should you write *Brad* on the license plate, then?" I said, trying to play along.

"That doesn't make any sense, Mara. You never call him Brad."

I wondered if she made placing an order this difficult for all her customers.

I finally convinced her that one large chocolate chip cookie with "I'm sorry" on it would do. It might not have been original, but it got my point across better than the cryptic car idea.

Bradford got the gift the next day—my mother couldn't resist a bouquet of mini cookies instead—and the card, which my mother had taken liberties with, and inspiration from Elton John, by writing out half the lyrics to "Sorry Seems to Be the Hardest Word." Not exactly my style, but she did hold back on the Ford car.

She also had my father drop off cloud-shaped cookies with blue icing for me, with a card that read "Let the sky be blue—not you!" My father gave me enough money for first and last month's rent and offered to help me move once I found a new place to live. Surprisingly, neither of them suggested I move in with Victoria, and Victoria didn't call to offer her place. I hadn't heard from her since my party.

I told Bradford now that if I couldn't find a place by the end of the month I'd take him up on his offer and his apartment. But I knew I'd find a place. I just had to focus.

"Well, if you don't want the handouts, you've got to move to the east side," Bradford said. "Rent drops $200 once you cross the Don Valley Parkway."

I thought about it. It actually made sense. If I moved to the Danforth, I would be closer to yoga, and right now that was perhaps the one steady thing in my life, the one constant that was giving me confidence and pushing me forward.

And then I realized what I could do.

After yoga the next day, I asked Sofi if she would consider having me work reception more often, which would give me something to do and a paycheck until I found a new job. "I know I'm not very good at yoga, but I want to get better."

She laughed and laughed, and I wondered if she thought the idea of me even working reception at all was too much. Then she shook her head. "I've been so preoccupied with Libby and the baby that I totally forgot to think about who's going to cover reception when I start teaching more of Libby's classes. Can you start tomorrow morning?"

—

The next morning, as I was filing the 9:30 a.m. class member invoices, Lisette Liposuction walked into Mok, and for a moment I experienced temporary displacement.

"Hey, I know you," she said and snapped her manicured fingers. "Mara, right?"

I nodded. I wondered where she remembered me from: the place where she claimed to get skinny or the place where she *really* got skinny.

"I didn't know you worked here," she continued. "I just switched. I tried the surfercize or whatever it was, but it was just so ridiculous, so I started shopping for a new yoga studio, and one of my friends"—she pointed to a dark-haired girl, who was taking off her shoes on the bench—"told me to come here. So, you don't work at Face Value anymore?"

I shook my head no.

"Well, in that case, maybe you can help me. I really want bigger breasts to offset my hips. I read something about a pill, only I can't remember what the pill was called or where I read about it. Do you know what I'm talking about?"

"A pill to make your breasts grow?" I wondered just how many pills Lisette was already taking. It sounded like a Sea-Monkeys mail-order scam to me. I shrugged. "Sorry."

"Hmm, oh well. I thought I'd ask. I figured you probably couldn't tell patients about stuff like that when you worked for a plastic surgeon, but now . . ."

She had a point. Wasn't that what I truly enjoyed doing— finding products for Marjorie's clients? That was actually the *only* part of the job I'd enjoyed. That, and researching the products when Marjorie wasn't looking.

Still, Lisette was skirting the issue.

"Why don't you just get implants?" I said. It wasn't subtle, but neither were implants.

She looked around her. There were still three women in the reception area, but Lisette didn't lean closer or lower her voice.

"I didn't really have a very good lipo experience," she said. "And I had to keep getting touchups to try to even out the pitting. I'd rather not get surgery if I don't have to, you know?"

Maybe I did know. Wasn't Lisette just like the women I thought existed? Women who didn't want to get surgery even though they wanted to change their bodies? And now, even someone who had gotten surgery was falling into that group.

Lisette picked up her yoga mat and pointed to the clock. "I better get up there before they close the door."

This is my chance, I thought.

"I'll look into it for you and let you know next time I see you," I called quickly after her.

She turned around on the stairs and nodded, then smiled.

Then I logged on to the reception computer and started my pill-hunt while the nine-thirty class was in session.

⌐

At 3:30 p.m. Sofi gave me a form to fill out my hours and a schedule for the next two weeks.

"Is it too many shifts?" she asked.

I shook my head without even looking. I needed the distraction and the cash. And I was so grateful to Sofi. But also, I was just happy with myself for making one good decision. Plus, with so many shifts, I'd actually have no excuse not to work out daily, since I'd already be at the studio.

That afternoon, I felt steady in Tree Pose for the first time.

"When you're really focused, you find that you're no longer attempting to hold Tree Pose," Sheri, the new instructor, said calmly as she walked around us. "Instead, you move into a deeper center of concentration, and you are the tree, the whole tree, including the trunk, not just a leaf, wavering in the wind."

Sheri came over to me and tapped me on the shoulder. I didn't move, didn't wobble. "Try moving into Toe Stand."

And I did. I had to put my hands down on the ground, and I couldn't move them into prayer position, but I was balancing on the toes of my right foot.

"Use every single toe to help you," Sheri guided me.

Instead of focusing on the people, the walls, the heat around me, I was focusing on every toe, every part of my body, using it all to support myself. To make me stronger. And I felt calm.

After class, I treated myself to a pair of Rawganique crop yoga pants and a fitted T (with my new fifty-percent-off staff discount). Then I picked up a newspaper at the stand outside and headed next door to Suck It Up to grab a smoothie and get down to the business of finding a home. I had two weeks until the first of September, when I had to break out of the dungeon.

As I ordered my favorite—the Banana Berry Blaster— I grabbed a purple pamphlet from the counter and flipped it open. It contained a chart that cross-referenced calories in each of the smoothies. I quickly scanned down to the Banana Berry Blaster smoothie.

Six hundred and fifty calories?

"Is this right?" I asked, thrusting the open pamphlet at the skinny counter guy with the goatee and Gorillaz concert shirt.

He nodded. "You know, you should try one of the fresh-fruit smoothies. They're actually tastier, and they have half the calories of the ones with frozen yogurt."

I couldn't believe I was just finding this out now.

"Let me add a shot of flaxseed oil, too," he continued. "You won't even taste it. I promise. So you're getting something healthy and fun. Middle ground," he added with a wink.

Stuck in Downward Dog

Maybe that was the key, I thought, as I flipped through the apartment ads and took a sip of my fresh-fruit smoothie.

Finding an apartment wasn't as easy as I'd thought it would be. Since I'd gotten full-time hours at Mok, I didn't have much time to look at places. And Bradford had been right—the east side of the city was cheaper—but given that I didn't want to rent a place in the suburbs and couldn't afford a place that cost more than I made all month, my choices were limited.

The first place I went to look at said it was a bright, clean one-bedroom with access to the subway. What it didn't say was that it was brightly lit because of the neon flashing safety light beside the entrance to the subway that was *right outside* the third-floor apartment window. And although the access to the subway *was* convenient, the roar every three minutes was hardly calming.

The next place turned out to be a furnished room rather than an apartment, and while I appreciated that I wouldn't have to buy or move any furniture (given that I owned only a futon, dresser and TV), it seemed rather discomforting to know that I'd be sleeping on someone else's bed and sitting on someone else's couch. Perhaps I could've gotten used to the idea, except I was sure once I stepped into the room that I couldn't get used to the ants—which were everywhere.

"Oh," said the elderly man showing the apartment, "the place comes with ant traps, so don't worry."

I wasn't concerned that there were ant traps. I was concerned that there were still ants leasing the place.

The next apartment was in a brown brick building on Broadview at the start of Greektown. I knocked on the superintendent's door, which was adjacent to the lobby, and a three-toothed man handed me a grubby key.

"You the chick that called?"

"That's me," I said, nodding.

"Nine-oh-one. Ninth floor," he said, and then nodded at the stairs. Both elevator doors had yellow tape across them, blocking them from use, turning the eleven-story building into a walkup.

I reached the top floor winded and sweaty. The stairwell was grungy and had been spray-painted by either renters or trespassers (I wasn't sure which was worse) with tags I couldn't begin to decipher because I was too old and too uncool. The carpeting in the hall was black, although the edges showed that it was intended to be a light shade of gray. The walls were streaked with yellow stains that smelled like pee. At that point, I wasn't sure why I kept walking toward the apartment, but I did. When I reached it, I could only assume I had the right apartment, because while the other doors had 9's on them, this door had just the 01. I stuck the key in and turned, slowly pushing the door open. The stench was unbearable. I quickly plugged my nose and pulled the door shut, but not before noting the smashed mirror from the sliding closet door. I pulled on the key, but it was stuck, so I twisted it and turned it, and then it snapped. In half. I didn't know what to do, so I dropped the half in my hand on the grimy carpet and raced down the hallway in my flip-flops.

Then I went home to wash my feet, deciding that only closed-toe shoes would be acceptable for apartment-hunting from then on.

"What price range are you looking in?" Bradford asked when I called him to discuss (not complain about) the situation.

I told him.

"What?! Mara, you go from overpaying for a basement to completely underpaying for above ground. You need to find a middle ground," he counseled, sounding just like the smoothie guy.

Bradford convinced me to consider at least $200 higher than what I was looking at, and I promised I would.

And it made a huge difference, but still, nothing was quite right.

The choices were better, and each apartment had a feature that impressed me, but I was determined not to get swayed by another faux fireplace. So I passed on the apartment with the shoe closet that was bigger than the bathroom, and the loft with the marble-top kitchen counter.

Two other places were passable but wouldn't allow pets, and one that did had two Newfoundland dogs capable of swallowing Pumpernickel whole.

I refused to give up. I was tired but not too discouraged because I knew I'd eventually find the right place. I just hoped it would be within the next three days. I had really gotten used to the idea of living on the Danforth. I liked the area. It was a mix of singles and multi-generational families, Greek restaurants and all-natural food stores, home decor shops and share-a-bike depots, holistic centers and hip boutiques. It was a perfect combination of trendy and traditional.

At least I'd had success in finding one-hundred-percent shea butter for Rhonda. Strangely enough, there wasn't a single store on the Danforth that sold the stuff. The closest I could find was seventy-six percent, and I knew from asking the naturopath in the Carrot Common that only the one-hundred-percent kind was completely irritant free. Finally, I'd learned that L'Occitane en Provence carried a pure shea butter product that would be perfect, so I'd headed to the Bloor Street West boutique to pick up a jar for Rhonda.

After leaving L'Occitane, I was walking west past the next set of lights to get a Diet Coke at the convenience store when I saw a small sign in a window. It was advertising an apartment on Bowden Street, which I was almost certain was practically across the street from the Carrot Common—and Mok—on the Danforth.

"I just put the sign up this morning," said the woman behind the counter. Her name tag said Alice, and she was a slightly pudgy woman in her fifties or sixties with jet-black hair and a natural flush. "My husband and I live on the first two floors, but we'd like to rent out the top floor. My husband said no one who shops on Bloor West would want to live in the east end, but I guess he was wrong, wasn't he?"

That evening, I met Alice at her house on Bowden Street, and we walked up the stairs to the fire-escape balcony, where the door to the third-floor apartment was located. Technically, it was an attic, but I loved it instantly. After looking at apartments with large kitchens and parquet flooring and marble-top counters and minuscule bathrooms, I'd found a place that had the features I needed and that I knew would make me happy.

There was a really small kitchen with just barely enough space for the small fridge and microwave. And there was no stove. Alice said if I wanted a stove I could put one in, but without it I had more space. And between the microwave and my toaster oven, I wasn't sure I really had a need for a stove. There was also no room for a kitchen table. Instead, there was a breakfast bar, complete with four high stools, eliminating the need for a table, which I didn't want, have or need. The bathroom had an oversized bathtub and a full-length mirror, and although I could hardly imagine staring at myself naked, there was hope that I might one day be comfortable enough with my body to do so if I chose. Now that I was cutting out the frozen yogurt smoothies, I was sure I was going to lose a pound or two.

The rest of the place was also tiny, but it felt spacious because all the rooms had interconnecting doors that could be left open. And while the bedroom wasn't big enough for a double bed, my father said he would deliver my twin-size bed from my childhood room back home.

But the best part was the room off the bedroom, which led out onto a miniature balcony. That room could have been a walk-in closet, but when I saw it I immediately pictured it furnished with an old-fashioned desk and chair and a computer, set up in front of the window where I could look out at the large oak tree in the front yard. Maybe not this month or next, but in the long term I could see myself having an office in that room.

Chapter Ten

KAPALBHATI PRANAYAMA: A BREATHING TECHNIQUE.
This succession of rapid breaths is used to cleanse the mind.

Originally, I'd planned to lug my unwanted belongings to the Goodwill, but given that I didn't want to make the trip to the area where I'd spent three years even one more time, I decided instead to sell my few remainders by holding a yard sale. Sure, I had only a futon, a roaster and the rest of Sam's junk, which was still stashed in the closet, and sure, Victoria probably thought yard sales were low class, but I figured selling the items would be therapeutic. It wasn't about the money, it was about the sense of finality it would bring, and the chance to really cleanse myself of the past—while I sat outside for a few hours enjoying the last days of summer.

I told Victoria I could drop off her furniture and the other items she'd lent me after our dad and I moved my things. But I think she was concerned that I would mistakenly sell off her stuff and pocket the money, so she arranged for a mover to come the morning of the sale. She also drove over herself to check on the movers (or to scope out my sale—I wasn't sure). She seemed thinner than I remembered, and not just in her thighs, where she had gotten the liposuction.

She didn't say much, but when she turned to leave, she stopped for a moment, her hand on the car-door handle.

"You seem self-sufficient." It seemed less like a compliment than like a sad statement. Either way, I decided not to let it bother me.

I thought about asking Olivia whether she wanted the roaster back, but it was likely she'd bought two more since, or moved on to a congee rice cooker or some other appliance I couldn't imagine a purpose for. Besides, I'd paid for it, so it was mine to do with (or not do with) as I pleased. And since I hadn't spoken to her since the party, I hardly thought the roaster was a good conversation starter.

While I sat on the front steps watching the occasional passerby check out one of Sam's old cassette tapes, I snacked on a package of trail mix, which seemed a lot healthier than jujubes, even if it did contain fat. I had a flash of regret that I hadn't moved when Sam had dumped me. Part of me was upset about not taking action long ago, but I now realized that I had to want to change first. In spite of the OM list, I hadn't wanted—truly *wanted*—to change my ways. If I'd actually been interested in cooking, why hadn't I cooked myself dinner after work, rather than eating cereal or making a sandwich? But I hadn't really wanted to learn how to cook because I didn't enjoy the act of cooking. I just wanted the end result: a fancy meal that would wow my friends.

Trouble was, *I* wouldn't be wowed by a cooked meal.

I liked cereal. And I liked eating sandwiches. And I liked that I could be done with dinner and on to other things by the time some people were just finished chopping the vegetables for the stir-fry they still had to make. I wanted to do things I enjoyed, and cooking wasn't one of them. Neither was painting an accent wall in brown sections or reading political literature or *Moby Dick*. I liked reading magazines and doing yoga, and I liked helping people and meeting my friends once a week and catching up rather than trying to show them up. Those were the things I would aim to do in my new place.

$$\textit{\textbf{---}}$$

The next day my dad appeared in the *Cookie's Cookie Bouquets— Serving the Entire Niagara Region!* van. Besides hauling my childhood bed to the city, my mom and dad had contributed to my move by giving me the old sofa bed from the basement. Even though it was slightly stained, it was much, much better than the futon, which I'd sold for $20.

As my father and I carried boxes to the van, three pigeons sat undisturbed on the sidewalk. My dad tried to shoo them with his feet without losing his balance, but they didn't move. They were comfortable. Chests puffed out. Proud. And suddenly I had a new respect for them.

"We can just go around," I said, taking a deep breath and pushing forward with a box in my arms.

Two hours later, I was home.

As my father was about to leave, he remembered something and went out to the van. I followed him, just as it started to sprinkle, a warm, comforting rain.

"From your mother, of course," he said, handing me a box. I opened the box and looked at the bouquet. Each of the

five cookies had been decorated to look like a miniature welcome mat.

I offered one to my dad, but he declined. Then he looked
down at his shoes and back at me.

"This is from me," he said and grabbed me by the shoulders, pulling me in to his chest. He wrapped his arms around
me and squeezed me tight. "I'm always so proud of you. You're
such an independent girl," he said. "Though we could've used
some help with moving."

〜

After making myself a cup of tea at my new place, I realized I
had forgotten to leave the keys in the mailbox at Clinton
Street, so I made one last trip back. Which is when I found
Olivia on the front steps, sniffling and wet. Her hair had been
chopped into a Gwyneth Paltrow *Sliding Doors* haircut, slicked
to her head so it looked very dark, particularly at the roots. The
rain was dripping from her hair onto her anti-Olivia sensible
flat and basic black Mary Janes.

"What are you doing here? What's wrong? What—"

"You have a lot of pigeon poop out here," she said.

I sat down beside her, probably on pigeon poop.

"Pigeons'll do that," I said. "What's going on?"

"Can I come in?" she sniffed and wiped her nose on her wet
sleeve.

"Not really. I don't live here anymore. I just came to drop
off the keys. Pigeon poop and all, it's a lot more comfortable
out here."

"You don't *live* here?"

I shook my head.

"Since when?"

I filled her in.

"I'm so sorry. I've been a horrible friend," she said between sniffles. "I didn't even know. I could've given you my agent's name." She wiped her nose on her cotton sleeve, and I thought, *When you're unemployed, you don't need an agent.*

"So you found a place? You're sure you like it?" she sniffled on. "Have you thought everything through? And you want to rent? Because you really should consider buying if you're going to bother at all. It's too bad we sold our place. It would've been perfect for you."

Olivia was infuriating. I was about to explain to her that I had chosen the right home for myself when she began crying more heavily and curled forward, resting her head on her knees.

I grabbed her by the shoulders and pulled her in to me.

"What's going on?" I asked her again.

"Johnnie and I got in a fight. Actually, we've been fighting ever since your party, which is why I haven't called. I was so embarrassed. By him, by me. We just can't get along." She half laughed, half choked back a sob. "All because of a stupid dress I didn't want because it was maternity. It was just too insulting that the one time he buys me something, it's a reminder that I'm going to get fat—"

Olivia interrupted her own rant by hurling her head toward the azalea bush beside her and throwing up. I instantly leaned over and rubbed her back, since she didn't have any hair that needed holding away from her face. She turned to me and wiped her mouth with her sleeve. I opened my handbag and handed her a slightly used Kleenex.

"Thanks." She shrugged. "So, I'm pregnant."

I didn't have time to react.

"And I know what everyone says, that being pregnant is beautiful, but I just don't feel that way. I don't feel glowy or radiant. I feel fat and blotchy. And the last thing I want to do is go out in public, let alone wear designer dresses that highlight the fact that I'm pregnant. I just want to hide away until I'm not fat anymore. Because whether I'm wearing designer rags or not, I'm going to look like a whale. A whale with a stomach full of baby whales just waiting to hatch."

I was fairly certain whales gave birth to only one calf at a time (since they're *mammals* and don't lay eggs), but I figured now wasn't the time to show off my knowledge of zoology (where was that flair for random facts when I'd needed it during my dinner party?).

Besides, I'd just realized something.

"The dress..."

Olivia nodded. "The one you were wearing. Actually, I don't know why I freaked out so much. The dress just made me so mad because I wasn't used to the idea of being pregnant yet, and when I told Johnnie I was, he said he was going to be on tour when I'm due to deliver. It just really sucked, you know?" She sighed deeply, her shoulders rising then returning back to their original position. "And then, in my fit of rage, I pulled the tag out of the dress because I didn't want to look at the maternity label, and that's when I ripped the hole in it. I don't even know why I was upset with you. Hormones?"

I had been wearing a maternity dress? As a shirt? *That's* the reason it fit?

But right now wasn't about me. I couldn't make this about me.

"I thought you didn't want to have kids," I said gingerly.

"I don't," she said. "Or I didn't. I mean, I never did because, honestly, we're always fighting, except when he's gone with the band and I'm doing exactly as I please. And when he comes home, he's super-sweet, but then I think, why? Why is this guy being so sweet to me but he won't even marry me? And now we're going to have a baby and he still won't marry me? It's just so much. It's overwhelming."

All this information *was* overwhelming, I thought.

"But I thought you never wanted to be married," I said.

Olivia pushed her hair off her forehead then ran the back of her hand under her eyes.

"Of course I did. I do. I always did. But Johnnie never wanted to get married." She shook her head.

"But you bought your own ring, and you're always defending your feminist rights and—"

"I'm not saying I'm not a feminist. It's just that I don't think wanting to be married and being a feminist have to be exclusive. I've always wanted to get married. I've had the Vera Wang dress picked out since, like, 1998. But when someone doesn't want to marry you, what do you do? I mean, I understand it: his mother's been married four times. She's so L.A. So of course he thinks marriage is pointless. But I don't." She looked at me. "I guess it's better to just make yourself believe that's what you want, too," she said quietly. "Anyway, the point is that it's like all our goals are completely out of line, and it wasn't a big deal until this whole house thing. Johnnie doesn't want a house. He never did, and he certainly doesn't want to live in the suburbs, but I wasn't going to let him get away with it. I mean, I've lived in the city for years. Is it too much to ask that we have a house with separate rooms and floors and a driveway and *grass*?"

It sounded reasonable to me. It was what we all wanted, and Olivia was miles ahead of me on home ownership. What surprised me was that this was an issue now. She'd already bought the house in Port Credit, so obviously she'd done an adequate job of convincing Johnnie to move to the suburbs.

"Which is why I'm pregnant," Olivia continued. "Johnnie couldn't see why we needed a house if there was just the two of us, which is just so ridiculous. I have no doubt we can fill a house."

I had no doubt Olivia could fill a house with kitchen appliances alone, but I still couldn't believe what I was hearing. Was Olivia saying she'd gotten pregnant so that she could get the house she wanted? It seemed a little extreme, irrational. In fact, crazy. We weren't teenagers. We were talking about a baby, a life, not a means to acquiring a second story.

"I'm not saying I didn't ever want kids. Maybe I did, or maybe I was just too selfish to consider it. And I know I should be happy—Johnnie's happy, and we're moving, and who knows, maybe I can convince him to marry me, after all. But it's a lot to think about, and every time I try to focus on it all, I keep thinking about how those cellulite treatments were a waste of money, given that I'd be pregnant a month later and would have stretch marks, acne and a bunt."

"Olivia, it's not a bum-in-the-front when there's a baby there," I said softly. "It's a belly, and you're going to look beautiful. You're always going to be beautiful." Saying such words to some people would be lying, but necessary to make a friend feel better. In Olivia's case, though, it was true.

"And I have roots." She pulled at her hair.

It occurred to me that perhaps Olivia had always colored her hair, though she denied it. And though such a lie would've upset me in the past, as though I'd personally been deceived, it didn't matter that much anymore.

"Bet you thought this was natural. That's why I chopped it off." Then she turned to throw up in the bushes again. When she sat back up, she looked at me. "I thought at least this way my roots would be less noticeable."

"I thought morning sickness happened in the morning." I said, trying to make a non-judgmental statement while changing the topic and digesting all the other information before me.

Olivia looked down at her feet. "I may have had a drink. And a few drags of a cigarette at Mitz's bachelorette party."

"What?" Who had a bachelorette party ten months before their wedding?

"Don't be mad that you missed it. You didn't miss anything good."

I wasn't concerned about missing the party—or, at least, not as concerned as I was that Olivia was drinking and smoking while pregnant. I told her so.

"Don't worry, I didn't drive. I *walked* here," Olivia said proudly. "Thanks to my sensible shoes," she said, staring glumly at her feet. "Oh, and Mitz is mad at you for not showing up."

Not showing up? How about not being invited?

"I didn't get an invite!"

Olivia stuck out her bottom lip in a pout.

"I sent you an e-vite," she said.

E-vite? What kind of etiquette was that?

I told her I hadn't got it, though I thought Tiffany probably had, since the Face Value account was the only e-mail account I'd used for years.

"It was sort of last-minute," Olivia explained. "Amir ended up having a dental conference in Atlantic City, and Mitz was sure he was going to work a bachelor party into the weekend, so she made the brideslaves throw her a bachelorette party."

Olivia could've called me.

"I should've called you. Maybe you would've stopped me from drinking. I'm going to be a horrible mother."

I wanted to tell her she would be fine, but I couldn't. I loved Olivia, but I really wasn't sure what kind of mother she would be.

"The worst part is that I'm being so selfish," she said, reading my mind. "I mean, I know I'm a selfish person, but I guess I thought if I ever became pregnant I'd just turn into Supermom instantly. But I haven't. I've got all this selfishness kicking around in me. What if it doesn't go away?" She was sobbing now.

I wrapped my arms around Olivia and rocked her back and forth. "Maybe the baby'll kick it out?"

She snorted.

"Just think of all the things you're going to be able to do," I said softly, mentally trying to muster up a list before she could ask. "Like Mommy Mondays at the movies. And right now, you can sign up for prenatal yoga," I said, even though I knew she was done with yoga. "And people have to give you their seat on the bus or subway. You know, if you took public transit."

Chapter Eleven

SATYA: TRUTH.
One of the five *yamas* (ways to relate to each other), its actions speak louder than words.

On Friday night I met Olivia at the movie theater by her condo for an evening of girl bonding, though she turned it into girl bashing, with the topic of conversation being Mitz.

"You should be glad she's not speaking to you. Because if she was, she'd have assigned you a task, too," Olivia said, filling me in on the wedding plans. "She's all about *tasks* right now, and if she's not waiting on you to complete one, she has no use for you. She's like Corporal Barbie. Plastic, with no emotion. Just a lot of orders. It's not even about the wedding anymore. I mean, I could accept being a brideslave for a few months, but this is out of control. The other day she asked me to source scalloped cupcake pans for her. Now, I know I work at the Bay, but there's no way she was asking for cupcake pans for her wedding. I mean, cupcakes at weddings are so three years ago. Besides, I already know she's planning a caramel fountain, which means, she was asking about cupcake pans for her own business! As if I don't have a job. And I would've done it, but she gave me, like, five hours. Never mind the fact that she's having five bridal showers, which is just ridiculous, and I have to go to all of them. And don't even get me started on the dresses. By the way, I haven't told her I'm pregnant, since who knows what she'll do if she thinks someone's going to be fat in her photos."

"But you're due in March. You won't be pregnant by the wedding."

Olivia shook her head. "Didn't she tell you? She's bumped up the wedding date. It's going to be a winter wedding. Juri just got engaged, and there's no way Mitz will let her younger sister get married before her, and since Juri's on a student exchange in Italy until March, she'll be having her wedding as soon as she gets back home, so Mitz moved her date up to Valentine's Day. I actually think she's not so concerned that her younger sister will get married before her as she is that Juri would have her wedding in Italy, and it will be romantic, and all the relatives who can't come over for Mitz's wedding will be at Juri's and she'll outshine Mitz."

Which was why we were seeing a horror flick that had nothing to do with love, romance, weddings or friendships— just lots of annoying college kids getting killed in their sleep. And so that we could eat popcorn, which Olivia had an insatiable craving for.

After the movie, Olivia and I walked back to her place, and I remembered the gift I had for her.

I handed her a bottle of John Frieda Sheer Blonde Luminous Color Glaze from my bag.

"It's safe to use while you're pregnant, and will keep your hair blonde," I said, handing her the shampoo.

She took the bottle and smiled. "Thanks. I'll try it. But the minute that baby busts out, I'm going back to being a true blonde. I'll give the kid nine months of the all-natural me, but that's it." She stuck the bottle in her green suede handbag, then hugged me. "I didn't even ask you, how's your new place?"

"It's really great. I mean, I've just started to unpack, but I love it."

"Just started to unpack? You moved in days ago!" she laughed. "Sorry. I know you probably don't need it, but if you want any help, even with painting, let me know. Although, I don't think I'm supposed to paint while I'm pregnant, am I?" She was doing a good job of finding the perks to being pregnant.

Although I was grateful for Olivia's offer, part of me wanted to keep my apartment to myself for a while, to decorate it the way I wanted and make it my own.

"Maybe I could just lend you my Bay discount card in case there are any items you want to pick up," she said.

That was true friendship.

—

Before selecting my paint, I armed myself with a second opinion. Although I knew Olivia had a flair for decorating, I was beginning to think that maybe her style wasn't the same as mine, and I didn't want to make another rash brown to Post-it Note color decision. And while I wasn't trying to please anyone else with my paint job, I didn't yet quite trust my own opinion on all matters. What I was trusting was that some people were experts, and it was okay to rely on their expertise. So when I called Bradford on Saturday to request a cupcake date the following afternoon, I asked if he could bring Tobias along. Given that Tobias had a better relationship with paint than he had with most people, I wanted his perspective.

"I'm warning you now," Bradford said when he arrived at my new place (he wanted to see my apartment before we went for dessert), "he's learning his lines for the new season, so he's in full-on psycho-decorologist mode. I can't get through dinner without finding out why I'm eating my green beans before my red potatoes and why my meat is framing the edge of the plate rather than parallel to the veggies. I warned him to tone it down with you, but there's no telling what will come out of his mouth. Just so you know."

As we walked up the stairs, he grabbed my arm.

"You know, I'm really proud of you."

I looked at him and half-shrugged. I wanted to appear nonchalant even though I was secretly pleased.

"Really," he said. "I believed in you. You just didn't believe in yourself. I love you. Always." Then he pulled me into a hug.

I hit him in the arm. "Isn't that a line from *Pretty in Pink?*"

"Inspired by, modified for the situation. Whatever, it's true."

I hugged Bradford back. It was nice to have a true friend.

At the Cupcake Shoppe, Tobias had turned down the sales-pitch-o-meter.

"The key to decorating is to go with your heart," he said between bites of his James Brown cupcake. "The couples who are happy with their home makeovers and don't redecorate the minute we leave the set are the ones who decorated to their tastes and were honest about *why* they wanted a pink patent leather settee or a big-screen TV. The Oakville diva who wants a granite pedestal sink just so her husband won't leave his shaving kit on the counter, but says that it's because she's always loved the look of one, ends up being upset that her mascara keeps rolling into the sink, which wouldn't have happened if she'd been honest."

Bradford gave Tobias a look. "We have a pedestal sink."

"In the guest bathroom. That's so our parents don't get too comfortable and stay over more than twice a year," he said to Bradford, then turned to me. "See—honesty. And it works, doesn't it? The point is that if she'd just told her husband that his messiness annoyed her, then we could've helped them build a shelf beside his sink, where he could stash his stuff. Instead, they end up ripping out the pedestal sink after we finish shooting or, worse, getting a divorce."

A divorce over a pedestal sink seemed a bit drastic. And also, it had nothing to do with me. "I don't think I'll have that problem, given that I'm not one half of a couple."

"Which makes it easy," Tobias assured me. "Who cares what furniture fabrics are inspired by Stella McCartney's latest runway show? Or what colors are in? You know what you like, so go with that. You'll be fine. And if someone asks you why you don't have a piece of trendy furniture you can't afford, just tell them it's minimalist chic."

～

At a quarter past midnight, as I was putting away my painting supplies, I heard a knock at the door. I had just finished the first coat of my new Ocean Blue bedroom. Pumpernickel jumped off the pillow, and I followed him out to the door of my apartment.

Victoria was standing on the fire escape.

She looked at me wide-eyed, and then she started to cry.

I didn't know what to say. Victoria never cries. So I didn't say anything. I pulled her in to me and let her sob.

"My credit card was maxed out."

This was what made my sister cry? I needed strength to deal with this.

I pulled her inside and sat her down on the couch. Pumpernickel hopped onto her lap, sniffed her face and licked a tear streak.

"So I couldn't stay any longer."

"Stay any longer, where?" I asked.

"At the Marriott."

"The Marriott?" I pushed her back to look at her. "Why have you been staying at a hotel?" And what kind of hotel kicks someone out at near-midnight?

She tucked her hair behind her ear. "George dunwamme."

"What?" She was slurring.

"We've been fighting forever. He says he doesn't want to deal with me anymore. He doesn't even want to talk about what to do. So I've been living in a hotel ever since you kicked me out. But he stopped paying the credit card bill when he saw I'd put the liposuction on it."

"What?" I couldn't digest all this information. "How long has this been going on?"

She shrugged and looked down at her hands in her lap. "Months. That's why I came to stay with you during the week. On the weekends I went to the hotel."

"But what about the kids?"

"He lets me see the kids during the week. I take them to the park after school with Francie. He won't let me see them without the nanny."

"He actually said that?"

It seemed completely unfair of George, but at the same time, I couldn't believe Victoria had been avoiding her marriage for months. And getting your husband to pay for liposuction hardly seemed the way to win him over.

And then it all made sense. Victoria hadn't come to stay with me so she could help me. She'd come to escape her own life.

"Were you just using me?" I asked, pushing her off my chest.

She looked at me, alarmed.

But then I felt bad. She was crying, after all.

"If you two are fighting, why isn't he living in a hotel if he doesn't want to make your marriage work? You're their mother, you're home all the time—"

"And he's the boss. He's the breadwinner. He pays for everything, including the nanny. But now I have no money and I don't know what to do."

I realized how scary it must be to give up your career and become reliant on someone else. For a moment, I was thankful that I was a self-made woman, even if I could just barely cover my rent. But this was no time to worry about my own money issues. My sister needed me. It was my chance to take care of her.

"Do you know how horrible it is to live in a hotel?" she asked. "The way the hotel staff looks at me with pity, it's worse than being mistaken for a hooker . . . I'm sorry to impose on you, I really am."

I wrapped my arms around her once more. "It's going to be okay."

I wasn't sure if it was, but I felt like I should at least say the words.

If my mother had a sixth sense for sad times, she had a seventh for knowing just where to find her daughters. The next morning she called to find out if Victoria was with me. I told her she was testing out my spotless, sanitized shower (which Victoria didn't believe I'd cleaned myself, despite repeated insistences and confirmations on my part).

I wasn't sure what to do—keep Victoria's admission to me a secret or tell my mother what was really going on. Telling my mom that her oldest daughter, who appeared so perfect in every way, maybe wasn't so perfect felt cruel. And I didn't want to hurt Victoria, especially now, since finding out she was human after all made me like her much more.

"Well, it's time you know," my mother interrupted my thoughts. "Victoria and George are separated."

My mother not only knew best, but seemingly everything.

"That's why I sent her to live with you when Sam left. I thought you could take care of her," she continued. "You always land on your feet, and sometimes I think your sister could use a dose of reality to keep her in check. I thought the break might help their marriage, and she'd see that she had it good." I had to wonder if my mother was implying that a month of roughing it with me would make anybody else's life seem better. "And that she shouldn't be so princess-like."

That afternoon at yoga, Sofi told us the theme of the practice was honesty.

"Truly interesting people are honest. People who are not honest are uninteresting. They're doing everything they think they're supposed to do in the way they're supposed to do it, but they're not being true to themselves. They're not being themselves. Honest people make mistakes and fail, and that's what makes them fascinating."

When I left yoga, I thought about honesty. Victoria hadn't been honest with her husband, her children, our parents or me. But worst of all, she hadn't been honest with herself. My mother hadn't been honest with me. If she had, I would've felt better about myself. I'd have known she wasn't sending my sister to live with me because I was useless, but because I could be a good companion for my sister during *her* tough time, and not the other way around. I wondered if maybe my mother didn't come to visit because she knew I was doing okay, that I was strong, not needy. Maybe she felt I was fine on my own because when things went wrong, I didn't crumble.

When I got home, I told Victoria she could stay. This time, it was on my terms. She wasn't giving me rent money, and she wasn't donating furniture.

"You are a guest," I informed her, handing her a paintbrush so she could help me paint my kitchen a soothing shade of Warm Vanilla Cream. "Which means you don't get to boss me around."

"Lovely way to treat your guests," she said, putting the paintbrush on the counter and reaching for a glass from the cupboard.

"And if you don't like it," I continued, "you don't have to live with it. You can tell me, and then you can move home. This time, we're going to be honest with each other."

She insisted she hadn't been keeping her relationship (or lack thereof) a secret. "It just happened that Sam broke up with you when George and I were planning to take a break. So instead of staying at a hotel all the time, I thought I'd stay with you and have some company, and give you some company. And rent money. But when I decided to do that, George got even more upset. I suppose he thought that instead of trying to fix our marriage I was trying to avoid it by hiding out at your place and then at a hotel. So we agreed to separate. And now, after the whole liposuction thing, I don't even know if he'll ever talk to me again. And the funny thing is, I was doing it for him so he would find me attractive."

"But if he was upset that you got liposuction, doesn't that make you think he was happy with you the way you were, at least physically?" I said. "And maybe your problems don't have to do with appearances, but with your emotions."

I was impressed with my ability to really seize this whole honesty mantra.

Victoria nodded. "I don't know, I just thought if he desired me . . . You know, it's tough having three kids."

I wanted to remind her how tough it could be to have three kids *and* a job, without a nanny or a housekeeper, but instead I reminded myself that I didn't know what it was like to be her. Or have three kids. It was tough *not* having three kids or a husband or a nanny or a maid. It was tough being single. But that was life.

"When was the last time you and George had a real conversation?" I asked her.

Victoria shrugged.

"Maybe it's time?"

For the next few days I worked on securing products for my growing list of "clients." The one-hundred-percent shea butter had been a cinch to find for Rhonda—and she'd paid me an extra $20 more than it had cost just for finding it. The breast pills had been a bit more difficult, since breast enlargement pills were as common as penile enlargement e-mails, and it was looking to me like they were all a big scam. But I didn't want to give up, and after a few hours of searching medical research papers online at the library, I came across an article by one of the top breast surgeons in the country, Dr. Nancy Leroux, who mentioned one breast enlargement supplement that she believed actually worked. I used the pay phone in the entrance to call her and asked her for five minutes of her time.

"Are you writing an article?" Dr. Leroux asked me. I held my notebook in hand and my head high and admitted that I wasn't, though I hardly wanted to explain that I was simply researching it for someone who might pay me an extra $20 for doing so.

"Too bad," she said. "If you only knew the questions I get from women. I suppose women used to be able to get information from magazines before advertising paid for all the editorial content. You know, cosmetic enhancement is such a fast-growing industry, but it's changing so quickly it's no wonder women don't know what works and what doesn't."

Dr. Leroux was right. I didn't know how I could get a job doing this, because as far as I knew there wasn't a website or a magazine that told women about new products and procedures. But if there was one, it would be perfect. At least, it sounded perfect for me. Was there a company that would hire me to do this, and could I find one before I completely ran out of money?

If, without even trying, I had several women relying on me to track down products for their problems, how many clients could I get if I actually tried to advertise my services?

I realized what I needed to do.

I called Face Value and explained the situation (okay, not *the* situation, but a plausible one) to Tiffany.

"The truth is that I didn't use a personal e-mail system," I said, "so I don't have a lot of my friends' e-mail addresses, which are stored in the office e-mail system. I thought now that I've set up a Gmail account, maybe I could drop by and just forward everything to myself?" I made a mental note to actually set up a Gmail account.

It probably wasn't ethical to steal all of Marjorie's clients' e-mail addresses, but I wasn't attempting to lure women away from Marjorie by offering them cut-rate breast or lip implants. I was just going to offer them information on their alternatives—breast pills, creams and lip plumpers.

"What's in it for me?" Tiffany snapped her gum and waited for my response. For a moment, I felt the same satisfaction I thought I'd have felt had I quit, rather than been fired.

"A signed picture of Tobias Strolz?" I asked.

"The hot painter?"

It was that easy. Given my new policy regarding honesty, I felt a little guilty about lying, but it was going to be worth it. I was finally taking action in my own life. And it was just a small lie. Besides, I belonged to the Church of Cable TV, and I hadn't attended in over fifteen years.

"I suppose you could come in tomorrow when Marjorie's out at her hair appointment," Tiffany said. "Be here at noon."

Chapter Twelve

TRIKONASANA: TRIANGLE POSE.
This three-cornered position is the most stable pose in yoga.

I seemed to do my best thinking during yoga, and as we moved from Warrior 1 to Warrior 2, the instructor told us to slide into Triangle Pose.

"This is the most powerful pose in yoga," she said. "There are three solid forces driving in three directions but united as one. Nothing is more stable than the triangle."

While I was balancing in Triangle, I thought about how that idea related to my life and the business I was starting. I knew there was a need. It wasn't just about cosmetic surgery solutions or organic foods or relying solely on exercise. It wasn't about extreme measures; it was about finding a balance between the three worlds that helped women feel good about themselves—the worlds of beauty, health and wellness. And then, as I was lying in *savasana*, I figured out my business, including the name: Tuck Shop.

In the city, women were too busy to take care of the necessities—cooking, cleaning, walking the dog. They hired personal chefs to cook their healthy meals, housekeepers to clean their homes, walkers to exercise their dogs, nannies to care for their kids. If they couldn't accomplish these tasks, they likely couldn't take time to check out new beauty products—or felt too guilty to do it. But paying someone else to recommend and buy their products for them seemed reasonable. It could even work for women who had time to shop, but didn't have the selection— women who lived in the suburbs or country, where Sephora, Holt Renfrew and Delineation didn't exist. I could be the go-to girl. The personal shopper for their skin.

For the next week, I staked out the library between shifts at Mok, dividing my time between the small-business reference section and the computer terminals, researching products while trying to determine whether my idea could become a viable business. I had the complete client list from Face Value, which I loaded into the new e-mail account I had set up at my new computer in my new office (which doubled as the Yorkville Library's computer terminal 2, by the window). During the day, the library was quiet and the perfect environment for a small-business startup, with only the occasional interruption when someone bumped my chair with their bag, cane or hip. It was here that I brainstormed my business plan.

What if I sent out a weekly e-mail to women, highlighting the latest anti-aging cream for their hands or breast cream that would firm their post-baby B-cups without surgery? And what if I linked to sites where women could buy these products, or set up a service to source the items for them and ship them for a nominal charge? Between trade shows and consumer shows, I could track down little-known products most women would never find themselves, and then supplement these products with popular ones sold at drugstore beauty boutiques and specialty stores women didn't have time to get to or lived too far away to shop at. Even better, I could be their reliable source, a person who had tested the products and knew whether they were worth the money before they bought anything.

As I was sending Lisette the information on the breast pills, an e-mail came through from Heather, one of Lisette's friends, asking me about stretch mark creams. As I sent her back a list of suggestions and an offer to pick up a cream for her, I realized that Olivia would likely be interested too. Given her less-than-enthusiastic attitude toward her new body, I knew I could find lots of products that she'd probably want to know about while she was pregnant and once she was a mom. And if she was interested, other moms might be as well.

But how could I target those moms and moms-to-be, particularly if they didn't have time to read my website? And then I knew.

What if I started throwing Mommy Makeover parties instead of baby showers? Decadent Divorce parties instead of bridal showers? Fabulous at Fifty parties instead of retirement parties?

I was sure that my idea was brilliant, original and profitable. I felt so confident that my family, too, would think my idea was great that I wanted to share my news with them right away.

"Sounds like Mary Kay," Victoria said when I explained the fix-it parties.

I glared at her.

"Just being honest," she said with a smirk.

I picked up the phone and called my mother.

"Like Mary Kay?" she said enthusiastically.

"Put Dad on."

"Ahh . . . like Avon. Million-dollar business," my father said, and I realized I would never be his million-dollar baby.

I was an idiot. Of course my idea was brilliant, but it certainly wasn't original. Mary Kay, Avon, Tupperware . . . I didn't have an entrepreneurial business plan. I had a suburban housewife idea for making extra money.

I couldn't believe how stupid I was.

~

"There are no new ideas, Mara," Bradford said when he showed up an hour later to take me out for cupcakes as part of the crisis intervention plan. We walked outside, and although it was only the first day of October, the temperature was hovering just above zero. I'd pulled on a new, chunky sweater with tiny ruffles around the edges that I'd picked up at a small, inexpensive boutique across from Mok. Without trying (and because shopping in boutiques was actually easier than heading to a Gap inside a mall), I felt I had created my own style—casual yet girly. I stuck my hands into the pockets of my jeans—jeans I could fit into once again, with room for fingers—and that took a bit of the guilt off the emergency cupcake session. I wasn't a size 2, but I wasn't a size 12 anymore. I was back to a solid size 10.

Instead of turning right to go to the subway station, Bradford turned left and then right, leading me onto Fairview.

"I thought we were going for cupcakes," I half-moaned, trailing him.

"We are," he said, grabbing my hand and leading me down the street toward the Loblaws at the other end of the road.

"I figured we'd just get cupcakes here," he added with a shrug, looking me in the eye.

"At the grocery store?" I said, sure I was missing a vital fact.

"Mmm. It's closer and cupcakes are cupcakes, right?" The automatic door let us in.

I shook my head. "Not really." Though the path through the bread section to the bakery counter was clear, this exercise was not.

"Really?" he said, as we came to a stop in front of the glass case.

I looked at the cupcakes behind the glass.

A woman beside us was ordering a dozen, all the same— vanilla cupcakes with white icing. There was no chocolate buttermilk batter or lemon butter-cream icing.

I exaggerated a frown and looked at Bradford.

"There's no variety. I like all the different flavors and colors and cute names. Don't you?"

And then I got it. We walked out of the store toward the subway station to head to The Cupcake Shoppe.

Half an hour later, Bradford took the last bite of his James Brown cupcake, said "Get up offa that thing" and sent me home (with an extra Sleepless in Toronto cupcake to keep me going) to get to work.

⌒

I considered Monday morning a success-in-the-making when I woke up at five-thirty to do my first-ever 6 a.m. yoga class.

"Got yourself a paper route?" Victoria complained when I turned on the light to find my sneakers.

Exercising this early might not have been my norm, but it was necessary if I was going to be at the library by nine, when it opened. If I wanted to be competition for those other at-home parties, I needed to find out what made all of them successful. So after yoga I spent the day online, researching various companies.

Then I started calling.

It turned out to be quite easy to figure out how to compete with an Avon, Mary Kay, Stampin' Up, Tupperware, Fantasia or Tealightful Treasures. They told all if you said you were interested in becoming a rep. Even if it wasn't true.

Bette Kraque was my first job-shadow. She had been a Mary Kay rep for thirteen years, so she was a wealth of information when it came to the financials and how to make more money and target different types of clients.

I created a document comparing all the home-party details and gave it to Bradford. He'd agreed to analyze it for me, then help me figure out the finances—from prices for parties and product markups to percentages I would take off Web sales, as well as sponsor ads, links and other Web related ways to make money.

And then I did the unthinkable. I willingly went to the Enhancement Expo.

Just two months earlier, I would've dreaded attending, even when I was getting paid to do so. Now, I *wanted* to attend and was prepared to use my own money to get in. And I would have paid if Marcie, the show organizer, hadn't recognized me from the past three years' worth of shows and let me in for free.

Now that I had my own goals, the expo was the ideal place to build contacts and find products and resources for my business. Certain companies—like No Needles, a line of wrinkle-reducing creams, and Fat Cat, a collagen-based brand of lip plumpers—were at the show looking for distributors or medi-spas, boutiques and clinics to carry their new product lines. And help with distribution was exactly what I—with my new business—could provide.

I spent seven hours roaming the show and watching demonstrations, and the only uncomfortable moment was when I bumped—literally—into Marjorie coming out of the bathroom. She looked at me blankly, as though she couldn't quite place me, and then, when she recognized me, her blank stare turned into a look of pity, as though she thought that perhaps since she fired me I had lost all sanity and was wandering aimlessly in a world I no longer belonged to.

"Well, it's nice to see you're wearing shoes!" Marjorie said and whirled past me, scarf fluttering slightly off the nape of her neck.

Then the moment was over. I reassured myself that it hadn't mattered. That she no longer mattered because I didn't need her approval.

By five o'clock, I had set up meetings with distributors and product owners, gotten business cards, made notes and stuffed two bags full of samples and a folder full of order forms for more than three dozen potential products.

I stepped out of the convention center onto Front Street and took a deep breath. Everything was falling into place. The next step was to test the products and come up with a list of recommendations for the ones I thought worked. I'd give out samples at parties and set markup prices for my personal beauty shopper business.

Now all I needed were clients.

Stuck in Downward Dog

~

"A party in my honor is just what I need," Olivia said when I called to ask her if I could throw her a faux baby shower to test-run my business. "Did you know I'm far too fat to be a brideslave?"

Apparently, Mitz had fired Olivia for being too "ornery, overbearing and opinionated." Though Olivia thought it had more to do with the tables Mitz was renting, which seated only ten, not twelve, so two of the wedding party members had to go, since Mitz wouldn't consider any other configuration.

I wasn't sure which reason was more plausible.

"It was me or a sister," Olivia said. "I was the easy out, since I was going to be fat. I know she thinks it's a hassle, since I can't get my dress yet. Who knows how big I'll be by February."

For once, I didn't wish that Mitz would ask me to be a bridesmaid now that Olivia was out. Because even if she did, I wasn't sure I'd want to be one. Olivia was right; being a bridesmaid was a job, and I was busy enough trying to start my own career—I didn't need another job. If anything, all I wanted was for Mitz and me to talk again, though now that I'd moved, I realized it was up to me to call her.

"Anyway, now I don't have to buy a dress," Olivia continued, "or worry about fitting into one, since I never work out anymore. I guess part of me says, what's the point in working out when you can just get surgery for every part of your body you hate?"

"Well, you know, being pregnant is very trendy," I told her. "So you'll always have that. At least, for the next six months or so."

"Are stretch marks trendy?" she asked.

I told her I could get her some creams.

Chapter Thirteen

SETHU BANDHASANA: BRIDGE POSE.
The active version of this position calms the brain and creates a
safe passage between the mind and surrounding influences.

$\mathcal{I}$ spent the next few days trying to construct the bridge position—not just in yoga, but in life. I needed to be the bridge
that connected Olivia, Mitz and me back together.

If I was going to throw a successful party, I wanted Mitz's
help.

"What are you calling to apologize for—not speaking to
me in over a month or missing my bachelorette party without
even RSVP'ing?" Mitz said when she heard my voice.

"Both," I said. Then I tried to change the subject by telling
her about the party and asking if she would help co-host. I
told her I'd take care of all the details, if she would agree to
cater it.

"I don't have time for a shower. I barely have time to plan
my wedding, never mind handle my business. I don't need to
donate my catering services to help you—or make Olivia's

ridiculous un—baby shower better. And I don't have time to go.
I don't even have time to talk."

My bridge was falling down, but I was determined to find
an alternate route to making things work.

Olivia had given me the guest list (a combination of
friends, co-workers and her mother's friends). Mitz wasn't on
the list, but I added her. I sent everyone else an e-vite, then
coerced my mom into baking a container (without the stems to
form a bouquet) of heart-shaped cookies. She attached the
invite for the Mommy Makeover party, which I'd e-mailed her
and my dad on the new computer they had finally purchased. I
didn't think bad behavior deserved special treatment, but Mitz
had been my friend for sixteen years, and maybe now, more
than ever, she needed a friend.

Olivia was on board with the anti—baby shower (she'd been
dreading the thought of receiving army-fatigue overalls or
faux-Robeez she'd be obligated to put on the tiny Closson-
Cutter whenever the gifter was around), so my e-vite explained
the gift-giving plan to the party guests. With the Mommy
Makeover party, there was no risk of giving unwanted gifts.
Instead of baby clothes, Olivia's friends could buy Olivia products at the party that she would love and that would make her
feel good about her changing body.

Of course, I needed to come up with the right products, so
while I rounded up a suitable selection, I recruited the rest of
my family to help me with my business. If I'd learned anything
from the OM list, it was that I couldn't expect to be an expert at
everything, and it was okay to ask for help from someone who
was an expert at something I wasn't. The plan hadn't worked
with Mitz, but I had to believe my family would be different.

Victoria was in charge of legalities. I needed to make sure I wouldn't be held responsible for my opinions on my website and couldn't be sued by companies for personal shopping for my clients. She also said I'd need insurance for running a business, particularly if I ever hosted a party in my apartment.

Then I got my father on board. With the Cookie's Cookie Bouquets website under his belt, he was ready to take on another project. He said he'd find a web host and register the site for me. Obviously, the new computer was inspiring him.

"You'll need a forum," he said, "so women can ask questions, discuss products and leave feedback on products they've tried. It'll keep them coming back to your site." While my father rambled on, I smiled.

He also said he'd create my business cards and promotional brochures, and then my mother, who'd been listening in on the conversation, said she'd make sure they weren't on orange paper.

The plan was to update the site daily with honest reviews of products I liked. Advertisers already wrote what they wanted us to believe; I would write what women wanted to know. Like that I loved using Cake Beauty Satin Sugar Hair & Body Refreshing Powder on days when I didn't have time to wash my hair, and that Clinique Derma White actually got rid of my freckle mustache last summer. And that Lip Flip really did make my lips look fuller, but that kissing was out of the question (I assumed, though I hadn't yet tested the theory) because the gloss made my lips so tacky that even holding a subway transfer in my mouth made it rip and cost me an extra fare.

By providing an honest review of products, I'd project integrity and gain the loyalty of readers, who would return to the site every time they wanted info about a new product. This, as my father had explained, would increase my site visits—the key to getting advertisers—as well as boost my "street cred," which made me think he'd been watching a little too much MTV.

And so, the next task was to dominate the computer station at the library until I'd written a bank of snappy, useful articles for my readers-to-be.

Freaky Friday

Between the breakouts and the frown lines, do you feel like you're 15 going on 50? You're not alone. You've got two choices: freak out or Face Up. We tried Face Up, the latest dermatologist-approved skin care line, recently and fell in love with the top seller, Wrinkle-Zit-Zap, an anti-blemish, anti-wrinkle overnight cream. Within two days, the glacial zit was melting and the crow's feet had flown the coop. And the ultra-light texture means your skin can breathe, so you can too. Now, if only we could get the confidence of Jamie Lee Curtis with a perky butt like Lindsay Lohan. A girl can dream . . .

Want to fall in love with Face Up? E-mail me to order.

I gave Victoria, who'd been keeping me company at the library, my article to read. She was in between the stacks, sitting on a chair covered in red fabric, studying *Civil Procedure: A Modern Approach*, the same book she'd been poring over for the past two days.

"I didn't know this was going to be so much work for you," I said, and meant it. I really thought she'd whip up a standard clause that I'd bring with me to parties and post on my website that would say I was not responsible—for anything.

"It's no problem," she said and shrugged.

As I returned to my computer station, it occurred to me that Victoria probably didn't need to read that book—or any legal book—cover to cover to get the information she needed to ensure I wouldn't be sued. It dawned on me that Victoria *liked* law.

"Are you sad you gave it up?" I asked her, when she brought the article back to me. She started to raise her eyebrows to give me a quizzical look (as though she couldn't understand what I was asking), but then she stopped, mid-expression.

"It's the thing you do when you live where we do."

And though I couldn't relate, I understood.

Victoria handed me back the article, then insisted I give her a sample of Wrinkle-Zit-Zap to try. She still didn't understand how I'd make any money, but a few days later, she too was hooked on the Face Up product and asked if I could get her a full-size bottle.

She had just proved that my reviews could work.

When I approached Sofi with my brochure on Tuesday morning to see if I could post one at Mok, she was hesitant. She said she didn't think it was in the moksha values to promote cosmetic enhancement and other unnatural forms of beauty, but she'd turn a blind eye if I put one on the bulletin board by the door. I gave her an eye cream as a thank you, which she said would definitely help cloud her vision.

A few days later, I had a list of twenty mom-friendly products, from Dermaglow Up-Lift Breast Firming Gel to OPI nail lacquer in Mother Road Rose.

The only unfortunate part was that Mitz wouldn't be at the party.

I'd left her several messages after sending the cookie bouquet, trying to convince her to come, but I hadn't heard anything from her. She obviously had no interest in co-hosting the party, catering it, attending as a guest or even returning my phone calls. The party was only five days away, and I had to focus on making it a success, even if I'd lost a friend. Still, I felt empty.

"Move on," Bradford told me.

"She's not a true friend," Victoria said.

"Want me to make cookies?" my mother offered. I couldn't have been more thankful. "How about a bunch of balloon animals?"

I didn't think Olivia was a balloon-animal kind of mom-to-be.

"What about something understated..."

"So no big knockers to symbolize breast-feeding?" my mom asked.

We settled on shortbread storks with pink icing.

⤷

I'd booked Buff Nails—an adorable pink-and-brown nail bar on Front Street—for Olivia's Mommy Makeover party. My own gift to Olivia was a year-long membership to the salon's Mommy Mornings, so that once a month she could get a manicure while her baby was entertained by the on-staff babysitter.

The spa was the perfect location for my anti-Tupperware party. Instead of plastic containers, I had tiny jars and tubes of creams and serums for the girls to try. Instead of kitchen gadgets, I had breast-firming creams.

As I walked past the St. Lawrence Market from the subway on my way to Buff, which was only a block farther east, I remembered it was just over two months earlier that I'd been here, frantically trying to pull off my dinner party. Compared with the dinner party, this event was far more important. The party wasn't just a gift to Olivia but a test to see whether I had a viable business.

An hour later, more than twenty of Olivia's friends, co-workers and family members were crowded into the nail bar, spread between the manicure and pedicure stations, sipping cocktails and testing products.

I'd invited my mom to stay so she could get a mini-makeover for all her hard work, and she'd brought the tray of stork-shaped cookies, which everyone adored. What I had never considered was that some of Olivia's guests would be moms-to-be or moms themselves. So as they sniffed and smoothed on the products, they weren't interested in placing orders only as gifts for Olivia. They also wanted products for themselves and their mothers, friends, daughters and co-workers, and they asked me how they could host their own parties. I had my work cut out for me.

I looked up just as she stepped inside the nail lounge. She looked different. She had chopped off her amazing long red hair, and now she had half-curls all over her head. If she were anyone else, she would've looked like an auburn Weird Al, but because she was Mitz, she looked like Ashley Judd—beautiful even on a bad hair day. Still, she'd never had more than a trim in the sixteen years I'd known her.

She looked around, and for a moment the thought flashed through my mind that she had just happened to stop in for a manicure—and had no idea this was Olivia's party.

She saw me and made eye contact, walking toward me.

I took a step forward too.

"Hi." She smiled and held out a plate of homemade cupcakes.

"What made you change your mind?" I asked.

She moved a hand as though to push a lock of hair behind her ear, but then stopped herself and gave a half-smile, turning up the right corner of her lip.

"Bradford. If you can believe it, we had a conversation longer than our typical two sentences," she said, and then nodded. "He's a real friend to you. And he reminded me that you're a real friend to me. And I was a real jerk."

Bradford had convinced Mitz to come?

I put the cupcakes down on the reception desk and pulled her in for a hug. When we unlocked arms, she cocked her head and focused her eyes on my hair.

"He also told me everyone was showing up with their hair chopped off as a gift to Olivia. To make her feel better about her own crop cut."

Mitz looked around at the other women, many of whom had long, luxurious hair. Then she looked at me expectantly. The explanation was obvious. *Bradford*. I tried not to laugh, and Mitz clenched her teeth, looking as if she was about to lose it.

Then she pulled her lips together, smiled and let out a half-laugh. "I guess I deserved that."

Epilogue

DHARANA: CONCENTRATION.
Disengaging oneself from outside distractions, one can finally achieve fixed inner awareness.

A few weeks later, I hosted my first girls' brunch: a breakfast bar buffet that included four kinds of milk, a tray of cereals ranging from super healthy to super sugary and a selection of toppings, from fresh raspberries to Raisinettes.

I nixed any type of formal invitation and invited Olivia and Mitz over by telephone. Mitz warned me that she was in a bad mood because her sisters were creating a bridal catastrophe by messing with linen colors, chair textures and unfortunate song selections, which included the Backstreet Boys.

"I know that I should focus on something else, but I *can't.*"

I expected Olivia to be somewhat smug about Mitz's bridesmaid chaos, but she wasn't. She arrived first, having driven in from Port Credit, where she'd moved into her new house the previous weekend. I'd offered to help, but she'd convinced Johnnie to hire first-class movers, who packed and unpacked all their belongings and organized them, from cookie sheets to bed sheets, into specific drawers and cupboards. Now she was glowing, and she attributed it to the jar of Kinerase cream, which was supposed to ward off pregnancy mask, she'd received at her shower.

Being pregnant had its advantages, she explained, and not having to worry about trying to be something she wasn't or do things she couldn't—for example, fitting her swelling body into a bridesmaid dress—was allowing her to embrace her pregnancy. She'd gotten over looking fat and was using her condition as an excuse to buy new outfits. I offered her the Diane dress/shirt back, but she shook her head.

"It looked great on you."

It looked even better now that I'd given up the high-cal smoothies (though I was still wearing it as a shirt), which I recommended to Olivia, who was having trouble gaining as much weight as her doctor wanted her to.

I gave the girls the tour of my place. I expected to hear them rattle on about what I should and shouldn't do with it and offer tips about useless accent pieces like empty bird cages or music stands, but neither did.

Olivia did try to move the DVDs off the top of the DVD player (she claimed it was bad feng shui), but when I explained that the set-up was functional, she put them back—in somewhat neater piles.

Mitz had decided that she did want a cupcake tree and did not want to cater her own wedding, so Olivia offered to give her a list of caterers—since she'd never cooked for a dinner party and had a whole host of reputable chefs to recommend. But she added that helping out didn't mean she wanted to be a bridesmaid again, especially since she'd found a knockoff of the black floor-length Gucci dress Gwyneth had worn when she was pregnant with Apple that went perfectly with her short hairstyle, which was much blonder than it had been when she'd first chopped it.

I wondered why I'd thought my friends were perfect. They had always seemed like they could do it all, but maybe I had just been blind to their struggles. I was now fairly sure that was the case. I'd been so hung up on labeling people as certain types— from the women who got cosmetic surgery to the women who did yoga to kept wives, like my sister, to my friends. I'd even avoided brands of yoga pants because I thought they were trendy and pretentious.

I thought about this as I took the milk—soy, added calcium, skim and chocolate—out of the fridge and placed the cartons on the breakfast bar in front of the girls, next to the six kinds of cereals and the lineup of toppings (fresh raspberries and strawberries, dried cranberries, marshmallows, Raisinettes, coconut and banana chips). The old me would've been stressed out about inviting my friends over for any sort of meal, worried that I'd screw something up or that what I was serving wasn't chic enough for company. But the changing me was attempting to be confident with who I was and wanted the best part of the breakfast to be not the menu (though it was fairly fabulous), but the bonding moment I hoped we'd have. So I served exactly what I liked to eat, and what I thought was just right for our girls' get-together. The best part was that I didn't have to worry about which ingredients needed to be cooked, cleaned, steamed or seared. The Craisins were dried, the berries were ripe, the milk was cold, and the cereal boxes were sealed for freshness, just like the label said.

Stuck in Downward Dog

As for my newfound career, I had come up with a use for my years at the slavery clinic. I was attending the trade shows I'd always despised and actually looked forward to spending hours roaming them now that the companies who bought booths were my prospective clients.

At the annual Skin Care Symposium, two amazing things happened. I got my first site sponsor—a one-woman-run company called F.B. that had created a line of products including my favorite, F.B.Eye, a gel that promised to "deflate the poof but not your spirits." Felicia Banner's products weren't yet in shops, and she needed to drive traffic to her online store. Every time someone clicked through from my site to the F.B. website or called the toll-free number and mentioned my site, I got a free sample that I could give away at the next party I hosted or in a contest on my site.

At that same show, I ran into Marjorie again, and she told me she'd heard about my website. I was worried that she'd find some way to sue me for stealing her client list—or at least threaten to do so. But to my surprise, she asked if I'd be interested in working on a freelance basis for her, updating her website with information about the treatments, machines and products she used at the clinic, and setting up a forum for her clients to share information. Apparently, Tiffany wore shoes—not flip-flops—but wasn't web savvy. Not that I was either, but I had a dad who was. I made a mental note to call him.

Olivia had gotten me the distributors' contact list for all the beauty brands that had pitched to the Bay but had never made it in, and now I was reviewing products that weren't yet available in stores or were offered only through smaller boutiques. After Sofi got sick of giving members a pen and paper to write down my information from the sign whenever I wasn't there, she agreed to let me put a stack of business cards and brochures on the desk. By the new year, she'd agreed to let me host an Antioxidant party at the studio. I was researching products that contained fruit and vegetable extracts; though they weren't all-natural, they would probably garner interest from the yogis anyway—as we both knew but rarely discussed, they weren't so all-natural themselves.

Mitz asked me to create beauty-themed favors for her bridesmaids and hired my mother to make cookies for the dessert table—she'd loved the hearts I'd sent her—as well as miniature wedding cakes and bell-shaped shortbread.

After the success of the shortbread storks at the Mommy Makeover party for Olivia, I'd recruited my mom to bake cookies for all my parties. Whenever my dad made a delivery, he'd stick around to teach me how to update my website and give me other tips I could use to take on the job for Marjorie. My mom had even tagged along with my dad twice, which I thought was a good effort. She'd promised to make the drive herself sometime when she wasn't too busy, though I didn't think that would happen now that her own business was doing even better. Once I'd convinced her that not every batch of cookies needed to be in a bouquet, she'd created a whole new sideline. Baking fancy biscuits for my parties had inspired her to create and sell cookies for baby showers and wedding receptions, as well as edible marketing tools for small businesses, from sewing studios to spas. Cookie bouquets might not have been cool in the city, but my mom's un-bunched confections shaped like lips, wedding cakes, stilettos and dresses were the trend of the year in Niagara and beyond. I had started handing out her brochures at any parties I hosted.

Victoria and George ended up staying separated, though it wasn't clear if they would divorce. I figured it depended on their therapy sessions—and whether they'd go to them. George kept the house and the nanny, but Victoria had arranged to get the kids from Thursday night through Monday morning. She rented the main floor of a house in High Park so she could be close to the kids' school but far enough away to make a fresh start. She got a job at one of the law firms on Bay Street, and although she was busier than ever, we started making an effort to get together once a week.

I was still working the reception desk at Mok, and I'd signed up for the first course to become a yoga instructor. I wasn't sure if I'd ever complete all the courses—you could do more than 2,000 hours of training, and I wasn't convinced I needed to know Yogic Numerology (which was one of the courses)—but I was going to start and see how it went.

I'd also started shopping at the Big Carrot, the natural food market inside the Carrot Common, which until this point I'd boycotted on principle alone. I'd figured that nothing that healthy could taste good. Turned out, I didn't need to wear hemp to shop there, and although the store stocked the staples I expected—tofu, beans and fruit that cost three times what it did at the regular grocery store—there was also a little takeout section with precooked healthy yet tasty meals, such as veggie samosas, tabbouleh, hummus and seven-grain salad. And even though the cereals were sort of bizarre (Where was the Cinnamon Toast Crunch? Where was the Golden Grahams?) the store had a huge bakery, filled with freshly baked pumpkin spice muffins (there were also turnip and sweet potato muffins, which I felt I had to steer clear of) and a whole row of fresh, single-wrapped cookies: chocolate chip and oatmeal raisin and cranberry apple. All made with natural ingredients, so surely they were better for you than the regular kind.

Maybe I wasn't ready to eat fruit from the earth—free of pesticides, crunch, shine and flavor—but I was embracing natural sugar and unrefined wheat flour (even if it was in a cookie).

Bradford and I were still meeting for cupcakes, but we'd counterbalanced the frequency of those dates with trips to the Lettuce Eatery. And I hadn't totally banned smoothies from my diet, thanks to the Suck It Up counter guy, to whom I'd given free rein to add supplements to my shakes as long as I couldn't taste them and didn't know what they were. He promised they'd restore balance to my system, and that didn't sound so horrible. After all, balance was my new mantra.

⌒

It used to be that my favorite pose in yoga was *savasana*— Corpse Pose—because all that was required was to lie very, very still. More importantly, it indicated the *end* of the workout. Then, when I started going to Mok, where *savasanas* were scattered throughout the series, they didn't signify the end anymore. As I began to enjoy the whole workout, rather than just the end of it (with the hope that I'd lost a pound or two), I discovered another segment with great benefit: *kapalbhati pranayama*, the breathing technique that ended the class.

Stuck in Downward Dog

At first, I hated the exercise. It was just breathing, but there was a technique, a right and wrong way, and I couldn't breathe deeply enough to maintain the slow pace the instructors set—and everyone else in the class seemed to follow. Then one day I stopped focusing on everyone else's breathing and instead turned my attention to my own. And, eventually, my pace slowed. And I just breathed.

Acknowledgments

My amazing agent, Suzanne Brandreth, believed in the book—and me—right from the start, and gave me endless encouragement, advice and beauty banter. I can never thank her enough. Thanks also to Dean Cooke, Samantha North and Mary Hu for all their support.

My editor, Janie Yoon, has been wise and honest, and helped me make this book the best it could be. Also at Key Porter, I thank Jordan Fenn, Marijke Friesen, Rob Howard and Daniel Rondeau.

I am so grateful to those who read the book and offered their advice and expertise: Kendall Anderson, Neal Burstyn, Christina Campbell, Jody Daye, Roger Gillott, Alvaro Goveia, Karen Hanson, Sarah Hartley, Laurie Mackenzie, Jeremy Rawlings and Gillian Tsintziras. Thanks to my friends, who were the best cheerleaders a girl could ask for and got excited at every tiny detail I shared with them. You know who you are.

My family has been wonderful. I am most indebted to my dad, Michel Guertin, for thirty-one years of love and support—

emotional, financial and always unconditional—and for never saying that being a writer wasn't a real job or a real dream. I wish my mom, who always believed in me, could be here to share this moment. Thanks also to my stepmom, Susan Guertin; my Manitoba mom and dad, Grace and Gary Simmons; my sister, Danielle; my sister-in-law, Melissa; my stepsisters, Sarah and Janet; and my cat, Mr. Baz, for his welcome distractions.

Above all, this book would never have happened if it weren't for Brent: hubs, best friend, reader, editor, motivator, biggest supporter and constant source of inspiration. Thank you for helping me get unstuck.

Author photograph: Alvaro Goveia

CHANTEL SIMMONS is the publisher and editor-in-chief of *Elevate*, Canada's premier cosmetic enhancement magazine, and a columnist at Sweetspot.ca. After a brief foray in book publishing, she was the assistant beauty editor at *Elle Canada* and assistant editor at *TV Guide*. She has written for *Reader's Digest, MoneySense, Faze Magazine,* the *Toronto Sun,* HGTV, Slice, W Network and Food Network. In 2007, Simmons was named one of the *National Post's* "Ones to Watch." She lives in Toronto, Ontario, with her husband and their cat.